Determined to take a break million dollar Winter Ha. money and more on dreams. Building boats was a childhood she's determined to pursue. With a love for Viking shipwright skills, she constructs a small scale longship. What she doesn't anticipate is an unexpected call from the past.

Of dragon blood, Viking King, Naðr Véurr Sigdir 'the bold' knew that the bargain he struck with the seers would likely lead to an unpredictable outcome. What he didn't foresee is a beautiful, headstrong woman from the future washing up on his shores.

Caught between twenty-first century America and ninth century Scandinavia, two souls connect. Both determined and willful, their battle soon becomes not one made of the eras separating them but all the unexpected moments that drive them closer together.

Anger. Need. Distrust. Hope. Never-ending desire. All merge, warring and passionate, when a modern day woman and a Viking king surge forward together to conquer not only their enemies but what lies within their hearts.

1

Viking King

The MacLomain Series-Viking Ancestors
Book One

By

Sky Purington

Dedication

For my fan turned dear friend, Jamie Ness Rodrigues. I might come from a Navy family and you were career Army, but wow did we hit it off. This one's for you because I believe in strong women who face all that life throws at them and still supersede. You are amazing. Thank you for your endless support, your service to our country and for your dedication to the Wounded Warrior Project.

Acknowledgments

Many thanks to Phoenix D. for always being available to give pointers on Norse Mythology and Viking history. Not only did you educate but inspire me.

Edited by *Cathy McElhaney*
Cover Art by *Tamra Westberry*

Published in the United States of America

Chapter One

Winter Harbor, Maine
2014

Mid-October never held so much appeal. Some might say it was the picturesque sunset splashing over Frenchman Bay at high tide. Others might say it was the riotous autumn colors surrounding her house. Or, those who knew her best might guess it was the nearly finished boat in her garage.

They would all be wrong.

Megan sat down at her sturdy oak desk. She didn't bother with the view of the rocky, windswept shoreline beyond multiple floor-to-ceiling windows. Instead, she plunked her feet on the desk, took a sip of icy cold locally brewed beer and eyed something she hoped would shed light on a mystery.

"Is that what I think it is?"

So Veronica made it after all. She hadn't heard the front door open. Megan looked at the clock. Five forty-five. "I gave up on you hours ago."

"You give up on everyone who's a few minutes late," her sister pointed out as she strolled over, heels clicking on the hardwood floor.

"Hours late," Megan muttered.

"Hug hello then?" Veronica prompted.

Megan hugged her sister. "Good to see you. Wine's in the fridge." Then she looked down and frowned. "You're not in New York anymore. Lose the stilettos."

Veronica blew her salon-perfect bangs out of her eyes. "That'll be the day."

Never had three women been more different than her and her sisters. Not to say she didn't love them. She did. With all her heart. But right now she was regretting having them up for the week. A *whole* week. What was she thinking? Yet when she'd made these plans she didn't know she'd be getting ahold of this manuscript. Or most of it. For some reason, parts were missing.

"You never answered my question." Veronica headed for the kitchen. "Is that stack of papers what I think it is?"

Megan quickly pocketed the item her sister clearly had not seen. "Sure is."

Veronica arched a delicately plucked eyebrow as she poured a glass of Sauvignon Blanc. "I'm always amazed at how many connections you have. Not easy getting manuscripts like that pre-publication."

Before semi-retiring, Megan had a knack at investing in real estate and currently owned various properties and businesses all the way from Manhattan to upstate Maine. Now thirty, she was an exceptionally wealthy woman. Which, thankfully, allowed her considerable time to do what she loved best…boat building.

Realizing it was unlikely she'd get more details about the origins of the manuscript, Veronica continued. "Have you heard from Cadence?"

"No." Megan frowned and took another sip. Cadence was a close friend who had vanished a few months ago. All she left behind were legal papers granting the ownership of her bookstore to Megan. That was the sole reason she was determined to get her hands on this manuscript. The agent behind its publisher was none other than Cadence's sister, Leslie. Not only that, but Cadence had been a ghost-writer for this book after her cousin, McKayla, its author, *also* disappeared.

"How did it go when you went to see Leslie?" Veronica asked, thumbing through the manuscript.

"Dead end." Megan put a hand on the papers and shook her head. "Leslie knew nothing. In fact, she's living in the old New Hampshire colonial alone now. Or should I say family free."

Veronica cocked her head in question.

Megan shoved her hands in the pockets of her hoodie and clucked her tongue. "She's got a Scotsman living with her."

"Scotsman?" Veronica mouthed.

"Mm hmm. Tall, really good-looking. Brogue so thick I barely understood a word he said." She curled up the corner of her lips. "But I didn't miss the looks he and Leslie exchanged when I was drilling her about Cadence."

"What kind of looks?"

"Like they knew a whole lot more than what they were saying."

"Ah." Veronica eyed the manuscript. "And naturally she doesn't know you have this."

"Nope."

"Again, how *do* you have it?"

"Like you said, I have connections."

"Have you read much of it yet?"

Megan pulled her hair out of its ponytail to rewrap it. "Bits and pieces."

Extremely interesting bits and pieces.

Bone-chilling in fact.

"Allow me." Veronica took the hair tie, shook her head and pulled back the thick, unruly curls. "I know I've said it before but women would pay thousands for your hair."

Megan grumbled under her breath and started flipping through the papers. Her hair was a curse. Golden with wisps of white blond, it had a mind of its own. All it needed to spread its frazzled wings was a humid day. "The gods only know why I was given this mess when I've a love for the sea."

"Right, your Norse gods." Veronica chuckled. "I'll bet they've already labeled you a Valkyrie. All crazy warrior woman with the wild hair."

Megan sighed. Her sister tried but she'd never gotten the hang of Norse mythology. "The Valkyrie chose who would and wouldn't live after battle. Those who were lucky enough to go on to Valhalla. Not so much warriors themselves."

"Either way." Veronica tied up her hair with one fluid motion. "There. Gorgeous as always."

"Says the part-time model." But Megan grinned. She wasn't the jealous type. Her looks got her by when she needed them to.

"And this coming from our infamous tigress," Veronica admonished.

"Ugh. Going to grab some candles. There's a storm brewing."

Megan shook her head and went upstairs. Her sisters had taken to calling her tigress years ago for two reasons. The first, her cut-throat, my-way-or-the-highway attitude in business. The second, her almost unnatural eye color. Most men had trouble holding her gaze. Like her locks, they were golden. In truth, they were pale chestnut mixed with even lighter tones. Some called them wild, untamed eyes.

No matter, nowadays she wasn't overly worried about holding any man's gaze, nor did she particularly care what they thought of her. Married once. Divorced. Done. She dated on occasion but was by no means looking for Mr. Forever. That boat had sailed.

"Oh, you got the manuscript!"

By the time Megan made it back downstairs, her sister Amber was already leafing through it.

"Hey sis." Megan spaced out candles on the wide mantle.

Amber instantly wrapped her up in a heartfelt hug, words warm. "Good to see you. Sorry I'm so late."

Veronica was already on the massive suede couch, legs curled under her and wine glass in hand. "It wouldn't be you otherwise, sweetie."

"You should talk." Megan lit the candles.

Amber's multi-layered chocolate brown eyes flashed at Megan. "Traffic."

"Sure." Megan shrugged. "Just glad you both got here before the bad weather."

Veronica pointed one long fingernail at the window. "Doesn't look it."

"Trust me. It's coming."

"If Megan says it is then it is." Amber headed for the kitchen. "She's never been wrong."

Megan grabbed her beer, the manuscript and sat on the opposite facing couch. After a quick sip, she set aside her drink and started thumbing through the pages. The truth was she'd already looked through it once. While she found it interesting that Cadence and Leslie's names were used in the book, it didn't explain in the least her disappearance. Maybe the missing pieces did.

"I couldn't help but notice there are several Scottish heroes in that," Veronica mentioned. "Interesting considering Leslie now has a Scotsman living with her."

Amber spoke from the kitchen island dividing the open-concept living area. "Does she really? That aside, was she able to shed further light on Cadence's disappearance?"

"Negative." Megan kept leafing through. "The whole thing's fishy."

"Well, if Leslie isn't concerned then you shouldn't be either." Wine in hand, Amber sat next to Megan. "So what's this book about anyways?"

"Time travel. Fantasy. Modern day women traveling back to medieval Scotland."

"Not really your cup of tea, eh?"

"Actually, some of it is," Veronica said softly.

Megan met her eyes. "You were busy while I was upstairs."

"Enough to figure out there was a Viking in there."

"Ohhh." Amber grinned, eyes twinkling and dark brown hair glistening beneath the recessed lighting. "Pray tell?"

Where Veronica was the willowy one with perfect lines, Amber was the one that dripped sensuality. Slender but curvier than her sisters, Amber attracted all men, young and old. And she adored every last one of them. Where Veronica made an enviable living magazine modeling, Amber was the struggling artist with an unequivocal talent at painting and playing numerous instruments.

Amber tapped Megan on the shoulder. "Still waiting."

Right. Vikings.

While she might have an unmatched admiration for Norse shipwright skills, it was purely in a non-fictional sense. A Viking in a manuscript held no interest for her.

Not really.

"The Viking's just a character in a nonsensical book," Megan answered. "And we never actually meet him. He's just a picture in a tapestry and then a voice in one of the heroine's head."

"Well, well," Veronica said. "Sounds like you've had time to really look through this."

No. Not until she realized there was a Norseman in it. Then she'd just skimmed looking for him.

Naðr Véurr.

She'd never heard of such a name so looked it up…nearly a year ago.

"Serpent protector," Veronica murmured.

When Megan's brows shot up, Veronica held up her cell phone. "Googled it."

"Serpent protector?" Amber grinned. "Now that *does* sound fantastical."

"And he's a king." Veronica's lips hovered over the edge of her glass as she eyed Megan. "He definitely sounds like your kind of guy."

"Very funny," she said dryly and continued looking through the book. Her sister, of course, was referring to the type of man Megan typically attracted…or at least had before she tucked herself away in Winter Harbor. "They were just the sort who ran in my circles. Now it's all about fishermen."

"Quite the leap." Veronica shook her head. "From power hungry men to—"

"Decent hardworking men who wouldn't rip your throat out to get ahead," Megan interrupted.

"Or heart out," Amber murmured. "How is Nathan?"

"I'd imagine he's sitting in his high rise office looking down on the rest of us little people."

"I read he's buying up a lot of marinas between Massachusetts and here." Veronica's deep green eyes watched Megan closely. Some might think her stunning features meant a dull mind but few were as brilliant as her statuesque sister.

"So it seems," Megan said.

Her ex-husband was ridiculously successful, his handsome face splashed in the newspaper far too often. She'd always had a certain type and he fit the bill. Tall, chiseled, driven and in-control. But those were back in the days when she'd preferred Dom Perignon and black-tie affairs to a cold beer and good, down-to-earth company at the local bar.

Back when getting ahead was more important than pursuing her dreams.

"Well I think a fictional Viking king sounds much better than that jackass any day of the week," Amber announced.

Megan raised her beer. "Heck yeah."

Yet Veronica wasn't quite ready to join the party train. "I also read that Nathan bought a monster of a house across the bay in Bar Harbor."

Megan buried a growl in a swig.

"Not surprising," Amber said. "We all know he's not good at rejection. Still." She frowned at Megan. "I can't say I like this move considering it's been three years since you left him. What gives?"

"He's just reminding her that he's still around." Veronica narrowed her eyes. "But be careful nonetheless, honey. No offense because you married him, but there's always been a little something off about that one."

That was an understatement.

Nathan was nothing less than a hedonistic, borderline sadistic bastard. Though he'd never hit her there was a darkness in him that simmered just beneath the surface. Add in the whole total lack of fidelity thing and she'd be fine with never crossing paths with him again. So it was best not to waste time thinking about him when there were better things to contemplate.

Out of instinct, she clasped the stone in her pocket and wondered at the symbols carved into either side of its flat surface. On one side, a Spirit Ship. A Norse symbol oftentimes referred to as the Ship of the Slain. It represented the journey to the afterlife. The picture itself very much resembled a Viking longship. On the other side, a Vegvisir. A Viking rune stave, it was a magical device used to aid in sea navigation.

"Alrighty, why don't we lose the negative talk and focus on food." Amber's full lips quirked when she looked at Megan. "Our local hottie still deliver lobster to your front door?"

"I already told Sean to stop by with his usual." Megan snorted. "I'm sure he knew the minute you drove into town."

Sean was not only Megan's best friend and fellow devotee of all things nautical but was also her sister's part-time fling when she visited. Smitten since he met her; Sean would no doubt weather the dangerous waters off central Nova Scotia during a category five hurricane to spend time with Amber.

"Should I get my phone?" Megan asked.

"Nah." Amber winked. "I got this."

"So Cadence going M.I.A. remains unsolved because that manuscript can in no way, shape or form explain it." Veronica finished off her wine and went for a refill. "Are we all in agreement with that?"

"I can't say either way as I've yet to read it," Amber reminded. A wide smile split her face as a text came through. "Look at that. Sean's here."

Megan couldn't contain a small grin as her sister bounded toward the door. Men didn't love her sister because she played hard to get. No. They loved her because she never for a second held back exactly how she felt, which as it turned out was always rather lustful.

Sean had no sooner walked in the front door with an armful of bags when Amber threw her arms around him and gave him a big kiss on the cheek. Meanwhile, Megan took the bags from her discombobulated but very happy friend.

Veronica laughed and gave him a quick hug after Amber let go. "Good to see you, Sean."

"Same to you," he grinned at Amber, "both."

Tall and rugged, Sean had the bearings of a boat captain and the charm of a rock. Bless him, but charisma wasn't his thing. Gruff and handsome in a sea-weathered way, he'd been born to live life off the choppy shores of Maine and would likely die here. The same age as her, fine lines already stemmed out from the corners of his golden-flecked green eyes. But she always suspected it was his haunted gaze and the light layer of stubble forever on his square jaw that attracted Amber. The artist in her sister was endlessly drawn…especially to those she surmised might need saving.

A lot of good that did those in need when she left…because she always did.

Amber didn't do dependable.

That was Megan's forte.

"You already cooked them." Megan pulled out the lobsters and plopped them into a pan. "Nice."

"Yeah well, I knew you were having company." He hung his coat, eyes never leaving Amber. "Brought Mema Angie's homemade apple pie too."

"Sweet. Hand-picked apples I'll bet."

"Yup." Sean made himself at home and set to lighting a fire on the hearth. Thunder rumbled in the distance. "Storm's nearly here."

Megan nodded and pulled more items out of the bag. "Oh! She made her potato salad too."

"Anything for you, Sea Siren." Sean lit the fire then returned. "Beer?"

"You bet." She tossed him one. "See what I did to our boat?"

"*Your* boat." His eyes warmed. "No. Show me later."

"Though it's sexy as hell, are you gonna wear that wool Beanie all night?" Amber said, voice an octave lower than normal as she eyed his hat.

Sean twisted off the beer cap and took a long swig, eyes never leaving her. "Depends, sweetheart. You want me to?"

Amber sidled over next to him and fingered the material. "I think maybe I do."

"Even if he's sweating his ass off in it?" Veronica echoed from the couch.

"True. I don't want you sweating too much." Amber trailed a finger down his arm. "Yet."

Sean's arm snaked around her lower back and pulled her against his side, promise in his eyes. "I'm looking forward to 'yet.'"

"Me too," she murmured, hiding behind her ridiculously thick eyelashes.

Megan chuckled. "Feel free to get 'yet' out of the way now so we can all enjoy each other's company."

Veronica nodded. "Agreed."

Amber waved away their suggestion. "Half the fun is in all those moments leading up to 'yet' right?" She pulled him toward the couch. "Come. Sit. Let's catch up."

"And that's my cue to help *you* out," Veronica said as she joined Megan in the kitchen.

"Right." Megan nodded at the cabinet. "Plates." Then at the drawer. "Forks and lobster crackers in there."

"So how are you doing sis?" Veronica set four plates on the island, sharp eyes swinging her way. "Really."

"Let's not talk about Nathan again."

"I wasn't referring to your ex." Her eyes swept over Megan's gorgeous house then out onto the bay. "I mean this life of seclusion you've chosen."

"It's not *that* secluded." She pulled out a stack of napkins and frowned. "I've made good friends and keep busy."

"But it's so different than how you lived before," Veronica argued softly. "So different than *who* you are."

"Actually, it's better. Before I was unhappy. Now I'm happy." She met her sister's eyes. "Sort of like you modeling when you have a law degree."

"Bad comparison."

"Is it?" Megan grabbed forks while Veronica pulled out lobster crackers. "I did one thing to make money but always loved another thing. You model to make money but your great love has always been defending those without much money. Which, by the way, won't make you much money either. So how are we different except that I've pursued my ultimate goal?"

"As long as I'm young enough I might as well keep making money," Veronica said.

"Pfft." Megan shook her head. "You already co-own one of the top magazines in New York and have made tons of money modeling. You're in a good enough financial position to make a career move. If for some reason you're not, I'll give you the money."

Veronica looked as though she'd been slapped. "You'll do no such thing."

Before she could respond, her sister started setting the table. The oldest of the three, it wouldn't be the first time Megan helped out her sisters financially. Whereas before Veronica may have accepted such an offer, things had changed over the past few years. Her sense of self-worth and pride had grown tremendously. Amber on the other hand had no issues 'borrowing' money on occasion. Or at least she'd never said otherwise.

If Megan had her way, she'd have both sisters set up in their dream homes doing whatever they liked for a living. She'd always made that clear. So when she joined Veronica at the table she said, "Sorry, didn't mean to…"

When she trailed off, Veronica met her eyes. "It's all good. Just not this week, okay?"

She nodded and said nothing more. Her sister had rebuilt her life since losing a child nearly eight years prior. And though immensely proud of how far she'd come, Megan still worried on occasion. Heartbreak like that never truly went away.

Another rumble of thunder shook the ground and the lights flickered.

"Not much longer then," Sean murmured from the couch, his words loud enough but still tucked into Amber's ever-eager ear.

"Food's here and ready." Not about to force anyone away from their moments of happiness she grabbed a fresh beer, drawn butter and sat at the table. "Eat if you're in the mood."

Amber grinned over her shoulder. "Be right there."

Megan smiled as she cracked her lobster. Not so much for Amber but for Sean. While most best friends would say a girl who came and went was bad for him, her sister always put a smile on his face. And smiling wasn't something he did often. While she'd gotten aggravated with her sister in the past, they seemed to have an agreement. One that she'd learned to steer clear of.

"Let's eat while it's hot," Sean said, a steady grin on his face as he pulled Amber after him.

Now that was unusual. Typically, he'd do anything to keep her couch bound.

Amber seemed to sense the shift as well because she pouted as they sat. Regardless, she was gracious. "Thanks for all of this, Sean." Her eyes met Megan's. "And for having me this week."

"No need to thank me." Megan smiled and nodded at the potato salad. "It's your favorite. Eat up."

Conversation became common and comfortable as they cracked their lobsters and ate. All the while though, Megan's eyes flickered toward the manuscript on her desk.

While she understood the flow of the story she still couldn't wrap her mind around the Viking king, Naðr Véurr. He belonged but didn't. The manuscript was based around a medieval clan called the MacLomains and their love connections, the Brouns. Yet in the midst of all that was a Viking who claimed he possessed the blood of a dragon.

A *dragon.*

Yes, the mythological creature could be connected with the Orient, British Isles and maybe even Scandinavia but it bothered her. She wanted him to be a simple Viking king. A strong man who stepped away from all the fantastical nonsense that seemed to lace the pages of what Leslie was calling The MacLomain Series: Next Generation. She wanted him to be a seafaring man not made of magic and odd creatures but of brawn and honor as history suggested of the Vikings. If a man as renowned as Naðr Véurr was in a book, shouldn't he be appreciated for what he truly was?

"And what is he again?"

"A man determined to win over my heart," Veronica said.

Megan blinked a few times. They weren't talking about her Viking king. Of course not. He didn't exist.

"And why is that?" Amber shook her head and shrugged. "Because he was good looking and said he'd make you a movie star."

Veronica snapped her lobster claw so sharply juice squirted. "I only met the guy a few weeks ago and by the way, I've no desire to be a movie star. *Please*."

Amber rolled her eyes and arched a brow at the same time. "Of course not."

Another clap of thunder rumbled and the lights flickered again.

"I guess Thor is busy tonight," Veronica said, eyes on Megan.

It had become a thing now. Her sisters had gone beyond teasing her for her love of Norse mythology and now often included it in conversations. While she usually thought it cute, tonight she was feeling edgy. About her sisters being here? Not really. About the incoming storm? Never. About the manuscript?

Definitely.

Sean nudged her elbow. "You okay?"

She met his eyes, calmed as always by his easy presence. "Yeah. Sure. Why wouldn't I be?"

"Here." He plunked a few pieces of shucked lobster on her plate then grabbed her unshelled lobster. "Why don't you relax and drink."

Relax? Even he knew that was something she wasn't good at. There was always something to get done. Mostly to do with her boat lately. "I can shuck my own lobster."

"Sure." The corner of his lip inched up a miniscule fraction. "But I can do it faster."

Some things a girl couldn't argue with. Offering a shrug, she leaned back and sipped her beer. Truth told, she wasn't much in the mood for family, alcohol or good food but tried her best. And Sean knew it.

An hour later, they remained at the table. All of them had eaten and drank heartily but her.

"What's the matter, sis," Amber said, eyes concerned. "You're not yourself."

"Not in the least," Veronica seconded.

Megan clenched her fist in her lap. They were right. She wasn't. Something was niggling at her and she couldn't put her finger on it. Like a door hadn't been closed. Or she'd forgotten to say thank you to someone. There was an uneasy feeling creeping up within her and she simply couldn't define it.

Sean handed her another beer. "You've barely touched the one you had. Drink a cold one and relax, okay?"

Was she tense?

Megan swigged the beer, eyes on the raging storm. The lights again flickered but didn't go out. Soon though. She could almost time it. "Two more minutes. Max."

"Huh?" Amber started then stopped. "Right. Electricity. I forgot how well you had that figured out."

"What?" she asked.

"The electricity." Amber notched her chin down as she looked at her. "Megan, are you with us? You seem a little out of it."

"She's fine," Sean muttered. "Just spooked."

"Spooked?" Veronica frowned. "By what?"

"Nothing," she assured.

Sean's eyes narrowed and he nodded out the window. "It's back again."

"Odin's sacred bird," she whispered.

Amber and Veronica looked out the window, eyes widening.

"Why is that huge bird sitting on your deck railing in the middle of this weather," Veronica murmured.

"It's a raven." Megan shook her head and started clearing the dishes. "They're getting confused lately. Climate change or something."

"Climate change?" Amber helped her gather up the dishes, eyes to the window. "Sure. Fine. But that bird seems to be…"

A loud clap of thunder crashed overhead. The lights flickered then went out.

"Looking right at Megan," Sean finished.

"Okay, I know you love Norse mythology and the Vikings sort of go hand and hand with your love for boats and the sea but," Amber looked from the raven to Megan, "Am I missing something? Because this is sort of creepy."

"No, it's fine." Megan turned to grab more plates. "It's just the weather."

Heavy gusts of wind blew yet the raven didn't budge as it watched her.

The same couldn't be said for the dozen or so ravens behind it.

Ping. Ping. Ping.

Birds started to slam into her windows in a rapid tangent.

17

God not again…
The ravens had come.

Chapter Two

"Your sisters would've understood."

Megan remained crouched, head bent, arms wrapped around the helm of her small boat.

Sean twisted the cap off a bottle. Then silence. He would wait her out at this point. Which suited her just fine. The storm had come and gone. Nothing but a cold wind and errant drops of rain were left.

"You didn't show them it, did you?"

Rolling back on her heels for at least the hundredth time in the past hour to disperse her weight, she gave no answer but pressed her cheek against the cool wood.

"God knows I can't help you with this but maybe they can, Meg." Sean sighed. "I've stood by you for the past few months but this is getting out of control."

A long silence passed. She wasn't ready. "It's past midnight. You shouldn't be drinking."

Low laughter preceded more silence until he relented. "I live my life at sea. There's no such thing as the right time to drink."

Megan murmured, "I know."

"So tell me." Sean's voice was soft and gruff. "Why am I out here worrying about you when I could be warm in bed with Amber? What happened with those ravens tonight? Because there are at least two dozen who managed to fly off despite hitting the window. Yet that big one is still perched there. He hasn't budged an inch."

"She," Megan whispered.

"All right. *She*."

Megan kept her cheek pressed against the wood and hoped with all her heart he'd go back to bed. Then she heard the heavy thump, thump of his boots propping up on the table. She clenched her jaw. She might've hoped for a lot. Sean leaving her in peace? Not a chance.

"Wait until you see the sketch Amber did of her."

"Okay, I'm just going to say it," Megan muttered. "Go away."

A piece of paper slid across the floor and hit her foot.

"You know Amber. She gets a thought in her head and watch out, she's gotta draw."

Megan bit her lower lip. That was Amber for sure. Which made her wonder how fulfilling Sean's night had likely been thus far. She lifted tired eyes to him. "Sorry, did I ruin it for you?"

The corner of his lips inched up slightly. "What do you need to hear right now, Sea Siren? Amber's my free flying girl till the day she dies."

So Amber slept with him but he was still out here worried about her. Thank god for best friends. Still, she hurt for him. Sean got that Amber was fly-by-night. He accepted it, probably always had. But it was hard for Megan to wrap her mind around. She'd been devoted to her ex, Nathan and no one after.

"Listen—"

"No," Sean said. "Not if it has to do with Amber." He arched both brows. "Right now I need to know what's up with you. Lotta crazy stuff happening lately."

"Nothing I can't handle." She really wasn't up for a heart to heart. The etching Amber drew caught her attention and she whispered, "*Jesus.*"

"Not bad, eh?"

"Haunting to say the least. She depicted the raven well." Megan stood, unable to tear her eyes away from it. "And drew a Viking ship into the background."

"Yup, floating the bay, riding those waves better than most I've seen out there."

Amber had done an amazing job. She'd used the pencil in such a way that it appeared a ghost ship swung toward the shore... almost as if it was steering directly toward her house. "Odd how it almost seems the raven is calling the ship forward and all the other birds are getting caught in an incoming gale."

"I thought the same thing," he murmured. "Your sisters know you've got a thing with Viking ships. You should share what's been going on lately." He nodded at her pocket. "And tell them about that."

Naturally he knew the rock was there. She carried it everywhere. Megan set aside the drawing, pulled out the worn stone and absently trailed a finger along their newly constructed boat.

Though she'd meant to keep it to herself, Megan couldn't help but share with Sean. "The Viking's name is in that manuscript."

"Yeah, I know."

She perked a brow. "Since when do you go anywhere near a book?"

"Since you spent more time staring at it than eating lobster."

"Ah, well." She sighed. "Couldn't be helped."

"Sooooo," he watched her closely, "I'm at a loss here. Must be some strange coincidence that his name popped up in a book."

Megan opened a drawer and pulled out the small, ancient metal box she'd found almost a year ago. This is what held the stones. Each had a runic symbol carved into either side. She dumped the other rocks into her palm and held out the box to him. "Seriously, what are the odds? The same name is carved into the inner lid of this. Naðr Véurr. Identical."

Sean took the box, eyed the words and shook his head. "Sorry. I got nothing, hon."

"And what about the whispers I've been hearing on the wind since the ravens went haywire?" She resumed trailing her fingers along the smooth edge of the boat. "Always the same name. *His*."

"Are you sure this manuscript was written recently?" Sean frowned. "Maybe it's been sitting on a back burner and you somehow saw it years ago." He shrugged. "*Or* it could be a name used before by other people and someone buried this box as a game or something."

"Yeah sure I guess both of those scenarios are possible but neither explains me hearing voices or why the ravens are going nutty."

"I wouldn't overly worry about the birds. I've seen 'em do strange things this close to the shore." He shot her a pointed look. "They get caught in wind shears, especially during hurricane season."

"And the voices?"

"You know as well as me that sound travels differently here. Voices carry over the water sometimes from miles away. No offense but you've been pretty hung up on that rock and his name since you found the box." Sean shook his head. "Sometimes we just hear what we wanna hear, sweetheart."

"Why would I *want* to hear his name," she mumbled and took a sip of his beer before returning it. "That's crazy."

"Hey, I understand more than most the whole idea of hearing what a person wants to hear instead of the reality of things," he said. "And while I love the hell out of you being here, I know damned well you made some pretty big life changes when you moved to Winter Harbor."

Megan looked skyward. "Don't you start on me too." Then she narrowed her eyes. "So what are you wanting to hear instead of the reality of things?" She regretted it the minute she said it and sighed. "Awe, shoot, Amber?"

Sean swigged his beer and nodded at the boat. "We gonna put her in the water soon?"

Megan sat next to him and knocked shoulders. "Way to evade the question." She softened her voice as she eyed him. "I thought you were good with your arrangement with my sister?"

"Most days I am," he said, voice rough. "Doesn't mean I don't want more sometimes."

The sadness was obvious in his voice and she did well to keep pity out of her response. "Who knows maybe one day down the line…"

"Naw, not Amber." He stared at the boat. "She needs more adventure than I can offer her. More of a challenge."

If nothing else, he knew her baby sister well. But she wouldn't drown all hope. "People change."

"Not her," he promised and shrugged a shoulder. "And honestly, I wouldn't want her to."

Megan set aside the box and rested her head on his shoulder. There were all sorts of comforting words she could offer but he'd see through them. The truth was he'd cast the line dead on when it came to Amber. Best to lead the conversation out of troubled waters and back to calmer seas. "They're calling for good weather. I thought we'd take our boat out tomorrow morning."

"No can do," he said. "I've got to work. How about the day after?"

"No good. Nor'easter coming in. Saturday then?"

"Nope, made plans with Amber."

She lifted her head and frowned. "You'd go on a date with my sister before taking our new baby out for her first swim?"

Sean chuckled. "Heck yeah. Besides, the storm won't be clear of us by then."

"Maybe not," she conceded and started to walk alongside the boat again, running her palm over the hull. "But you know a little bit of rough weather doesn't faze me."

Sean crossed his arms over his chest. "We've built a miniature replica of a Viking ship and everyone in Winter Harbor knows about it. You row this thing, which by the way is far different than anything you're used to, alone into turbulent water you'll make the local newspaper in a *bad* way." His lips pulled down. "Besides, I should be with you for its maiden voyage."

"Then tell Amber you have plans and we'll take it out." Megan grinned. "Give her a dose of her own medicine. Make *her* wait for *you*."

He shook his head. "If only I were that strong. Nope, I get her a few times a year and intend to take advantage."

"Ugh." There'd be no gaining ground here. "Fine, we'll aim for early next week."

Sean nodded, swigged the last of his beer and stood. "Enough moping out here. Come inside and get some rest."

"Safe to assume you're sleeping over then?"

He chuckled. "Where else would I be?"

"Right. Go on then. I'll be in soon."

"Will you?" Sean nodded at the boat. "Or am I going to find you sleeping in that tomorrow morning?"

Megan shot it a contemplative look. "Not such a bad idea." Then she winked at him. "Kidding. I'll be in soon. Go on."

Sean eyed what she suspected were her bloodshot eyes for another long moment before he nodded and turned away, saying over his shoulder, "I'll be back out in ten if you haven't turned in."

"Yeah, yeah," she muttered under her breath and tucked the metal box back into the drawer. Leaning against the workbench, she continued to eye the boat. Though Sean had certainly helped, she had put in most of the work building it. Regardless, it would always be *theirs*. And though he said it'd make the local paper if she went down in a storm, Megan knew it'd make the paper no matter what. It was a work of art. With clean, smooth lines it was built historically accurate.

Made of oak, they'd fastened the boards with authentic iron nails to a single sturdy keel and then to each other so that one plank overlapped the next. The Viking's had called it the 'clinker' technique rather than the more conventional method of first building an inner skeleton for the hull. Then they'd affixed evenly spaced floor timbers to the keel and not to the hull. This insured resilience and flexibility. After that, they added crossbeams to provide a deck and a few rowing benches, and secured a beam along the keel to support the mast.

Yes, it was all done on a much smaller scale but she was proud.

Though she'd dabbled in making model ships, this offered a whole new sense of accomplishment. It provided more fulfillment than those cut-throat real estate deals in her past. Sure, she'd felt a certain amount of pride back then but it always had more to do with her competitive nature rather than anything else.

But perhaps age and her relationship status had something to do with that. After all, half the reason she pursued real estate like she did was because Nathan had. Right out of college, they'd made a contest out of it. They were young and ambitious…and talented.

Megan ground her jaw and flicked off the lights. About the last thing she wanted to do was think about her ex-husband. She wanted thoughts of him nowhere near this beautiful boat and all the love she'd put into it.

While she had no trouble pushing thoughts of Nathan aside, Naðr Véurr continued to haunt her through the night. It was too damn uncanny that his name was in that manuscript. And though she'd gone along with Sean's theory that his name might've been mentioned before, she'd spent a great deal of time researching it. When she had no luck on the internet beyond the actual meaning of the name, she'd hit the local libraries. Nothing. But there *had* to be something out there. So not for the first time, Megan tossed and turned restlessly through the night until the sun cracked over the horizon.

A few loud woofs made her sit up in bed. *Uh oh.* She flung the blanket over herself moments before a Husky/Shepard mix burst into the room and jumped on the bed. With a hearty laugh, she flung her arms around the excited pooch. "Hello my sweet girl." Burying her face in the thick fur, she smiled. "Welcome home, Guardian."

She'd only been in Winter Harbor a few months when a local suggested she keep a dog around for protection. Though relatively crime free, it was rather isolated. *Absolutely not* had been her initial response. Megan didn't do dogs. Then she relented…okay, maybe a small one that wouldn't get in the way too much. Instead, she ended up with a light tan little mutt with a gray racer stripe down her back. As it turned out, the pup grew into a great beauty that currently weighed ninety pounds.

Amber sauntered in and flung herself down on the bed beside them, laughing as Guardian smothered her in kisses. Around heavy licks, she said, "Sean picked her up from the groomers before he went to work."

"I figured." Megan lay next to Amber as Guardian cuddled down between them. "God, the sun has barely risen. Did you two sleep at all?"

Amber grinned as she patted the dog. "Oh, here and there."

Megan shifted onto her side facing Amber and yawned. "Let's go back to sleep."

Amber lay on her side as well. "Not all that tired."

Megan shut her eyes. "Then go cook breakfast."

A weighty silence passed and she cracked open an eye. Amber was staring at her.

"What?" Megan mumbled.

"I'm worried about this guy Veronica just met."

Not 'I'm worried about Sean because I keep tugging on his heartstrings'. But Megan knew better. Eyes again closed, she said, "Veronica can take care of herself."

"Veronica's playing the same game you did."

Megan didn't take the bait but focused on breakfast. "I seem to recall you had a talent with pancakes."

"He's pressuring her to do things she has no interest in. Apparently he's been in the business for years and truly sees star potential in her," Amber said, a frown apparent in her voice. "But we both know that's not the direction she should go in."

She got where Amber was going with this. Megan should have never pursued real estate because Nathan did. "I was a lot younger than Veronica is now. She's got a good head on her shoulders. If she wants this go with it, sis."

Yet Megan was concerned as well. Veronica had made no mention of this guy to her and after their brief conversation last night about her being a lawyer…

"I know you're worried too," Amber said softly.

Megan put a hand to her forehead and opened her eyes. "If there's one thing that's been proven time and time again with us three, when it comes to men we're going to do what we want to do."

"True." Amber continued to pat Guardian. "But that doesn't mean we stop worrying about each other."

"Of course it doesn't." Apparently there would be no more sleeping. Megan swung her legs over the side of the bed. "I'll talk to her while she's here."

"I'm sorry to put this on you but you're the only one she'll listen to."

Her little sister truly had no idea how much Veronica had changed the past few years but there was no point in concerning her. "It's okay." Megan looked over her shoulder. "Now that I'm officially up, pancakes?"

Amber patted the bed. "Sure. Lie back down. I'll take care of it."

Megan shook her head and padded into the adjoining bathroom. "No. I'm up. Couldn't really sleep anyways."

"You all right, sis?"

Megan braced her hands on the granite top sink and stared at her red-rimmed eyes and drawn skin in the mirror. "Yeah, I'm good. Be better with pancakes."

A brief silence ensued before Amber responded. "You got it."

When Guardian sat next to Megan, she knew her sister had left. With a deep breath, she met the light blue eyes staring up at her. "Shower time, sweet girl." She nodded at the door. "Go follow Amber. You know she'll spoil you rotten."

Guardian shifted as though excited to follow Amber but kept her eyes trained on Megan.

With a quick ruffle on her head, she nodded at the door. "Go on now or you'll miss out."

That's all it took. Guardian bounded after Amber. Megan smiled and hopped in the shower. Regrettably it did nothing to clear her stressed and far too tired mind. Veronica didn't overly worry her. She'd feel her sister out like she always did and see where she was at. No, what continued to eat at her was the manuscript, the Viking Naðr and all the odd things that had been happening lately in regards to it.

Megan closed her eyes as the hot water met her chilled flesh. While her practical side continued to search out a logical explanation for all this, another side was all too aware of what else had been happening. More and more, especially since she began working on the boat, she'd been experiencing a physical reaction when she 'heard' the Viking's name on the wind. Heck, when she even *thought* about him.

A faceless man.

It was almost as if she had forgotten about someone she'd been in love with and was only just remembering him. The bouts of arousal were intense but the growing sense of heartache more so. She didn't get emotional often if ever so what Sean saw last night in the garage was a rarity. But in her defense, all that had been happening was getting to be a bit too much.

And if she was going to be truthful with herself, that her ex had bought a house across the bay didn't help things any. Getting as far away from Nathan as she could was a good move. But now he was close again. That definitely threw her off kilter. Add the manuscript and Naðr to the whole mix and forget it; she was working hard to keep mentally stable.

In record time she'd showered, pulled on jeans, a white turtleneck sweater, practical boots and headed downstairs. The smell of bacon already wafted through the house, a cozy addition to the pinks and purples of the sun cresting the bay. Guardian bounded over and danced around her as she accepted a steaming hot mug of black coffee from Amber.

"Morning, sister," Veronica said from behind her newspaper.

Megan shook her head and slid onto a barstool at the kitchen island. "Wow, you're *both* up. Amazing."

"How could anybody sleep in this house last night?" Veronica lowered the paper and rolled her eyes before sipping coffee.

"Say no more," Megan murmured into her coffee mug.

Amber issued a wide, toothy grin. "Not my fault Megan's million dollar house doesn't have sound proof walls."

"Like I said, say no more," Megan reminded then gave Amber a pointed look. "There's a loft above the garage. If you and Sean are keeping Veronica up all night, consider it yours this visit."

Amber scrunched her nose. "It's drafty and smells like the stuff you use to tarnish your boat."

"Varnish."

"Whatever."

Megan arched one brow while lowering the other, a look that no sister dare challenge. "If you're set on being inconsiderate then that's your new home away from home, Little Dove."

"When you whip out that nickname you've got me by the throat." Amber hung her head then continued cooking. "Done. I'll take the loft."

Veronica smirked then hid behind the newspaper again. The three of them were settling into being around one another as easily as they always did.

"I'm not used to seeing you read the newspaper," Megan commented to Veronica.

Veronica shrugged one borderline bony shoulder, folded the newspaper and set it aside. "Oh, just catching up on the local news."

Megan hadn't been so successful for no good reason. A bit of the 'old her' kicked in as her eyes flickered between the two. Amber was flipping the pancakes before the batter bubbled and Veronica's OCD, *obsessive compulsive disorder*, was lacking in her not-quite-perfect folding of the paper.

They were hiding something and she'd bet it had to do with what Veronica had been reading. Megan stood and wiggled her fingers at her sister. "Give me the newspaper."

Veronica breathed heavily through her nose. "Bad idea, sis. Why not do breakfast first?"

"Newspaper." Megan nodded at it. "Now."

"Hell," Amber said and shut off the griddle.

Megan took the paper from Veronica. No need to flip it open. Everything she needed to see was right there on the front page. Nathan shaking hands with who-the-heck-ever. The caption above it read… "Local billionaire buys Winter Harbor oceanfront property."

She'd no sooner released a steady stream of curses when a knock came at the front door and Guardian started barking. Tongue in cheek, furious, Megan strode down the hallway fully expecting to see Mema Angie. A dear friend eager to explain what was going on and how they might fight it. Yet when she swung open the door, ready to vent on someone who would sooth her with scones, she got someone else entirely.

Nathan. Her ex-husband.

Though every muscle in her body urged her to slam the door in his face, she stood there stunned and motionless.

Good thing for sisters.

"Are you *kidding* me?" Veronica held back Guardian.

"Get the hell out of here." Amber tried to shut the door.

Nathan's foot met the door jamb as he stared at Megan. "Ready to talk now?"

Megan hadn't actually seen him in person for nearly three years and was embarrassed by her immediate response. This guy didn't deserve a gawking stare. He deserved a punch in the face.

She shook her head. "You need to go. Now."

"I've been trying to call you for days, Megan." Though his words were passionate his eyes were deadly calm. "I take it you saw the newspaper."

He'd changed little in the looks department but then she knew that by the newspaper article she'd just seen. "It's safe to say everyone in Winter Harbor has."

"There's more to this." Nathan's eyes flickered between her sisters then down to Guardian before meeting her eyes again. "I remember how much you once loved Viking history. Has that changed?"

Megan might have imagined a thousand different words coming from his mouth but not those. And while she still wanted to slam the door so hard it chopped off his perfectly aligned nose, she was far too interested in what he'd said. "Talk fast or this door shuts."

Amber and Veronica made sounds of frustration.

"Viking treasure." Nathan's eyes remained locked with hers. "Off your shore. I'll let you lead the first team down."

"He's full of shit," Veronica said.

"I second that," Amber said.

"Not gold." Nathan's eyes narrowed. "But genuine artifacts."

"How do you know?" Megan said.

"We talk alone and I'll tell you more."

"Heck no," Amber said.

Guardian growled.

"I think the dog sees through your crap, Nathan," Veronica said.

Amber put a hand on Megan's shoulder. "Don't fall for it, sis."

"I totally agree." Veronica put a hand on her other shoulder. "Don't."

Megan clenched the doorjamb as she looked at Nathan. "You've had divers offshore?"

"You aren't the only one who loves sea treasure, Megan," he said through clenched teeth. But he soon masked his aggravation and smoothed his features. "Yes, I've had divers exploring the Maine and New Hampshire shorelines for years now."

"And?"

He tilted back his head slightly and looked down his nose at her, a gesture she recalled far too well. "And we've found stuff but nothing like what's in the waters in front of your house."

"Don't listen to him," Veronica said. "This one was always good at saying what you wanted to hear."

"Boy, was he ever," Amber echoed.

But Nathan had already grabbed her attention and well he knew it.

"Wipe that smug look off your face and walk around back," she said softly. "I'll meet you on the deck."

Before he could answer she shut the door and leaned her forehead against it.

"*What* are you *doing*?" Amber said.

"Damn," Veronica muttered.

Still, their hands were on her shoulders, a never ending support system.

Though it felt like her legs were sinking into the floor, Megan knew she could only ever show them strength. *That* was her role. *That* was what they expected of her. They needed someone stable and that had always been their oldest sister.

So with a deep breath, Megan pulled away from the door and strode down the hallway. She shouldered into a jacket and grabbed her coffee. "Veronica, keep Guardian from barking. Amber, keep cooking."

Not giving them a chance to respond, she stepped out onto her spacious back deck into the chilly air. Megan chose to lean against the railing overlooking the bay rather than sit when Nathan joined her. As she suspected he would, Nathan stood a few inches too close. He nodded at the ocean. "It's several thousand feet out."

"Tell me exactly what you found," she said.

"Tell me exactly why I should."

Jackass. Megan met his eyes and clenched her jaw. "Tell me or get the hell out of here."

His steely gray eyes held hers for a long moment before he spoke. "They're late ninth century artifacts. Even you know that's a groundbreaking discovery."

Her heart leapt. Viking artifacts were few and far between in these parts. They'd been too busy setting sail for closer conquests such as the British Isles and Ireland. "I want proof."

Nathan's level gaze never left hers. "Yet I'm the one with *all* the bargaining power."

Regrettably, that might be true. But she'd turn him down if he didn't handle this transaction correctly. Or so she kept telling herself. Megan rested her arm on the railing and kept his gaze. Yes, she'd love to look away but not once in all their years had she done such and wouldn't start now. "What do you get out of this."

She hadn't offered it as a question because Nathan didn't speak that language.

He only understood demand.

"Not a second chance because that's passed for us both." He looked at the shore then back at her. "I want you with me when we start pulling it up."

"Why, Nathan." She frowned. "Never once have you done a thing for the joy of another so please share. What's this really about?"

"Your expertise." He shrugged and arched his brows. "Believe it or not, you have a little bit of everything I need for this project. A love for Viking history, over three years' worth of familiarity with these waters…"

When he trailed off she narrowed her eyes. "And what?"

"A *need* for this," he stated softly but firmly.

Nathan might be standing there in khakis and a designer wool jacket but she could only see him in an expensive business suit. He'd have a leather briefcase in hand and a 'we'll just see who wins' look in his eyes. Yet he knew to this day what she strove for and it was no longer the next great real estate deal.

No, things had changed.

And no matter how much she told herself otherwise, the need to further explore beyond the metal box she'd found only grew stronger. Especially in light of the manuscript and Naðr Véurr's name being repeated. *Over and over.* The need to learn more about him made her mouth water. And if she'd found that metal box in the rocks on her shore, then chances were good that the sea treasure had something to do with him too.

More and more was coming together that brought *him* closer.

What was his ghost trying to tell her?

Megan almost groaned. Ghosts? Yeah right. Not part of this. Not part of reality. But still she felt herself reaching out to something...someone. It was similar to the feeling she'd had the night before when they'd all been eating and the raven showed up. There was an angle to all of this, a baser feeling that she just couldn't seem to grasp.

"Like I said, you'll be part of the lead team going down," Nathan said. "You and I."

Ah, there's the catch.

They would be a team.

But...what if Nathan's discovery actually existed?

Megan looked to the sea. "I know what *team* means to you. So do I lead this expedition or not?" She dragged her eyes to his. "And again, what's in it for you?"

"Yes, you'd lead, mainly once we pulled the artifacts up." His deceptive eyes never left hers. "What's in it for me? I think that's obvious. Treasure."

"Viking treasure should go to museums," she said.

His unwavering eyes sparked with something she didn't much like. "So you *do* think the idea of Viking treasure off these waters isn't too far-fetched."

Megan didn't miss a beat. "Very unlikely. But I honestly don't think this has anything to do with treasure." Her eyes narrowed on him. "You bought all the land on either side of me. Why?"

"You especially should know the answer to that, darling. It was a good investment."

And she had little doubt that he intended to build up around her and rip away half the charm of the area. "I haven't been your darling for a long time so lose the endearments. You bought everything around here and intend to navigate for treasure in front of *my* house. Sounds meticulously well planned."

Nathan had the nerve to smirk. "It does, doesn't it?"

Grasping the railing, she ground her jaw. "You don't give a crap about treasure. You just want another 'one up' on me."

"Is that what this is," he said softly.

Before Megan could respond he grabbed her wrist and yanked her against him, hand grasping her chin as his eyes bore into hers. "*Is* that what this is? Maybe I want something entirely different from you this time."

Megan was about to respond and tell him to shove it up his ass when a raven landed on the railing beside them. Though startlingly large, it didn't faze Nathan in the least but she knew...the raven meant to support her.

She was safe.

And she needed to see this through.

Though her teeth were still clenched, she felt an undeniable nugget of hope surface. One that most certainly had nothing to do with the tyrant pressed against her. Though tempted to rip her chin away she didn't. But she did narrow her eyes. "I want in."

Nathan's eyes held hers for a long moment before he slowly nodded and pulled away. "Good. My men are ready. We'll anchor offshore soon."

He gave her one last look before he strode off the deck, firm words thrown over his shoulder. "We go treasure hunting today."

Then the raven gave her an equally long look before it launched into the sky and released a loud cry.

Chapter Three

Three hours later, Megan stood on the bow of Nathan's hundred foot fully equipped Luxury Steel Dive Yacht. She should have known he wouldn't go small. Her sisters, mortified that she agreed to go anywhere alone with him, had decided to join her.

Face to the wind, Amber closed her eyes. "Though I'd rather your ex wasn't part of this, I've got to admit it's pretty cool." She opened her eyes and grinned while patting Guardian. "And we've got our girl along too."

"I wasn't giving him a choice about my dog," Megan said. "She goes where I go."

Veronica's narrowed eyes remained pinned on the men below, mainly Nathan, as she zipped up her white down jacket. "Hellishly cold if you ask me." She shook her head. "So Viking treasure off the shores of your house is it." Her sister slanted dubious eyes at Megan. "A little too convenient, wouldn't you say?"

Definitely…if she hadn't found the metal box.

But she had yet to share that with them.

"Viking artifacts have been found throughout New England so it's not an impossible concept," Megan said.

"Maybe." Veronica's eyes swung back to Nathan. "But I don't like the idea of you going diving alone with him."

"We won't be alone."

"Right, a few of *his* men are going with you."

"I wish Sean was here." Amber pouted. "I'd love to see him in his element."

Megan frowned. "His element is captaining a fishing boat, sis. Tad bit different than sailing a million dollar yacht and sipping cocktails before an afternoon dive."

Amber eyed her glass of wine. "Hey, Nathan offered and I needed a little something to keep me calm so I don't push him overboard. And I'm not the one diving, *you* are."

"Hence me not drinking." Not that she would within a hundred yards of Nathan. She wouldn't just push him overboard but chain a few cement blocks to his ankles first.

When he waved that she join him, Megan nodded. "All right ladies, time for me to suit up." She glanced at Amber. "Keep a tight hold on Guardian's leash or she'll jump in after me."

Amber nodded. "Of course, sis. Stay safe, okay?"

Megan nodded.

Veronica's face soured. "I seriously don't like this."

"I'll be fine." Megan patted her on the shoulder. "I've done this plenty of times. I know how to handle myself."

"Oh, I don't doubt that." Veronica nodded at Nathan. "It's his part in all this that worries me."

Megan gave no response but headed down. She didn't particularly like his part in this either but she had no choice. There *was* something below this boat. Megan had sensed it when the raven flew in this direction earlier. Since then the feeling had only grown. And the closer they got to this area, the more intense the feeling became. She suspected once she dove it would only increase.

Nathan nodded below deck. "Your suit's in the cabin."

The water temperature was below sixty degrees Fahrenheit so she'd be wearing more than usual when diving. Having had plenty of practice, it didn't take her long to get on the thicker-than-usual full bodysuit with wrist and ankle seals. Megan had made sure she'd tucked the small Viking stone in her cleavage. By the time she joined Nathan again he and two others were already geared up. She donned the rest of her suit including a mask, fins, BCD, *buoyancy control device*, weight system, dive light, regulator, tank and several other items.

As Megan came alongside the guys on the backboard she eyed the sky out of habit. The winds had shifted and the water was choppier than it had been earlier. Though the sun still glittered icy gold off the steel blue sea, the Nor'easter would be coming in sooner than forecasted.

Nathan and the others wasted no time but slid off and vanished beneath the water.

Megan twisted and gave a final wave to her sisters on the upper deck before she followed. Though her excitement grew, she kept a cool head, breathing steady as she sank beneath the Atlantic. As it turned out, this location was fairly deep considering its proximity to the shore. They'd be going down a little less than eighty feet which was twenty feet or so shy of what would be considered a more dangerous deep dive.

It was nearly noon so the sun was at the best angle to provide visibility. The storm the night before had stirred up the sea but luckily they were dealing with more of a rock bottom at this distance out. Had they gone further it would have turned to mud and visibility would lower sharply. But they weren't here to admire the underwater landscape.

They were here for treasure.

Megan followed the men and snapped on her dive light about halfway down. Who would have ever thought she'd be trailing her ex-husband into the depths of the ocean to pursue more knowledge of another man. Because she was downright eager at this point...she wanted, no *needed*, to find more connections to Naðr Véurr.

Nearly to the bottom, she slowed when Nathan came alongside and nodded for her to follow. The waters were pretty dark at this depth but her light made navigation fairly easy. There was a rocky outcrop on the bottom that the other two were already swimming around. Though Megan asked, Nathan had told her nothing of what to expect down here except that it was profound. She knew there would be no remnants of a ship. Even buried beneath a silt or sandy ocean floor, wood was unlikely to remain intact much over a century.

Yet something *was* down here.

Roughly strewn, some sort of debris was scattered along the rock crevices. Upon closer inspection she realized it was mainly metal pieces. Her eyes widened when she shone her light down. These were remnants of Viking weapons! Double edged blades, broad leafed iron spears, and crescent shaped axe blades amongst other deadly metal devices. But that's not what had her blinking several times in disbelief. Damn it. These weapons lacked any signs of corrosion which was downright impossible.

She'd been duped.

Or better yet Nathan had.

But he was too smart for this bullshit. So she went back to the theory of being duped. But by *him*. Bastard. She should have known better. What they viewed was clearly dumped here recently by whomever. Based on the gleam of the weapons and wooden handles attached to most of them, it wasn't all that long ago either.

Megan almost rolled her eyes as the other divers gathered up some of the weapons. Were these guys a bunch of idiots? Unlikely. No, this was obviously all part of Nathan's elaborate hoax. Yet he wasn't looking at her with a triumphant gleam in his eyes. Instead, he kept swimming, shining his light as if looking for something.

She was just about to call it quits when a strange sensation rolled through her, an almost indefinable feeling of anticipation. Shortly thereafter, a pulse of water pressure rippled over her. It was almost what one would feel far closer to the surface when a good sized wave passed above. In fact, the water even pushed her forward until she saw around the next bend of rocks.

Megan aimed her light down and squinted.

What the hell?

Though she knew it was against diver protocol, she didn't bother to let Nathan know where she was going as she swam downward, eyes growing wider and wider until she stopped, stunned. Again, she blinked several times. She couldn't be seeing clearly. But then maybe this explained the well-preserved weaponry.

Close enough that she could already see the dragon-headed prow was...a Viking longship?

Megan swam down the remaining distance and started traveling alongside the boat. It was in amazingly good condition, its sail recently torn and billowing in the water. Her heart thudded heavily as she did her best to get measurements. By the time she made it to the stern, her breathing was irregular. Larger than any recorded in history, this thing was over one hundred and thirty feet long and not only gorgeously made but remarkably preserved. Even the intricate Nordic carvings lining the hull were fresh and visible.

For all appearances, this ship had gone down days ago if that.

Frenchman Bay and all its many harbors reported constantly on the latest news. Anyone sailing a ship like this would've been the talk of not only Maine and the Eastern seaboard but the entire United States if not worldwide. Every historical nautical society worth a grain of salt would have reported this the moment it hit water. In all honesty, a ship this well-made *might* have sailed here from Scandinavia.

If it had the right crew and more importantly the right captain.

Where did that thought come from? Obviously that wasn't the case with this boat. News outlets would have covered such an undertaking. Her mind was spinning and her breath so irregular that Megan knew she had to get a grip fast. She was nearly eighty feet down and depending on an oxygen tank. Overexcitement had no place here. So she carefully made her way back to the prow, studying the construction as she went.

Absolutely astounding.

As research suggested, the ship had no big, vertical keel. That meant this piece of perfection was highly maneuverable and could easily penetrate shallow surf. A chill went through her as she thought of Amber's picture. This particular ship could easily navigate close to her house. If chuckling was an option she would have. There was no way around it, if this thing came anywhere near her house she would have known and snapped a ton of pictures. She could only imagine how impressive it would have looked on the horizon.

But wow if it didn't look *exactly* like the ship her sister had drawn.

Megan checked her oxygen level. Pretty soon she'd have to head back up. She turned and looked around. No sign of Nathan and his men. Though she knew better, she was rather enjoying this time alone with such a beautiful ship. She didn't care if it was a replica or lying in the graveyard of the Atlantic, there was a certain peace here. Nathan and his team would find her soon enough.

So she continued toward the bow, smiling as she drifted alongside the monstrous billowing square sail. Now *this* was the life. Sure, looking up at this sail on the open seas would likely be more exhilarating but there was a haunting beauty in seeing it in the dark depths and privacy of the ocean's floor. Yet no sooner did she think it than an overwhelming sadness filled her. People had built this beauty and clearly loved it as much as Megan did her own small Viking boat. They'd labored and adored, because nothing this grand was built without a great deal of pride and meticulousness.

Then there were the men who sailed her.

Though Megan knew they'd been modern day sailors she could only envision Vikings of the past navigating this great beauty through the Norwegian Sea then past the north of Scotland and Ireland into the riotous and unpredictable waters of the Atlantic. They'd be sea weathering men made of steel and more honor than most guys possessed in one testicle nowadays.

Naðr Véurr.

Or as the manuscript said… *King* Naðr Véurr.

Megan stopped at the dragon-headed prow and turned back. As she looked down the length of the ship it almost seemed a dull whitish glow lit everything. This allowed her to see clear to the end as its sail billowed beneath the black sea.

This was a ship that could conquer any ocean.

This was a ship that could be captained by Naðr Véurr.

She gripped the prow as an unexpected rush of lust tore through her and breathing once more increased. Christ, this was about the last place she should be having erotic thoughts. But she was. And they were far more intense than any before. Megan slowly traveled down the long length of the prow. Thoughts of what she'd read in the manuscript surfaced as readily as bubbles from her oxygen tank.

Naðr had dragon blood in him.

He could shift into a dragon.

History told that the dragon or serpent head on the prow was typically detachable. Superstitious, Vikings believed that the head would frighten away sea monsters. They'd then remove the head when approaching land so they didn't scare off friendly spirits.

But not this ship.

Wherever it went, so too did its dragon.

Megan stopped, ran her hand along the dragon-prow neck, closed her eyes and drifted down. There was no such thing as dragons. That part of Naðr was purely fictional. The stone nestled between her breasts, *that* was real…and somehow most definitely part of him.

When her feet at last hit the ship's floor, she opened her eyes. It was as impressive if not more so from this angle. Megan tilted back her head and looked up at the mast and what looked to be about thirty-eight hundred square feet of sail. God, what had this looked like above water as it crested waves with the sun bursting over it?

She sunk until she sat at the prow's base and simply stared in awe. How many men had oared this ship? Better yet, how many knots did she travel with the right wind? Yet even as Megan stared, the white light faded away. She shook her head but remained calm. To see the ship in its entirety in this darkness shouldn't have been possible to begin with.

Flipping the dive light into her face, she briefly focused on its glow before looking away. She knew damn well that if a ship sunk to this depth it'd more than likely land on its side not belly up as though intent to keep on sailing. Though entirely mesmerized by the ship she was beginning to comprehend its very absurdity.

Megan took a deep breath. It was time to surface and clear her head. Would she tell them about this ship? Not if they didn't mention it. But her tank was getting low and it was time to go. She set her hand down to push off but met with something that rolled away from her. Curious, she angled her light down.

It was a metal cylinder.

About the circumference of her arm and maybe a foot long, it was, like the ship, covered in Nordic symbols. Megan picked it up and studied both ends. It was tightly sealed and obviously encased something. Well then, this would be *her* treasure this time down.

The ship?

Her secret until she found out exactly how much Nathan knew.

Tucking the cylinder under her arm, Megan launched upwards into the darkness. Though it hurt to leave such a ship behind, she was eager to see what she carried. She didn't know how she knew, but there was something very important in this. Yet even as she worked toward the surface a part of her speculated it was likely a log kept by the modern day sailors who'd lost this vessel to the sea.

But what if it was something more?

What if it had to do with her Viking king?

Megan stopped swimming for a second and drifted in the sunlit waters beneath the surface. When had she started thinking of Naðr Véurr as *her* Viking king? She swallowed and looked down into the darkness and the peace that it had offered. No, Megan, there was no Viking king down there…she looked up…nor there. She clenched the metal tube tighter as she surfaced the water. This was hers and nobody would look inside it before her. Intent to say as much when she boarded the yacht, Megan tore off her mask and gulped fresh air as she looked at the boat.

Or not.

Treading water, she turned a few times. Where was Nathan's yacht? Better yet…why was there a mountainous shoreline? She licked her lips. When a splash resounded behind her she turned. Guardian? Crap! Her dog was swimming toward her. What was going on? Where was the boat and why was Guardian out here with her?

Happy face intact, Guardian swum to her but Megan navigated her in circles around her. *Hell.* They were way too far offshore and a dog, never mind a human, had only so much strength to stay afloat in waters that were slightly colder than what they'd been before. If that wasn't bad enough, she'd somehow managed to tear her wetsuit. But she couldn't worry about that right now.

Megan stopped over thinking and went into survival mode for them both. She lost the oxygen tank as well as all extra gear, kept the wet suit and swam fast, saying, "Come on my wolfy girl, let's race!"

Whenever she used the command word 'wolfy,' Guardian knew it was genuine competition time. 'Wolfy' was her go word. It meant act fast and think twice as fast. It meant listen. So when Megan started swimming not recreationally but professionally, counting between breaths, Guardian would smooth sail too. She even tossed aside the cylinder. It would only slow her down. They were out *way* too far in waters that would cripple a dog fast and swimming swiftly might be her dog's only hope. Good thing Guardian was her world beyond boat building and she'd trained her well or they both might be screwed right now.

Guardian could have outpaced her quickly but kept with her. She could have, *should have*, left Megan behind but she wouldn't. And that made Megan swim all that much harder. She'd be damned if her dog died trying to save her. But it wouldn't go that way. If Guardian sank, so would she.

Megan tuned out the fact her surroundings made no sense and swam for Guardian's life.

They were only a few hundred feet out when her dog's pace changed and she slowed, nose just above the heavier swell of waves as they drew closer to the shore. So Megan started the pep talk first. "Let's go girl. You can do it!"

Every muscle in her body burned at this point so she could only imagine what her dog was feeling. When Guardian slowed more and more, her desperate eyes on Megan, she paced alongside, command sharper. "Come on, wolfy girl. Let's go!"

Guardian got a little extra pep but it didn't last long. The waves were getting rougher and rougher to handle especially since they were already exhausted.

It was best for them both that she remain stern and keep swimming. Be a good trainer…and friend. So Megan kept going. "Now or never, wolfy girl. Let's do this!"

This seemed to give Guardian renewed strength.

Until it didn't.

When she looked back her dog was plunking her paws down in the waves, desperate to keep up, wild eyes locked on Megan, before a big wave caught her and pulled her under. The moment she saw her dog go down everything went numb.

Hell no.

She wouldn't leave her behind.

The tear in her wetsuit had grown. Now it was a hindrance that would likely slow her down beneath the water. Though hard as heck, she managed to get out of the thing faster than most. With limited time before hypothermia set in, she dove.

Arms and legs pumping hard, she pushed down into the murky depths of the wave-churned water. The sea was getting far rougher. Still, she kicked hard and ignored the sting in her eyes as she searched for Guardian. She *had* to be here somewhere.

Yet the more she tried to swim, the more the waves tumbled her.

She was going to lose her dog.

But there was no way Megan would surface until she had her. So she searched and searched, desperate. Even when her lungs burned and her vision started to dim, she searched. But there was no sign of her and the panic she refused to acknowledge was surfacing.

Suddenly, an arm grabbed her around the waist and started pulling her. Megan tried to flail against whoever held her but she'd grown too weak. By the time she was dragged onto the shore she had no fight left in her and flopped down on the grainy dirt. Sea water stung her eyes so badly the world was a blur.

"I'm coming lass," a man's voice said as it grew further away, as if heading back for the ocean.

Lass? Megan coughed out some water and rubbed the water from her eyes as she struggled to sit. Her words were a weak croak. "My dog. *Please.*"

The world swayed and tilted but slowly righted itself as a woman's voice came closer. "I've got the wolf."

Wolf? A surge of hope shot through her as Megan's vision cleared. Guardian!

"Thank you," she said hoarsely as Guardian was set down beside her. Though clearly weakened and bedraggled, her dog was breathing. She stroked her fur and whispered reassurances in her ear.

Megan was about to thank whomever had saved them but the words died on her lips. Was there some sort of medieval costume fair going on in the area? There *had* to be. With pale blond hair sporting numerous small braids, the woman wore a long linen dress ripped off at the knees. She suspected it was done to make swimming easier. And while she knew the woman's clothing wasn't right, it was the man's appearance that had her completely confused.

Bare-chested, he wore nothing but…a kilt?

Clearly seeing her confusion, he crouched and nodded. "I'm Valan." Then he gestured toward the woman. "That's Meyla. She saved your wolf." Then he nodded at Guardian. "She's tired now but do we need to worry about her attacking once she gains strength?"

Megan shook her head and had to listen closely to understand because his brogue was so thick. Was there a Scottish festival in the area then? No. She would have heard about it. Regardless, she was grateful if nothing else so she looked at Meyla. "Thank you so much." Then her eyes returned to Valan with his dark hair and notably good looks. "And thank you for saving my life."

They nodded and Meyla wrapped a fur over her shoulders. Beyond numb and more worried about Guardian than anything else, she'd forgotten she wore nothing but a one piece black bathing suit. A moment of panic went through her. The stone. She pressed her hand against her chest. *Phew.* It was still there.

She was about to thank Meyla for the fur when her eyes were ensnared by the horizon.

Better yet, what was *on* the horizon.

A ship.

But not just any ship. She rubbed her eyes and blinked several times. She *had* to be seeing things. Because what was sailing inland was truly impossible, truly baffling…

The same monstrous Viking longship she'd just left behind at the bottom of the Atlantic.

Valan's eyes turned to the ocean. "Och, he's back."

"What the hell's going on," Megan said, so confused she could barely think straight. "I just saw…I mean…on the seafloor…how is that ship…"

"Enough." Meyla's tone changed entirely from moments before. "We need to get back. Father will be expecting me."

Huh? Father will be expecting her? That ship must have been another built alongside the first. And she must have drifted a ways north in Maine to a more mountainous area. But even Megan knew that nothing along Maine's coast looked like what she'd witnessed when she first surfaced from the ocean. She grew more and more stunned as she tried to make sense of everything.

Maybe she was in some sort of shock induced coma.

Maybe she'd died beneath the water and this came after death.

But none of it really mattered in the least when Valan muttered his next words...

"Aye, Meyla, we *must* get back. After all, King Naðr Véurr has returned."

Chapter Four

Scandinavia
877 A.D.

"Naðr Véurr," she whispered, heart thundering in her chest as she gazed at the ship angling in toward the shore. "Impossible."

But had she not just met a woman named Meyla? A woman's name that had, in fact, been mentioned in the manuscript as being the Viking king's daughter? Megan tried her best not to hyperventilate.

"She sounds like your futuristic friends from Scotland," Meyla said to Valan as she helped Megan stand.

"Aye," Valan said, but his scowling expression remained locked on the ship.

Right. Scotland. The main setting for the manuscript. This was getting crazier by the moment but she made no mention of it. Besides, she didn't recall coming across the name Valan. But then again, pages *were* missing from the book.

Megan did her best to stand though her legs shook. While her muscle weakness was assuredly from her strenuous swim, she knew it had every bit as much to do with information overload and downright disbelief.

"I need answers," she said, voice as firm as she could manage. "Now."

Meyla cocked a brow at her as she wrapped a fur over her shoulders. "You think to demand answers?"

Megan squared off with the other woman. Well, really more of a teenager. Eighteen or nineteen max based on her appearance.

Yes, Megan was frightened but it wasn't the first time she'd felt this way. Too many times she'd gone up against powerful people in order to get what she wanted. The only difference now was that she didn't have the facts to make any sort of assessment let alone argument.

Somehow she'd gone adrift and wasn't where she belonged, so needed answers. Yet she wasn't about being overly confrontational without explaining her circumstances. "I went on a diving expedition off the coast of Winter Harbor earlier today. When I surfaced I was

45

here which is obviously not where I started. I need to know where in Maine I am...please."

Meyla's eyes had narrowed more and more as Megan spoke. When her answer came it was almost condescending. "Do you not know then that you've traveled through time?"

Megan opened her mouth to speak then snapped it shut. *What?*

"We need to go," Valan said. "We'll work this out back at the fortress, aye?"

Megan couldn't help but chuckle. "Fortress?" But then again, she was watching a Viking longship cruise ever closer. So whatever sort of dream she was having remained consistent...save a Scotsman being here. But that was the least of her concerns.

Meyla eyed Megan for another long moment before she started walking with Valan. "Keep your wolf well tamed or her fur will be put to good use."

Megan stared after them as they strode along the shore. Maybe she'd gone about asking for information wrongly because clearly none would be offered. Or at least she thought as much until Valan stopped at a small rocky outcrop and pulled something from a satchel. He held out a pair of odd looking leather shoes. "Put these on. When we get to the village dinnae make any eye contact and keep your cloak closed or ye'll end up on your back with your legs spread."

Again she was speechless. Was he serious?

Meyla's blue eyes met hers, grim expression unwavering. "I'll give you honesty. Make of it what you will because I've no further time to explain right now. This isn't the first time Valan and I have dealt with your sort so I can tell you with certainty that you've traveled back in time. You're in ninth century Scandinavia."

Meyla paused and eyed Megan before continuing. "My guess is things are vastly different here than where you come from but only one bit of knowledge is important for you to remember. My father, Naðr Véurr, is king of this region and he's been in a foul mood lately. Or at least he was before setting sail two fortnights ago. So though you are with me do your best to fade into the background." Then her eyes again flickered up and down Megan. "Though it'll likely be impossible with your appearance."

Megan imagined quite a few expressions crossed her face at that moment. Was this girl serious? But she wasn't about being passive

46

and sitting back in the face of change so said, "Let me again say how grateful I am that you saved my dog. That said, are you out of your ever loving mind? Number one, don't ever threaten my dog again. Number two, you both have taken this reenactment too far. Number three, which sort of makes your reenactment fairly obvious…you're speaking English. If you were from ninth century Scandinavia, you'd speak Norse, would you not?"

"Again, I don't have time to explain this to her." Meyla started striding along the shore again, words thrown into the wind. "We're not speaking the same language. I'd guess we understand one another because of the stone in your cleavage."

Megan stopped, stunned as the two continued walking. There was no doubt that Valan had pulled her from the ocean and seeing the stone through her suit was possible. But how did Meyla know that? When Guardian whined, she ruffled her head and said softly, "It's okay, girl. At least as okay as it's going to get for now."

One thing was certain, she could stand out here dressed as she was on a shore so completely unfamiliar or she could follow these strangers. Never a fool, Megan slid on the shoes, wrapped the cloak tighter around her and started walking. Though she tried to analyze the towering mountains and thick spruce forest to her left, her eyes were almost magnetically drawn to the ship drawing closer and closer on her right.

When the sun moved in and out of fast moving clouds, it rippled shadows across the sea, tossing the ship in and out of light. As sea salt and wind brushed her cheeks, so too did it push the big square sail billowing over the ship. It was as mesmerizing as she imagined it. The idea that Naðr actually captained such a sight made her steps grow heavier and her mouth turn dry.

What if she *had* somehow traveled back in time?

Honestly, how else could she explain this?

But Megan tried to deal in logic before all else so tore her gaze from the ship and kept her eyes on her surroundings. Good thing because they'd just rounded the bend and what appeared before her made Megan stop short and gasp. Good sized and sweeping, a bay was back-dropped by sharp mountains steeped in white clouds and what was most definitely a Viking ring fortress with ramparts, otherwise known as *Trelleborgs*.

At least ten long docks stretched out beside large boathouses. A sizeable fleet of ships were already at port including numerous broader based *Knarrs,* or ocean-going cargo vessels. Floating alongside were *Byrding* ships, those designed for lighter cargo. Then there were three types of longships including *Snekkes, Drekkars,* and *Skeids* that ranged in size from seventy to ninety feet long each. Then of course there were docks upon docks of smaller boats meant for everyday life, mainly fishing.

Megan had never seen such an astounding display of historical ships so sunk to her haunches and stared. Guardian sat next to her and waited patiently. She patted her dog's head absently, dumbfounded. "I know this'll sound cliché but I don't think we're in Kansas anymore, Toto. If anything, with Viking ships like this, we've been dropped into my idea of Heaven."

"If ye dinnae stay with us, ye will find yourself in a verra bad position." Valan stopped and gave her a pointed look with his obsidian eyes. "And ye dinnae want to do such here, lass."

Right, so said the Scotsman who saved her in Viking waters. Forget Toto and Heaven, she'd landed square in Alice's Wonderland. Megan nodded and followed, deciding it best to keep using training commands when it came to Guardian. "Heel, wolfy girl."

Bless her dog, she listened. It was then that Megan truly took in the enormity of her situation. They were walking into a large village vastly different than what existed at home. Good thing she had a passion for Viking history or she'd be clueless. But even then, books didn't do much justice to what she witnessed.

A thriving community existed beyond the fortress with endless carts set up where people sold their wares. Megan couldn't process all that unfolded around her. In every sense of what she'd researched this *was* a Viking community. Women wore long linen dresses with woolen tunics, much like aprons, and a belt around their waists.

And the men? Jesus, if this was some sort of a festival it catered to a rugged bunch. More often than not, they were tall, bearded, well-muscled and weatherworn. They wore long woolen shirts, cloth trousers and sturdy leather boots. Though the colors and styles varied, they mostly wore sleeved jerkins or a three-quarter coat with a belt.

The air smelled of commerce. Seafood and smoke. Brine and sweat. Baked goods and breads. Altogether, the odor that permeated the air wasn't all that bad, just busy and different. Back home, if she'd gone into a place this congested it would smell of car exhaust, perfumes, colognes and far more varied foods.

Valan took her elbow and steered her through the crowd. "This way."

Megan was again thankful for all the hours she'd spent training Guardian because her girl never left her side. That said a lot considering all the smells that *had* to be drawing her in every direction. Many cast an eye at her dog but none seemed all that fazed. It appeared 'wolves' didn't bother Vikings all that much.

Or at least not this group.

If anything, the glances thrown their way were by men checking out Megan. They weren't discreet in the least with their straightforward appraisals and obvious approval. Good thing her hair was still tied back or she'd likely draw more attention than she could handle. Valan muttered under his breath and kept her close.

The crowd grew thicker as they made their way. Megan wasn't surprised in the least when they arrived at the edge of the crowd and stepped onto one of the docks. Her Viking longship was coming into harbor. At least that's what she was calling it because...what else would it be to her?

Damn, was it *beautiful*.

Most were stopped at the foot of the docks but not Meyla and Valan it seemed...and her. Yet where Meyla continued toward the ship, Valan and Megan only walked out a short ways then stopped. His voice was low. "We go no further, lass."

Megan was fine with that. As it was, she'd just been given a front row seat to history. Her mouth fell open a fraction as the ship came into port. Its sail had been lowered and the oarsmen were steering her in. She shook her head, impressed with the smooth docking despite the winds and choppy water. After all, these guys were working without the benefit of modern day engines.

The docks became busy as men made to tie off the great ship. Megan watched everything with an avid eye. These men were sailors to the bone and moved with a swift efficiency that she more than appreciated.

When a roar came from the ship, a louder roar echoed all around her. Excitement crackled in the air as three men left the boat and started down the dock. Megan narrowed her eyes as they drew closer.

Oh *hell.*

Tall, muscled, all were too damned good looking no matter the century. But only one gave her an acute case of tunnel vision. The one in the middle. A black fur cloak stretched over his broad shoulders. With a black, leather jerkin and long leather encased legs that led down to heavy boots, he had a confident, easy swagger that ignited hot heat between her thighs.

A searing burn broke over every inch of her skin and she dug her nails into her palms as he drew closer. Wind-blown, shoulder-length black hair brushed the nape of his strong neck and a light beard did nothing to hide his well-sculpted face. Her body started to tremble when he was only halfway down the dock. Clenching her teeth, Megan breathed deeply through her nose. Her need to *smell* his skin was so strong she put her hand on Guardian's head to ground herself.

When had she ever wanted to *smell* a man?

Valan pulled Megan aside as several women were allowed to pass. There was never a more torturous moment than watching the young, beautiful women swarm around him. Like any 'normal' red-blooded pirate, sailor, or *Viking*, who had been out to sea for days would do, all three men linked arms with the women so that they each had one on either side. Megan barely comprehended that the low growl she heard was coming from her own throat until Valan looked at her and shook his head.

Megan cleared her throat and continued to stare at the man approaching.

To look away was impossible.

Suddenly, he stopped. When he did the girls on either arm purred and leaned closer. But it didn't much matter. It almost seemed that he caught a scent on the wind because he leaned his head back slowly, closed his eyes and inhaled.

All went silent.

Megan watched, enthralled by the display. How did one man make so many people go silent in a moment? But somehow she knew deep down inside. A simple *man* couldn't.

But a *king* could.

It felt almost like the shock wave she'd felt eighty feet beneath the Atlantic once more hit her when his eyes turned her way. Megan dug her hands further into Guardian's fur as he untangled from his women and approached. His eyes flickered to Valan then back to her before he stopped.

Holy mother of any god listening was he gorgeous.

Skin darkened by the sun, his face was a masterpiece up close. A little over a foot taller than her, his lips curved so well they'd make a woman stare forever. His jaw line was a fraction off from being square and his eyebrows arched slashes. But none of that compared to his eyes.

They were his *everything*.

A light but bright cobalt blue framed by a bizarre circle of dark blue with flecks of silver, they were so unusual that it *almost* seemed a mirror was behind them. In fact, one nearly got the impression they were looking back at themselves when they looked into this man's eyes. Megan was tempted to look away from his unusual gaze but knew she couldn't…that she never would. He'd captained that Viking longship. Desire pounded through her blood so harshly it took years of dealing with powerful men to keep her body tremble-free and eyes locked with his. Because there could be no doubt…

He was her Viking king.

"Naðr Véurr," she whispered.

And she knew she was right.

Of course he wasn't fazed by his name on a stranger's lips. He'd likely dealt with it before. And unlike most men, he wasn't put off by her unnatural eye color in the least. Rather, he seemed to spend an overly long moment holding her gaze, so much so that she had to work at keeping a neutral face. No easy task considering the ever increasing burn between her thighs that nearly made her bite her lower lip. One thing was for sure, she'd never had such a strong sexual reaction to a man.

He smelled of sea and storms, of dark nights and even darker pleasures.

Thump. Thump. Thump.

Heck, was her heart going to beat out of her chest?

Megan worked at breathing evenly as though she was diving and never let go of his gaze. For a split second, she thought he sensed her nervousness. And it seemed she might be right.

His hand scooped beneath her cloak so fast that she made a small audible sound. Was he going to tear her cloak away? Because based on what she knew of Vikings that might just make sense. Instead, his palm pressed against the delicate flesh of her upper chest and warmth spread through her. Not arousal at first but…a sense of peace. The pain caused from the difficult swim vanished. And though he'd clearly done something soothing, her heart continued to hammer.

Then, naturally, arousal flared like wildfire when the tips of his fingers dusted her cleavage before he pulled his hand back. Megan knew that at some point she should have slapped this man's hands away but she never did, *couldn't*. There was something about his touch that was…unavoidable.

"She's with me, father," Meyla said from behind him.

Megan pressed her teeth together and swallowed. Then she was right. This was the man who had haunted her for almost a year.

His eyes never left hers as he responded, his deep voice a rumble that did nothing to help the raging inferno below. "Then she should *be* with you, Meyla. Not left with a traitor to defend her."

So that explained Valan's less than happy response to Naðr arriving. But wow, what kind of story was behind a Viking king hating a Scotsman but allowing him around his daughter? An interesting one she imagined.

Naðr's gaze finally left hers only to travel slowly over her features, lingering on her lips overly long before traveling down her body. Megan felt every slow inch of his perusal as if his hands touched where he looked. And while she'd admit to being on fire because of his proximity and languid visual roaming of her fur covered body, she wasn't used to being looked at like this without at least an introduction.

So she held out a hand to shake. "I'm Megan. And you are?"

The corner of his lips inched up slowly and a surprising glint of mischief lit his eyes. "*I'm* looking forward to seeing you with less clothing." Naðr took her hand. His rough thumb swept gently over the clattering pulse beneath the thin skin of the underside of her wrist. Enough to send sparks raging through her veins and shudders through her body. The mischief in his eyes turned to triumph. "Ah, you would like that as well."

Arrogance! But had she truly expected anything less? "I'd like you to give your name in return."

Naðr pulled his hand away, purposefully running his thumb over her palm and his fingers over the backside of her hand. The intimate gesture was made all that more profound by the way his eyes once more locked on hers. If she didn't know better, he was challenging her to show no response.

So Megan gritted her teeth and kept her expression blank. She'd say nothing more until he did. And though she knew the entire shoreline had gone silent and despite her body's reaction to him, she remained still…waiting.

Amusement flickered within his azure gaze before he softly murmured, "Why ask a question you already know the answer to."

Then he turned away, made a gesture to all and said, "I've been too long at sea. Time to drink!"

The second he walked in the other direction she released a long exhale and willed away body tremors. Damn, he looked as good walking away as he had coming. Megan again eyed his broad shoulders and wished he wasn't wearing a cloak so she could see his leather-clad backside better. Naðr flung his arms around the shoulders of the two big men waiting for him and walked toward the fortress with a trail of women following.

Valan shook his head. "Looks like you made an impression."

Megan glanced at the Scotsman as she patted Guardian. Meyla had already joined the three Vikings mainly because the blond turned back and threw her over his shoulder. Laughing, Naðr's daughter pounded him on the back as they vanished into the crowd.

"So I just met the Viking king," Meyla said. "Who are the two guys with him?"

"His brothers." Valan urged her to follow. "Raknar 'the hunter', the uncle with Meyla over his shoulder, is next to become king unless Naðr is killed by someone else. Kol 'the lucky' is the youngest brother."

"So they all have the last name Véurr?"

Valan snorted. "Nay, lass. Véurr is just part of the name they call the king. Sigdir is their family title. It means victory bringer."

He shook his head. "'Tis all bloody different than how we Scots name things."

Right. Megan understood a little bit about Viking titles. "So names such as 'the hunter' and 'the lucky' were earned." She slanted her eyes at Valan. "So does Naðr Véurr have a nickname?"

"Aye," Valan said as though surprised she needed to ask. "The bold."

Of course. What else would it be? Valan kept her close as they filtered through the crowd, mainly because far too many big men gawked at her. Though she should probably be concerned, she was far more interested in other things. "No offense but I'm too curious…why does the king call you a traitor though you're obviously privileged enough to be around his daughter?"

A little light lit Valan's eyes and a surprising touch of reverence deepened his voice. "Because Meyla and I intend to be wed."

"Oh." Megan couldn't help but grin as she thought about the father he had to contend with. "Good luck with that."

"Aye," Valan quipped. "More luck than I likely have."

Though astounded by her surroundings as they entered the inner compound, she couldn't help but say, "Not to be rude but I don't get how you're even here." Not that he couldn't clearly hold his own with his muscled build and height nearly as tall as the king. "A Scotsman in ninth century Scandinavia, if that's truly where I am. It makes no sense."

His brows rose. "Do you actually still doubt you've traveled back in time?"

Megan nodded then shook her head. "Honestly, it's easier for me to pretend otherwise or else I might not be functioning right now." She sighed and ground her jaw. "Definitely *that* scary."

"Aye." His voice was surprisingly compassionate. "Keep with whatever thoughts make ye strongest then, lass. Let the rest come as it will."

Hundreds of houses fanned out before her as they walked along a road down into the encampment. With long slanted roofs nearly touching the ground, they were exactly as history books depicted. Guardian kept pace alongside, never detouring for a moment. "So if I was to give into this reality and admit I've traveled back in time, is it safe to say you did the same?"

Valan wrapped his arm around her lower back and halfway unsheathed his sword as two men openly gawked at her, their eyes lewd as they passed. "Aye, 'tis safe to say as much. I traveled here from Scotland. The year was 1254."

"*Really?*"

"Aye." He put some distance between them once the threat passed, murmuring under his breath, "Ye'd think if Naðr has an interest in ye he'd see ye escorted safely."

Yeah right. "Assuming he had an interest."

"Och, he has an interest all right," Valan muttered. "But he likes to play his games."

"Typical man," she said, not overly concerned with Naðr's actions.

"Not all men are like that." Valan narrowed his eyes on more guys as they passed. "Had a highlander desired ye, ye'd be protected right now. Not walking with a lad he disliked."

While she got where Valan was coming from, something told her Naðr's games were more for show than anything else. If he wanted someone protected, they would be. Most likely by eyes and ears that no one saw. A man like she'd just met on the docks didn't come into all she saw around her by being less than vigilant.

"Well, I guess our Viking king isn't all that worried about me," Megan said, not entirely above wishing she had a knife in her hand. She'd taken a few self-defense classes. Though she knew most of the men walking past would have her down in an instant, she'd give them a good nick or two first.

Valan was about to respond when Kol, Naðr's youngest brother, appeared out of nowhere and strolled alongside her. Though as tall as the king, his expression was far less intense upon greeting. In fact, he acted as though he'd known her for years as he eyed her up and down.

Megan didn't know what to make of him as his darker than dark chocolate eyes assessed her with a little bit too much appreciation. He was remarkably handsome but in a different way than his brother. Where Naðr was fierce with an edge of mock humor, Kol almost seemed to have a charming air about him. When he remained silent, she said, "Can I help you?"

After a stretch of silence, Valan grumbled, "You're not your brother. Just speak already."

A low chuckle came from his throat before Kol didn't just speak but wrapped an arm around her shoulders and pulled her close, lips curving up. "I never could pull off the silent treatment like *The Bold*." His merry eyes hid behind thick black lashes as he peered down. "*Beiskaldi*, you're beautiful."

Valan ground his jaw. "Dinnae call her that, aye?"

"Call her what?" Kol said a little too innocently as he steered her along.

Megan stopped short and pulled free from him, eyes narrowed. "Not sure we know each other well enough for your arm to be around me."

Kol smirked, clearly enjoying her defiance. "Probably not." He shrugged. "Sorry." Then he eyed her up and down again. "But you *are* beautiful."

"She's bonnie enough." Valan's eyes cut to Kol. "And I'd guess if you're here now 'tis because your brother wants her watched over and *not* touched."

The Viking made an indiscernible sound and nodded toward what was definitely the main holding. "I'm here not there drinking like I should be." He started walking. "Come then."

Valan gave her a small nod as they continued and Megan realized that no matter where she was now, this Scotsman was an ally. As they trailed Kol she leaned close and asked softly, "What does *beiskaldi* mean?"

He shook his head. "Ye dinnae want to know."

But this brought her to another thing she'd been wondering about. "Meyla mentioned that the stone I carried helped me to understand these people. How? And why do words like *beiskaldi* slip through translation?"

The Scotsman didn't quite meet her eyes. "Let's just say that whatever magic is at work, the stone must keep certain words from touching your ears."

"Yeah, got that. Why?"

Valan gave a small shrug of his shoulder, uncomfortable. "'Tis likely because they are words that are unsavory."

Unsavory? "You mean like swears?"

When Valan looked at her confused, she rethought her explanation. "Like curses?"

He nodded. "Aye, precisely."

Naðr's brother had already sworn at her? Real nice. "Again, what does *beiskaldi* mean?*"*

"He's young and foolish," Valan explained.

"Not *that* young," she said. "I'd put him in his mid to late twenties."

But it seemed their talk was done as they approached the massive building. Built in a similar fashion to its smaller predecessors, tall wooden railings led to the inner courtyard. Yet unlike the houses built of *wattle*, or woven sticks, covered with mud to keep out the wind and rain, this main building had been constructed of stone. Talk of cursing vanished as she took in the scale of the building from this angle. What would it look like from the side? Her guess was exceptionally long.

"They dinnae do castles here," Valan mentioned as they followed Kol.

Castles? No. Something far better and more suited to the environment. But she knew she was prejudiced. After all, she wasn't ignorant when it came to Vikings. Or should she say, unstudied.

"Though smaller, there are good sized cottages through the backside of this for Naðr, Meyla and his brothers," Valan said. "That we're being led here means that Meyla is keeping you with her."

Well thank God for small favors. Megan almost rolled her eyes. "Then where *is* Meyla?"

"No doubt being chastised by her father once more for desiring me."

"Right. The whole Viking girl falls in love with the Scotsman from another time thing." Megan couldn't help but grin. "I'd almost feel bad for you if I wasn't here too with no real purpose or way to get home."

She had no choice but to play the part of a woman who had traveled through time…right?

"Och, me thinks if you're here then ye've a purpose, lass."

Megan couldn't stop grinning despite her dire circumstances. "And what is that? To be sworn at by the natives?"

Valan offered a crooked grin in return. "Try being in love with the king's daughter."

Yeah, *that* had to suck.

Yet talk of Naðr made her think about how good-looking he was. "So how old was he when he had her, twelve?"

"Meyla's nineteen winters so nay, he was fifteen," Valan said as though it was nothing.

But then kids were born to fifteen year old mothers back home so it wasn't such a far-fetched idea, just too darned young. Then again, this was the ninth century so fifteen was prime time for child bearing.

"So Naðr Véurr is thirty-four?"

Valan thought about it for a moment before nodding. "Aye, must be."

Megan put a hand on her hip and grinned at Valan. "So you're sorta robbin' the cradle with Meyla, eh?"

"Robbing the cradle?"

"Going after a younger woman?" She eyed him. "Because I'd put us close to the same age."

"I'm twenty-nine winters," Valan said, confused. "Ten winters is a common age difference."

Megan only grinned and nodded. Of course it was. "So in this day and age I'm ancient, huh?"

Valan's expression grew guarded and she almost laughed. No matter the century, men knew better than to comment on a woman's age.

"The king took notice of you," he said carefully. "That says something."

It was impossible not to chuckle at his safe answer. "I'm not sure I want it to *say* anything."

She was about to *say* more, just to get a rise out of Valan, when a young boy approached. His blue eyes were cautious but reverent. "I'm Heid..d..drek," he stuttered, gaze tossed between her and Guardian. "M..my k..king wants me t..to see to your w…wolf."

Megan's heart warmed to Heidrek the instant he looked at Guardian with adoration. But she was worried about letting her dog out of her sight. Unsure, she said, "Nice to meet you, Heidrek. I'm Megan. Where will you take my wolf?"

Heidrek pointed at a building behind her before once more meeting her eyes. "J..just over th...there."

The building was close and like all the others clean and busy. But releasing her dog to a stranger, a boy she didn't know? She wasn't so sure about that. Instead of referring to Valan who likely knew him, she crouched in front of the boy. Young, maybe ten at most, he stood tall, his blond hair sticking up at odd angles. Though tempted to tell him Guardian was a dog, he'd never understand. So she said, "What do you know of caring for a wolf, my friend?"

Heidrek calmed at her easy approach and his pale blue eyes grew remarkably stern. "I k..know it's a g..good wolf. You can s..see it in its e..eyes."

Megan quirked her lip and nodded, voice soft. "You're right. You can." She took his hand and smiled. "Do you often care for stray wolves?"

First a nod then a shake of his head before he declared, "They like f..food and w..water and to talk. Then w..we curl up together a..and sleep."

She nodded. Before Megan could say a word her dog smiled and licked Heidrek's hand. Smiling in return, he patted her. The next thing she knew her pooch was sidling up alongside the boy, swishing her tail. Grinning, Megan stood. It seemed a friendship had just been born.

Still.

This was her dog.

As if Heidrek understood the gravity of her uncertainty he lowered his head. "I w..will take g..good care of it."

"Her," Megan said gently. "She's a girl."

Heidrek nodded over and over. "Y..yes. A g..girl."

"Not an it."

He shook his head. "N..not an it."

She trusted this boy. And so did Guardian it seemed.

Megan put a comforting hand on his shoulder and met his eyes. "I'm going to trust you to take care of Guardian, Heidrek." She smiled. "Take good care of her, all right?"

Heidrek nodded so avidly his long bangs flopped in his eyes. "I w..will."

Turning her attention to Guardian, she said, "I won't be gone long, wolfy girl. Keep an eye on our new friend, okay?"

Guardian offered her a quick lick then bounded around Heidrek. Before she knew it the two were chatting and walking in the opposite direction. Watching them, she shook her head.

"'Tis a good friendship forged already," Valan murmured.

Megan stood. "So it seems."

"Come then," came a sharp feminine voice from behind. "Though my betrothed is not overly welcomed it seems *you* are."

Determined to keep a neutral face, she turned to Meyla.

Though she suspected the girl wasn't normally despondent, now she was.

With a flick of her wrist and a come-hither motion, Meyla said, "Let's go then. Time for me to dress you up so that my father can have his way with you."

Chapter Five

Naðr drank from his horn of ale and cheered another good raid.

Though he kept a smile on his face and a woman on his lap, he still fumed over his daughter's choice in men. There were plenty of strapping warriors here but instead she was determined to marry a traitor from the future. That he was Scottish didn't bother him so much, that he was dishonorable *did*.

He'd like to wring Adlin MacLomain's neck for somehow enabling Meyla to meet Valan Hamilton to begin with. But the past he and Adlin shared was a complicated one and now he was stuck with what he had. And it just so happened that it was a Scottish traitor determined to marry his daughter.

There was no doubting it…he'd gotten the raw end of the deal.

"We should have gone further, raided more," his brother Raknar said from his left as he drank from his horn and pushed away any woman advancing on him.

"Agreed," his brother Kol said from his right, trying to pile as many women as possible onto his lap.

Naðr absently stroked the thigh of the woman on his lap and tried to figure out how to turn Meyla's attention from the Scotsman. There was always a way.

"You give Rennir too much room with this move," Raknar muttered.

"To Niflheim with Rennir till we figure out what to do with him," Kol said, grinning before his lips dragged from one woman's mouth to another.

"We should have pushed on," Raknar continued.

Naðr ignored his brothers and kept an eye on the hall. His people were doing well and celebrating heartily. But that's not why he watched everything so closely. No, he was waiting for *her*. He ignored the woman purring impatiently in his ear as he again scanned the room. Where *was* she?

No sooner did he think it for the hundredth time then she appeared.

And his cock at last stirred to life.

Interested, the woman on his lap grabbed at it. He snatched her wrist and shook his head. But he didn't push her away. Instead, he watched the woman called Megan trail his daughter into the crowd. Naðr ran his tongue slowly over the roof of his mouth and eyed her. Never before had he seen a woman quite like her. Rolling his tongue slowly, he tempered his breathing.

She was gorgeous, wild...untamed.

He wanted to taste her from the inside out then start all over again. Her hair was longer than he expected. Somehow, somebody had managed to hold back her blond curls by roping them into a few braids on either side of her face. But though they tried to settle her hair, nothing could help the fiery rebellion in her eyes. Golden spears, they challenged all who dared look her way.

Naðr bit the corner of his lower lip as he leaned forward, imagining it was *her* lower lip beneath his controlling teeth. When had the gods gotten around to making a woman like her and why hadn't they told him about it?

So hard he could barely think, he stared at *Megan*. Though dressed like a proper Viking woman now, he knew far more existed beneath the less-than-revealing clothing. He again inhaled deeply and tried to reign in his need. But it wasn't easy. Naðr wanted to smell her more than he had at the docks. Hell, he wanted to inhale her very core. But then, what man wouldn't want to?

"She's a feisty one," Kol said, his eyes as thoroughly trained on Megan as most of the men's gazes in the hall.

Naðr ignored Kol. His brother knew damn well to keep his hands off her. He was a little surprised to see Raknar watching her as well so said, "It's been too long since you've had a woman, brother."

Raknar ignored the implication, his pale blue eyes contemplative. "Like Valan, she's traveled through time. From where do think she hails?"

Of course they all knew she'd time traveled. Their dragon blood gave them an incomparable second sight. Naðr allowed the woman on his lap to stroke him wherever she liked save his erection. That was being saved for someone else. "Far in the future I'd say."

But Naðr already knew she came from the twenty-first century. He'd felt it in the stone nestled between her remarkably firm breasts. After a slightly longer swig from his horn, he grunted as his pants grew tighter. The woman on his lap smiled knowingly and again went for the goods but froze when he shook his head. Frustrated but pleased to be on his lap regardless, she redirected her attention to his chest.

Tables lined the long outer edges of the room and the center was kept open for dancing. The music was a rhythmic, sultry mix of bodhran drums, falster pipes and lyres. His men had been at sea too long so Naðr was cultivating an environment of pleasure. There was plenty of fresh meat and fish as well as rye and barley breads, cheeses, and a variety of berries and nuts. Naturally, there was an abundant amount of ale and mead too.

Naðr debated his next move.

Though tempted to throw Megan over the nearest table and relieve his arousal, he wouldn't. He might be a lot of things but he didn't take women against their will. When her golden eyes locked with his across the room and a becoming flush stained her cheekbones, Naðr smiled to himself. Maybe he wouldn't have to take her *against* her will after all.

Kol chuckled. "You'll have no trouble conquering that one, brother."

Typically, his brother's lewd comments didn't bother him but something about the statement irked him. It didn't matter in the least if he'd just thought that very thing.

When Meyla glanced his way, Naðr made a gesture that she and Megan join him. As always, the Scotsman hovered around her. The king did his best to ignore how close the two had become. But his daughter knew better than to approach with Valan. Instead, she kept Megan by her side.

Naðr patted the hip of the woman on his lap. "Off with you now."

Though she pouted she knew better than to argue and left.

Expression neutral, he nodded at Meyla and Megan as they approached. Unable to help himself, he made a slow roam down the foreign woman's body. The crème colored dress suited her but as he determined earlier it didn't show off nearly enough of what he wanted to see. His brothers were watching Megan just as avidly. Though her eyes skirted briefly between them Naðr was pleased she seemed drawn to him.

Megan had a cup of ale in her hand and he knew damned well she'd downed most of it before he'd motioned them over. Good. He liked a woman who wasn't afraid to drink. But could she hold her liquor?

"Meyla, take your seat next to Raknar." Naðr's eyes locked with Megan and he patted his knee. "You. Come here."

Megan's eyes widened a fraction then her brows lowered sharply. "The name's Megan not *you*." Then she stood up a little straighter. "And *hell no* I won't sit on your lap."

She thought to defy him? His blood stirred and his cock turned to forged steel. Naðr slowly raised a brow. "Either you come here or I let Kol swing you over his shoulder and bring you here."

"Ah, yes." Megan's eyes narrowed between Naðr and Kol. "The brother who called me *beiskaldi*." This garnered a few hardy laughs. All of which died beneath Naðr's frown. *Beiskaldi?* He wouldn't acknowledge it now but Kol would likely feel Naðr's fist later for that one.

Naðr's words were soft with promise, eyes still locked with hers. "Your choice."

Megan swallowed and kept her eyes narrowed.

Meanwhile, Meyla sat next to Raknar.

After the moment had stretched longer than he would've liked, Naðr nodded at Kol.

When his far-too-eager brother stood, Megan put up a hand, shook her head and frowned. "Fine then."

Naðr nearly licked his lips with anticipation as she made her way around. When she drew close, he wasted no time in taking her hand, spreading his thighs and plunking her down on one leg. Her beautiful eyes widened when she felt his erection press against her backside. He couldn't help but murmur, "That's for you."

Most likely stunned by his easy admission, her sinfully full lips pulled down. "You've no shame, do you?"

More happy and aroused than he'd been in far too long, he smirked. "None."

But for all the fire and disbelief in her eyes, he didn't miss the slight shudder that went through her unbelievably sweet body. And it *was* one hell of a body. With his hand on her hip, he had a much better idea of what lay beneath the dress. It was firm yet curvy enough to likely entertain him for hours, maybe even days.

Megan polished off her ale and set down the mug. "This is barbaric."

Naðr chuckled, nodded at each brother and properly introduced them. "You've already met Kol." His eyes went to his other brother. "This is Raknar."

Megan and Raknar nodded at one another but said nothing.

When Naðr made a motion with his hand, a fresh mug of ale was brought over for Megan. After it was delivered, he looked from it back to her. "You should drink, woman. Seems you need it."

"Warm beer," she said without much enthusiasm but drank nonetheless.

Beer? Obviously what she called ale.

"How else would it be?" He couldn't contain a low growl of arousal as he watched her slender white throat work the fluid down.

Megan's lips stilled on the edge of the mug and she slowly lowered it. But he gave her credit. Instead of averting her eyes when a perfect stranger forced her to sit on his lap, her gaze bravely met his. And that's exactly where he wanted it to stay. A man could spend forever lost in her otherworldly eyes.

"Cold," she said.

Cold? Right, the ale, or *beer*. He continued to study her face, pleased that she didn't look away beneath his scrutiny. Her fine brows were arched and her lashes thick. Where her brows were slightly darker than her hair, her lashes were considerably darker, adding an interesting intensity to her pale golden eyes. The planes of her face were well-formed with high cheekbones and a nicely shaped jaw. Her nose was small and straight. He especially liked the sun-kissed smoothness of her skin. Yet it was easy to see that aging would not lessen but enhance her beauty.

Naðr was startled to realize he'd like to see fine lines form on her face someday. To see lines fan from the corner of her eyes because he made her laugh so much, perhaps a few on her forehead because he consistently shocked her. Maybe even some between her eyes because he managed to pull forth more scowls like the one she currently wore.

"From what year do you hail?" Raknar said, interrupting his thoughts.

His people knew their king and his brothers were of dragon blood and that Valan had traveled here from another time, so this was not an unusual question.

Megan, however, seemed a little surprised. But she answered nonetheless. "2014."

For the first time in ages, Raknar's eyes lit up. "Truly?"

"Yes." Interest sparked in Megan's eyes as she looked between the men. "Assuming that I really *have* traveled back over a thousand years in time, do you have any idea how to get me home?"

Naðr's body tensed and he tightened his grip on her hip. Her eyes shot to his. "What?"

He scowled. The last thing he wanted to consider right now was getting her home. His body hadn't responded like this to a woman in far too long. Not that he had trouble releasing his seed. But that's all lying with a woman was now. A necessary chore.

"What," she said again when he gave no answer.

"Yes, *what* brother?" Kol said with a sly grin on his face.

Naðr kept his attention on Megan and slid his hand up along the tight cinch of her waist. "You are *here* now."

Megan's lips pinched in even as her body again quivered in response to his touch. "Yep, I'm *here* but don't belong. I need to get home."

"Yep," Kol mouthed and kept on grinning.

"We will figure it out." Raknar gave a renewed look of determination. "Tell us about your time. Are there riches to be had?"

Megan looked at him cautiously. "Not sure what you mean by that."

Naðr narrowed his eyes on Raknar as he nodded toward the chests they'd brought into the hall earlier. "Are you not happy enough with our recent plunder?"

"For now," Raknar conceded, eyes never leaving Megan. "But I'd like to hear of new lands and new conquests."

"You only just got home." Meyla leaned forward, eyes on Valan across the way. "Not that you shouldn't go exploring again soon."

Naðr frowned at his daughter. She wanted him gone so that she could carry on with the Scotsman. "I don't intend to sail with them next time."

Meyla's eyes met his and she frowned as well. But she was smart enough not to say what she was thinking. Instead, she said something that would cut a little deeper. "I *am* marrying him, father."

Megan, so it seemed, chose her corner of this argument as she nodded at Meyla. "Valan seems like a nice guy. You should."

"Guy?" Raknar asked.

"Man," Megan said.

Naðr took a long swig of ale then decided to focus on Megan's lush body rather than his daughter's misguided notions. Running his hand up a bit further, he dusted the side of her breast, again pleased with its firm roundness.

"Easy, buddy." She brushed it away. But again, her body wasn't in agreement with her words as she shifted and pressed her thighs together.

When Naðr inhaled and grinned, her eyes went saucer round and she tried to stand. His arm wrapped around her small waist and locked her into position. Leaning close to her ear, he murmured, "You smell of desire," he brushed his lips lightly over the soft skin just beneath, "for me."

A small sound rumbled deep down inside her throat and he nearly closed his mouth over the delicate column of flesh to feel the vibration against his lips, to see if she tasted as sweet as she smelled. Her breathing increased and she released a tiny gush of air. Naðr wondered if she realized her backside no longer tried to edge away from his cock but instead pushed closer.

When his hand covered her slender thigh, she tensed. Yet instead of pushing it away, her hand clasped over his and her eyes again narrowed on him. "We need to talk."

"We *are* talking." He grinned. "Mostly."

"Alone."

"Soon."

"Talk, nothing more."

His grin didn't falter. "Once I've celebrated proper with my men I'll *talk* all night with you, woman."

"Megan."

"Megan," he agreed.

"And I don't need all night." Her expression was stern. "Just a few moments alone."

"Oh, he's good for more than a few moments." Kol winked. "Just."

This incited a round of chuckles from many nearby.

Naðr brought the mug to her lips. "Drink. Enjoy. Then we'll talk." His lips curled up with promise. "For more than a few moments."

Meyla rolled her eyes and sighed. "Enough with this. I want to go dance."

When his daughter stood, Naðr said, "Sit."

Exasperated but not about to defy him, Meyla plunked down, crossed her arms over her chest and released another gusty sigh.

Meanwhile, Megan took a good long draw from her ale and turned her attention to the thickening crowd in front of them. Raknar went back to brooding about lost conquests and Kol resumed tending to the women on his lap. But Naðr knew his brothers kept a close sidelong eye on Megan. How could they not? She was ravenous and far different than any woman here. They were all explorers and the lovely creature sitting on his lap was well worth exploring.

Overheated and so aroused it was on the edge of becoming painful, he decided rather than remove her from his lap, he'd remove his fur cloak. While not nearly the relief he needed, shimmying down to his sleeveless tunic was a good start.

Yet it seemed such an action would only worsen his aroused state.

Megan's eyes slid to the clingy material hugging his chest then down first one arm then the other. When her tongue slid out and moistened her plush lips, Naðr was a heartbeat away from straddling her over him and slaking his raging lust.

"Holy *Christ*," she whispered as her eyes at last stopped their appreciative roaming and locked onto one of the tattoos on his shoulder. "It's the same."

Naðr glanced at the ship etched into his skin. "The same as what?"

Caught off guard, Megan clearly hadn't meant to say such so tried to refocus his attention. "Where'd all your facial hair go? Or should I say most of it. You've still a good layer of stubble."

But Naðr wasn't king because he was so easily distracted.

Even by such a beautiful woman.

"You've seen the marking on my skin before?" he said.

It seemed his brothers were just as interested in her response based on their sudden silence.

"Sure," Megan said automatically, seemingly aware of the reaction her words received. "Out in your harbor. Lots of ships look like that."

Naðr fingered one of her buoyant curls to give her the impression that he was still entirely focused on lust. "There are no ships in my port that look like the one on my arm."

When she shifted her shoulders just a bit he knew. It was what he'd sensed when he first met her. The stone.

"Let me see it," he said softly, twirling a length of curl around his finger.

"See what?"

His eyes stayed steady on hers. "Either hand it to me or I'll get it myself. You choose."

Megan started to shake her head but he stilled her when he gripped her dainty chin gently. "I'd much rather get it from between your breasts so consider your answer carefully."

She stared at him for several long moments before she came to a conclusion. "Fine."

Naðr watched her hand with envy as it disappeared beneath the front of her dress. Clearly aware of too many watching, she made quick work of pulling something out. Fist closed around it, she straightened her shoulders and imagined herself in a position to bargain. "I'll let you see it as long as you give it back to me."

He held out his hand and gave no response.

"Do we have a deal?"

Naðr curled the tips of his fingers, urging her to hand it over.

Megan eyed him for a long moment then grumbled under her breath before dropping it into his palm. He instinctively closed his hand around the small stone and shut his eyes. The dragon within rushed up and its eyes stared back. Curious, he listened to what his other half told him. Astounded, he opened his eyes then flipped the stone until he held it between his thumb and forefinger.

The carvings on either side matched his interlocking tattoos.

"The seers," he whispered.

His brothers kept fixated eyes on him.

"Does the stone mean what I think it does," Raknar said, voice low.

"What does it mean?" Meyla said.

Kol's eyes flickered until they were harshly narrowed on first one side of the stone then the other. He cursed and drank long from his horn. Megan looked at all three men, alarmed when his younger brother ushered away his women.

Naðr eyed the stone for a long moment before he sighed. "We all knew what we agreed to."

"And what was that?" Meyla asked.

Giving no response, he handed the stone back to Megan. "Keep it safe."

Megan snatched it from his palm and eyed him warily. "Care to share what's going on?"

Not here. Not with so many paying attention. Naðr shrugged, pulled her tighter against him and plastered a cocky grin on his face as his eyes swung from brother to brother. "We agreed to a night of drinking and romping, yes?"

Raknar didn't miss a beat, a renewed light in his eyes as he raised his horn of ale. "So we did."

Kol, however, wasn't nearly as jovial. Still, when his brother's eyes locked on him, he slowly but surely raised his horn as well. "So we did."

The curious crowd roared with approval as the ale and mead continued to flow and drums pounded louder. Many were moving past drinking to dancing and the display was one born of men gone too long from women.

Megan kept still beside him, taking advantage of the loud crowd to murmur, "What does my stone have to do with seers?"

"We will talk later," he replied.

Her brows arched up in response to his serious tone. "I see. So now talking really *means* talking, does it?"

"Does it ever," Kol said, obviously a little too in his cups when he leaned over and relayed words that shouldn't be uttered right now.

"*Yep.* After all, we three brothers are committed to women from another time."

Chapter Six

Megan did her best to ignore the thick erection pressed against her backside yet failed.

But Naðr didn't need to know that.

It was still hard to believe that she'd been forced to sit on the king's lap. And she *had* been forced no matter how you wanted to dress it up. Despite how hard she tried not to, her eyes again went to his face. *Lord*, was he a beautiful man. She'd thought him well beyond attractive with the light beard but now, shaven as much as a guy like this could be with an instant five o'clock shadow, his strong jaw line and sculptured lips were all that much more obvious.

Before she'd arrived in the main hall, Megan spent several hours with Meyla. In truth, the woman was fairly pleasant as long as she wasn't around her father. More mature than most her age, she explained her society at length including Megan's current position within it. And though Meyla did her best to sugarcoat it, she understood.

Megan was a slave.

Meyla assured her that she, her father and uncles treated their slaves as family but it was still disconcerting. She didn't do the whole human owning another human thing. Yet she knew this was part of Viking culture. Still. It was a hard pill to swallow. So once they'd bathed and Meyla's other 'slaves' spent a great deal of time weaving braids into her defiant hair and pampering her skin with delicious smelling creams, they dressed and joined the celebration.

It was no easy thing to once more feel earrings dangling from her ears and a necklace hanging around her neck. She'd done away with all jewelry when she moved to Maine. But it seemed Viking women liked their baubles and for now, *she* was one of *them*.

The moment she'd arrived in the great hall things truly became surreal. She wasn't just looking upon a harbor full of boats or watching a longship dock but was surrounded by and immersed in a culture she'd only ever dreamt about. Metal, bowl shaped chandeliers dangled on long chains from the ceiling, fire crackling within. Not only round shields but a variety of weapons hung on the walls.

The music, food, smells and people saturated her almost as well as the steady gaze of the king. Only several moments into the great hall and she'd sensed his eyes on her. The moment her gaze turned to the head table, his eyes had locked with hers and everything else fell away.

The rest was history.

Now she sat on his lap with his strong arm wrapped around her.

And it all might have been halfway bearable in a, *'damn this man is hot and sitting on his lap is a very bad idea'* sort of way if he hadn't decided to remove the fur cloak from his broad shoulders. Ripped, muscles poured down his tattooed arms, chest and abs. Regrettably, *or not*, he was so overheated that his already snug tunic clung tightly and left little to the imagination.

If all that wasn't bad enough, he'd sported an overly impressive erection from the second she joined him. But then he'd had another woman sitting here just before her, didn't he? And she was determined to keep that thought at the forefront.

Naðr was a womanizing man just like any other.

Now he'd seen her stone and shared it with his brothers. Attention still focused on what Kol just said about all three brothers being committed to women from another time, she made to speak. When she did, Naðr's finger came to her lips and he pulled her closer, hot breath by her ear when he said, "Say nothing more. I will explain later."

Before she could respond he pulled away, leaned close to Kol and said something far more scathing in his brother's ear based on his response. Meanwhile, Raknar eyed her with more curiosity than before. This brother was far different than the others. Just as handsome with his classic blond haired, blue eyed Nordic features, he struck her more contemplative though still eager for adventure and conquest.

So Kol wanted women. Raknar wanted glory. And Naðr? Hard to say. For now, based on his never-ending arousal, she'd say he wanted *her*.

Megan continued to drink the strong, warm ale and tried to ignore the steely thigh beneath her. She tucked the stone back into her cleavage and mulled over his reaction to it. What did he know?

Because he obviously knew something and it was enough to make Kol do away with his harem and Raknar enjoy his drink with a whole new gleam in his eye.

For a split second, she actually relaxed into her situation until Naðr's hand snaked into her hair and his gaze once more focused on her face. Something about his undivided attention made her both wary and aroused. Wary because he was far too intense and sexual. In fact, she'd about had enough of the steady glares she'd been receiving from women since he'd pulled her onto his lap. And of course aroused because…well, that was obvious. The man wasn't necessarily made of charm but most definitely of tempered control and streamlined sensuality. Pretty lethal combo. At least for her.

Megan got the impression that he laid with women often, gave them far more than they knew they wanted, then moved on. He wasn't the sort to invest his heart and she wondered why. But then the very position he held might explain much. Being a king over men such as these would take a certain sort of nature. One made of grit and steel. Not of romance and love.

Now he seemed to be making a project out of digging his hands into her hair because her thick curls wouldn't allow for anything else. There'd be no sifting fingers through billowing locks with her. And she suspected the longer she remained in this cool, humid climate the worse it would get.

"You've the look of the goddess Freyja about you," he murmured, seemingly mesmerized by her hair and eyes. "Wild. Like sex and war all at once." As seemed to be his way, Naðr's startling blue eyes tried to crawl inside her soul. "But I wonder, were you deserted as she was by Od?"

Megan clenched her teeth and tried to ignore how close he came to her own personal truth with Nathan. Yet the stories told that Freyja leaned toward promiscuousness when mourning Od's absence. "Rest assured, if I was anything like Freyja I wouldn't turn to other men to bury my heartache."

Naðr's eyes stayed with hers, his gaze a little lost as he whispered, "No, I don't think you would."

It was the first time since she'd met him that Megan saw a smidge of vulnerability in his eyes and she didn't much like how it switched her breathing. Pulling her eyes from his, she took a long swig of ale and did her best to ignore the constant ache below her waist.

His hand left her hair and trailed down her back slowly, as though memorizing the contours of her spine. "You seem to know much of my gods, even my people. You're not afraid of being here. Why is that?"

"Just trying to blend in."

"I think it's more than that."

"Do you?"

"Yes."

Though it was likely because of the beer, Megan was growing comfortable so said more than she probably should. "I grew up in a place called Hampton, New Hampshire. My Dad ran a small fishing company so I was raised around a fairly hearty seafaring bunch." She shook her head and sipped from her drink. "My father had lots of ideas about how best to provide for his family. Most of the time it meant gambling away money but there was this one project that he thought might be the start of something."

Naðr said nothing as she drank again, lost in thought…in memories.

"We had this beat up house a few blocks off the beach with a sizeable yard." She again shook her head. "The truth was we had more yard than house. Far more. Inherited. Anyways, he decided to build a boat. I was ten at the time." She snorted. "He started to build this thing out of any scrap wood he could find and I'll give him this, Dad made it work."

She peered at the king. "Know what he called it?"

Naðr shook his head, eyes as always avidly on her face.

"The Viking."

His eyes warmed. "Ah, so started your fascination with Vikings?"

Megan quirked her lip. "Yeah, actually, it was that simple." Then she again got lost in thought. "At first." She sighed. "Yet the more he became obsessed with building this boat the more infatuated I became with being knowledgeable about what he'd named his obsession after. There was nothing as gratifying as eventually helping him build the boat while sharing what I'd learned about Vikings."

When her words trailed off, Naðr murmured, "And was your father proud of your knowledge?"

Not expecting his question, she involuntarily arched her brows as she stared without any real focus. "He might've been had he named the boat for actual Vikings."

Naðr frowned. "I don't understand."

"Neither did I." She took another swig of beer. "At first."

When the king continued to frown in confusion she said, "He named it for someone who not only loved the sea but evidently stole his heart. A woman he was having an affair with. He apparently called her his little Viking."

"I do not know the word *affair*."

"He was…" she paused, considering the best way to phrase this to a man that slept around. "He was having sex with someone other than my mother when he'd promised to be faithful."

The lighter cobalt in Naðr's eyes flashed a bit brighter. "I see."

"I'm sure you do."

Naðr ignored her innuendo. "What happened to the boat then?"

A man after her own heart in a way. Why bother with human emotion when a boat was at stake? Megan couldn't help but smirk as she remembered the sweet revenge that Fate took out on her father. "Though he survived, it sunk and my mother left him."

"Good." Naðr nodded. "A weak boat made by a weak man and a woman only stronger because of it."

Surprised by his response, she could only nod slowly. But he didn't have the full story and she'd already over shared. So if he was determined to keep her on his lap, she'd turn the conversation his way. "What about you?" Her eyes scanned the room before once more landing on him. "How'd you become king of all this?"

But it seemed Naðr wasn't the sharer she was or so said his redirected attention to her body. When he went to touch the side of her breast she grabbed his wrist and shook her head. "Pretty sure I just asked you a question."

His sweeping brows lowered but his lips twitched as though tempted to smile.

Naðr looked at her long and hard before he nodded. "Then I best share." But he wasn't above wrapping his hand over her vulnerable backside and squeezing before he continued. "I was born to a poor boat builder. He wanted to be in charge of all the ships he helped construct. So one day instead of building he volunteered to start sailing with the other warriors. My father paid attention to the winds, to the people they raided, to everything. Soon enough, his was the voice that led those raids."

"So basically your Dad succeeded where mine failed," she murmured. "But I know enough about your culture that eventually leading a Viking charge would by no means make him a king."

"No, it wouldn't," Naðr said softly, his intelligent eyes on hers.

Though they were interrupted by his brothers, Megan knew he wasn't going to say much more if anything. No more than she was willing to share the entirety of her story with someone she'd just met. Yet Megan wondered. Was what she'd read in the manuscript correct? Did Naðr Véurr possess the blood of a dragon? If so, would he have the power to see inside her mind and know her secrets? She almost chuckled. Figure the odds. But then she'd seemingly traveled back in time to the Viking period so…anything was possible, right?

The music and crowd were growing rowdy. More and more men seemed to be demanding Naðr's attention. Even so, when Kol stood, held his hand down to her and asked her to dance, she said, "You're joking, right?"

Before she could respond, Naðr grabbed her hips and made her stand as he eyed a warrior who was ranting about one thing or another. His towering body was inches behind hers as he stood and murmured in her ear, "Go dance with my brother. But no *sex*."

"What the hel—" she started but it was too late. Kol grabbed her hand and pulled her after him.

Sonofabitch.

The music was a heady mix of both drums and some sort of harp and flute as Kol dragged her into the crowd. Though his arm wrapped around her lower back and he pulled her close, Megan quickly realized it wasn't *that* close. Still, she put her hands on his chest and leaned back some. He might be hot as hell but Megan was having no part of the *'woman being tossed from man to man'* thing.

"I don't want sex from you." Kol twisted his lips wryly, not above smirking at her actions. "Besides, you belong to my brother."

Belong?

Kol wasn't finished. "I like a little more there." He nodded at her breasts, and then leaned his head so he could look at her backside. "And more there too."

"Jesus," she muttered and tried to push him away but he held tight and swung her into the crowd. "What's the *matter* with you?"

Kol clearly had no idea what she was talking about but assumed he had offended her based on his next statement. "You're damned beautiful, woman, but too slight." He made a fist and shrugged. "I like a little more to grab onto if you understand my meaning."

Stunned, speechless, Megan's mouth fell open.

Kol nodded, pleased it seemed with his explanation. "So you understand."

Yeah, that he was an utter dickhead.

But at least he wasn't trying to feel her up like Naðr had so *that* was something.

She supposed she was safe enough dancing with Kol and tried to ignore the strange reality she'd been thrust into. They'd just made the edge of the crowd when he slowed their pace and leaned his lips close to her ear. "Sorry about that. Naðr asked it of me. He's staking his claim on you." Kol pulled back slightly and grinned. "No matter the loot we came back with the men are anxious to travel further. The more they drink the more they complain."

She focused on the first part of what he'd said. Staking his claim? Megan shook her head, determined to remain focused. "I'm not any man's claim."

Kol didn't miss a beat. "So you'd rather be shared by Naðr's men this eve?"

"He wouldn't allow that." But the truth was she didn't know a thing about what he would and would not allow.

"He would have little choice in the matter if you turn him away," Kol warned. "His men would expect such a prize after a voyage."

Megan almost joked about it until she realized he was absolutely serious. "So I can only hope he respects my wishes behind closed doors."

Kol looked at her oddly. "Do you not desire my brother?"

"Whether or not I desire your brother has nothing to do with it. I only just met him."

Which wasn't entirely true. Not if one counted the year or so he'd plagued her mind.

"How long you have known him means nothing." Kol shook his head. "Not to the men and likely not to Naðr."

Terrific. But she wasn't about to show fear. "I thought I was Meyla's slave. Does she not have any say in what happens to me?"

"Perhaps," he said, offering a glimmer of hope then crushing it. "If it wasn't her father who wanted you."

Back to square one. Maybe there was another way. She eyed Kol then Raknar across the room. Though he said otherwise, she suspected Kol would have no issues sleeping with her. Raknar however? He didn't seem as interested. "What if I wanted Raknar instead?"

Kol chuckled. "Do not let Raknar's indifference fool you, woman. He'd lay with you as quickly as any other here." His eyes narrowed. "Besides, why would you want him when you look at Naðr as you do?"

Because he looked at her the same way and that wasn't conducive to the whole 'no sex' thing. "I look at Naðr like I do because he's damn intimidating."

"Then go with Raknar," Kol said easily. "But you will not make things easy on my brothers if you do."

This conversation was insane. "And why is that?"

"Do men not get jealous from where you hail?"

The king might strike her as a lot of things but someone capable of jealousy wasn't one of them. "I don't see Naðr getting jealous."

"Maybe not but Raknar would when Naðr eventually took you away." Kol went back to grinning. "Then I might end up jealous too because they both had what I did not."

Megan frowned. "I thought you didn't want sex from me."

Kol shrugged. "What else am I supposed to say when Naðr wants you?"

Ugh, these men were crazy but at least they were honest. Megan was about to respond when she felt another body come up far too close behind her. She didn't have to guess who it was based on the way her body hit overdrive. Kol didn't let her go but looked over the top of her head. "Brother."

Nothing was said as a pair of warm hands landed on her shoulders and lips came close to her ear. "Do you like being between two men?"

It didn't matter if Kol was still at her front. Her sole focus was on Naðr at her back.

"I'm typically more of a one guy sorta gal," Megan said, voice raspier than she would have liked.

"Typically? *Hel,*" Naðr said, humor obvious as his arousal pressed against her back. But she suspected he shot Kol a look because his brother pulled away. The next thing she knew the king spun her and walked her backwards a few steps until her back was against one of the large support beams. He braced a hand above her head and wrapped one of her curls around his finger as his eyes locked on hers, voice a deep rumble. "So you think to choose Raknar, do you?"

Her breath caught in her throat and her heart gave a few extra heavy thuds. They were close to one of the small fires and the flames almost seemed to reflect within his intense eyes. Had he been standing behind her when she was talking to Kol? She'd sworn he was across the room with his men. "Honestly I'd rather not be forced to choose to begin with."

"I would not hurt you." His finger continued to play with her curl and his knowing eyes fell to her slightly parted lips. "My guess is you would like it."

Oh, she didn't doubt *that* for a second. "I still need to talk to you."

"Later," he assured, words a soft murmur. "But until then."

Megan realized his intentions a second too late when he left the curl, wrapped his hand behind her neck and tilted his lips over hers. Possessive, hungry, his kiss was so well-executed she didn't stand a chance. Sure, she could have pushed him away but instead her traitorous hands twisted into his tunic and held on for dear life. The things he did with his tongue nearly had her melting into the floor. Far too eager, she followed his lead and laved her tongue against his before flicking then twisting.

Growling, he lifted her enough so that he could grind his erection between her shaking thighs. Megan was fairly certain she moaned as she gripped his muscular biceps. The rowdy crowd faded away as she was caught in the swift tide of his all-consuming presence. He tasted of a delicious mix between ale and man. Yet it was his scent that nearly drove her past the point of coherency. A spicy but sweet masculine heat seemed to radiate from his hot skin and permeate the scant air between them.

She *knew* that smell.

It was the same scent she'd caught on the wind back home when she heard his name.

Ignited by not only the powerful sense of connection but by the intensity of his mouth against hers, she gripped him tighter and rocked her hips forward. A small tremble rippled through his strong body as he pulled his lips from hers. Steeped in desire, his eyes fell to her lips before they slowly rose. When they locked with hers, she didn't misunderstand the possessive promise in his gaze.

You're *mine*.

Yet a small grin curled his lips without meeting his eyes as he slowly pulled away. Megan could barely stand never mind process that Raknar now stood alongside. Naðr inclined his head toward the other man, his soft words curious while somehow dangerous. "Now dance with my brother, Megan, and see if you still want him."

The way he said her name kept her eyes on him. It was almost as if he'd said it a thousand times before. Though she made to respond nothing came out as he backed away then faded into the crowd. Raknar, meantime, stepped in front of her, his pale blue eyes alive with something she couldn't quite pinpoint.

When he took her hand she drifted into his arms. There was something unusual about these brothers. Beneath their steely, lusty Viking mentalities simmered something not exactly sinister but dark and mystical.

Dragon blood.

The words seemed to whisper through her mind like Naðr's name had on the coastal winds of Maine. Raknar said nothing at first, simply held her a bit closer than Kol had as he studied her. But like it had been in Kol's arms, nothing stirred. Certainly not the blasphemous fire and desire Naðr harnessed when near.

Or across the room.

Or across time for that matter.

"He will not let you go."

Raknar's words pulled her out of a daze made of Viking king and unquenched need. When her eyes met his she was startled to see a flicker of contentment there. It was obvious he cared a great deal for his brother.

"I don't belong here," she whispered. "Any more than he belongs with someone from my time."

"Time does not matter when a connection is forged," Raknar enlightened. "He looks at you as he once did Aesa."

Megan worked hard to keep her face free of expression. "Who is Aesa?"

"She was his wife. Meyla's mother."

Was? Megan ignored a sharp sense of relief. "Where is Aesa now?"

"Drinking and battling alongside Freyja in Fólkvangr," he said with pride. "A great shield maiden, none were her equal."

So she had passed away. In Norse mythology, the Valkyrie led only the best warriors to Odin's, Valhalla. A great hall in Asgard, half of the fallen warriors then went on to Freyja's, Fólkvangr. Megan knew better than to say sorry for their loss. After all, it was a great honor to go to Valhalla and was why Vikings supposedly had absolutely no fear in battle.

Yet she couldn't help but notice the sadness in Raknar's eyes and recognized it for what it was. After all, she'd seen the same thing in her own eyes when looking in the mirror after her marriage fell apart. She couldn't help but whisper, "You loved her."

Renewed pain flashed in his eyes but vanished within moments. "We all loved her."

But she'd seen enough to know Aesa had clearly made a strong impact on Raknar.

His assessing eyes continued to roam her face. This brother had a mind that wasn't good at resting. Much like Veronica's. When her sister popped into her mind, Megan frowned. What was happening back home? She could only imagine how much her sisters must be worrying about her.

As if he followed her every thought, Raknar said, "Tell me of your home. Do all the women act as you do?"

How exactly did she *act*? Megan shook her head and chuckled. "No, like the people, everyone has their own personality, Raknar."

"But some have more fire within their souls than others," he murmured. "Do they not?"

"I suppose." Yet she felt as though he baited her, that he was seeking specific knowledge. "Precisely what are you curious about?"

"Your bloodline." His eyes pinned hers. "The women who are closest to you."

Megan wasn't quite sure she liked where this was going. "Why?"

"F..father, a m..moment?"

Alarmed, she pulled away from Raknar and looked down at the boy, Heidrek. "Is Guardian all right?"

Heidrek nodded, eyes wide. "Y..yes, *she* is v..very good."

Relieved, she watched as Raknar lifted the boy and rested him on his hip, adoration in his eyes. "What it is son?"

Heidrek was Raknar's son? Obviously. And, as any child should be, well loved by the looks of it. Megan couldn't help but be a little awed by the soft expression on the Viking's face. Heidrek wasn't a small boy but he looked fairly tiny in his father's arms.

Heidrek's face grew solemn. "The raven c...comes."

A chill raced through Megan. Obviously it wasn't *her* raven.

Raknar nodded, kissed his boy on the cheek and set him down. "Let us go get the king then."

Bereft, she watched Raknar and Heidrek vanish into the crowd. Thankfully, it wasn't long before Valan joined her. He shook his head and handed her a fresh mug of ale. "Looks like it has already been a verra long eve for us both."

Now *that* was a vast understatement. Relieved to be in the company of someone she was a smidge more comfortable with, she eyed his tartan. "I'm surprised you still dress like a Scotsman."

Valan scowled. "How else would I dress?"

Megan took a swig of ale and shrugged. "I don't know. Maybe more like a Viking." She cocked her head at him. "Aren't you trying to win over a Viking father so that you can marry his Viking daughter?"

"I'm not trying to win over anyone." He steered her through the riotous crowd. "I love Meyla. That should be enough."

Megan snorted. "And there's one mistake among many that you're making."

Valan eyed her, his gaze a fraction less moody. "Any Scottish Da would wish for a lad to love his lassie. 'Twould be his deciding factor when giving his blessing."

"Yeah, but you're not in Scotland any more than I'm in America." She gave him a pointed look. "So we both need to stop thinking like we're at home, eh?"

"'Tis no easy thing setting aside one culture for another," he grumbled.

"No it isn't," she agreed as she watched the rowdy Vikings around them. "But I have no doubt it'd be in our best interest to do so."

Valan offered a noncommittal shrug and drank from his horn.

"I'm curious," she said, sidestepping a couple swinging in a clumsy circle. "How did you meet Meyla?"

"She traveled to my time in Scotland," he began but was cut off by a towering man with a shaved head and two thin braids trailing down from his goatee. The massive Viking literally stepped between them, his lustful but distrusting eyes trailing down her body. She couldn't say he was unattractive. No, with deep-set eyes and a chiseled face, he was striking in an overly intense sort of way.

When Valan stepped around him and started to say something, Megan shook her head, never taking her eyes off the giant in front of her. Hands on hips, she glared up. "You have a problem?"

The Viking chuckled as he stroked one of his braids, lewd eyes on her breasts. "No problem that I can see, woman."

When he went to touch what he was looking at, Megan slapped his hand away and didn't back down an inch. "Don't even try it."

"Oh, he tried it all right," Valan said but she again shook her head at the Scotsman without removing her eyes from the Viking. If there was one thing she'd gleaned about this society it was that fear wasn't respected and actions spoke louder than words.

"Leave her be, Kjar," Meyla said as she joined them.

The Viking's green eyes went to Meyla before returning to Megan. "Is the king keeping her then?"

Meyla slipped her hand into Valan's and shrugged. "As long as he keeps any woman I'd imagine."

Megan frowned. *Real nice.* But not surprising. "Nobody's keeping me."

"Keep telling yourself that," Meyla said but didn't waste time getting into a debate. Instead she looked between the two. "Megan, meet Kjar, our master boat builder and my father's cousin."

"Master boat builder?" Megan said, unable to keep shock from her voice as she eyed his huge hands. Her eyes shot to his. "Hard to imagine those big mitts could create the masterpieces I saw out there."

The only response he offered was a flare of his pupils as he continued to eye her. Then, as if a cloud lifted, both lust and potential anger fled as he flung back his head and laughed. But it seemed Kjar wasn't into small talk because he turned and sauntered into the crowd.

"Beast," Meyla muttered and shook her head. But her exasperation didn't last long as she wrapped her arms over Valan's shoulders and kissed him soundly. It appeared neither of them were overly concerned with Naðr's disapproval. Yet Megan knew Valan would be better off showing the king respect rather than executing such a display with his daughter.

Megan drank her ale and watched the crowd. Many appeared to be trailing outside. About to follow, she stopped when Meyla put a hand on her arm. "Best that you stay with us for now."

"Not a problem," she replied. "If you two actually talked to me rather than made out."

Valan frowned. "Made out?"

Megan did well not to roll her eyes. "Kiss."

Meyla and Valan grinned.

"Why would you rather we talk to you than kiss?" Meyla asked, truly curious.

But Valan apparently had a ready answer. "Because she has no one to kiss too, lass."

"That's not what I was getting at." Megan sighed. "Never mind."

Meyla's eyes roamed the hall. "Uncle Kol is still in here. He'll kiss you." Then another grin crawled onto her face. "But my father won't much like it."

"Speaking of your Da." Valan's eyes narrowed. "Is he out with the raven then?"

"Based on the way Uncle Raknar left, yes."

Megan frowned as another odd chill passed through her. She needed to see this bird. This time when Meyla tried to stop her, she kept on going. Striding through the partying crowd, she made her way out into the chilled night.

Torches lined the yard then lit the road and village beyond. And though there were plenty of people about she didn't have to go far to find Naðr and Raknar. Given a wide birth they were near the outer gate. Raknar leaned back against one side of the exit with his arms crossed over his chest and head bent. The king was on the other side of the gate. Facing toward the sea, his white-knuckled grip held the railing. His head was also bent. But her eyes didn't linger on either man long. No, all she could look at was what perched on the post between them.

A raven.

One identical to that which had visited her back home.

Megan knew without doubt. It was *her* raven.

The bird cocked its head and stared at her for a long minute before it cried out, flapped its wings and launched in the air. Then, as it had done at home, it flew in the direction of the sea, toward the Viking longship, another loud cry echoing in the wind.

Chapter Seven

Naðr crouched, elbows resting on bent knees and stared out over the sea. The sun's tip had just crested the mountains at his back and spliced over the water in a riot of colors. But he didn't see the splendor of his homeland nor hear the whispers of the gods as he usually did.

"You need to claim her or allow the men to have her."

Offering no response, he contemplated Kjar's words as the boat builder leaned against the prow of his ship. Megan had been here three days and though tempted to take her, he kept his distance. "She is my daughter's slave. No man has a right to her without Meyla's permission."

"The woman appeared when we returned from the best raiding we have had yet." Kjar yawned and stretched. "She is beautiful and considered a gift from Odin for a good conquering. They grow restless."

They did. And they were not to blame. He would do the same in their position. Regardless. "There are bigger concerns."

Kjar sat forward and eyed him. "And they will grow bigger yet if you don't lay claim to the woman." He shrugged. "Or you could give her to them and be done with the strife that has arisen. It would be a good move, cousin. They will see you as more of a hero than they already do."

Naðr knew Kjar spoke the truth but he remained torn. When the raven came the first night Megan arrived he knew it was a message as readily given as the seers with their stones.

Always of kindred thought, his cousin said, "But perhaps your heart has already been affected. The woman from the future is strong and now it seems Aesa approves."

So it appeared but the situation was difficult nonetheless. Yet his people needed to come before his baser emotions and those were too thoroughly caught between the past and future right now. Which wasn't good for a man determined to lead.

"At least be around her. Your mood has been too foul even for me since she first came." Kjar stood. "It seemed you claimed her then pushed her away. It looks weak for a king unless you do not want her."

He stepped off the boat, his gruff words coming from behind. "But no man would not want her so it makes you look the fool."

Kjar didn't wait for a reply but left. Naðr felt the heavy vibration of his boots departing the dock as he continued to stare at the sea. Based on the stirring of his cock even at this moment there could be no doubt that he wanted Megan. And only Loki knew how much. Because his need ran deep and superseded even the desire he'd had for his warrior maiden, his *wife*, Aesa.

Naðr closed his eyes and clenched his fists.

He had promised her he would never love another as deeply.

Yet the raven came.

If that wasn't enough, so too did Rennir. Forever a thorn in his side, the rival king wanted this port, ships and his warriors. Like Naðr, he hadn't earned his current position but inherited it. Since then, he focused less on what he already had and more on conquering not foreign lands but those of his fellowmen.

Frustrated in more ways than one, Naðr headed for the shore. His daughter was likely awake and he needed to speak with her. She and Valan had not been shy with their affection for one another. Yet it had not gone unnoticed that the Scotsman seemed to be helping more with preparing the ships for their next voyage. Nor had it gone unnoticed that he'd started to wear leggings instead of his plaid.

Naðr had just made it to the gates of the main holding when Megan's wolf appeared. He knew it was no wolf but had not shared as much. Glancing around to make sure they were alone, he crouched and quirked his lips as the dog trotted over. "Good morning, Guardian."

Guardian licked his cheek and buried her nose against his chest. Naðr murmured in her ear, "Is Megan awake?"

He closed his eyes and listened to the response no human could hear. Ruffling Guardian's head, he stood and nodded. "Much thanks." He looked toward the building in which Heidrek slept. "Go wake him for food then."

When he made it into the main lodge it was to find what Guardian had shared. Megan was breaking her fast alongside Meyla,

Valan and Raknar. He suspected Kol was still on a rampage sleeping with every woman possible before his destiny caught up with him. Others sat in the hall eating. They lowered their heads and raised their mugs when he passed.

Naðr nodded back then sat down with his family…and Valan and Megan, at the head table. Megan seemed to have settled in well enough over the past few days.

"Brother," Raknar grunted as he ate.

"Father," Meyla acknowledged.

"King Naðr Véurr," Valan said, lowering his head.

Naðr narrowed his eyes at the Scotsman but said nothing.

"Good morning, King Naðr," Megan said, head lowered slightly before her eyes held his. "In a better mood today?"

Meyla snorted then buried her grin in a mouthful of mead.

Determined to push past his reservations and listen to Kjar's advice that he take action one way or another with Megan, he held up his cup. "Actually, I am." He drank deeply then dug into the food on his plate. "Megan, you will join me in my lodgings this eve."

The soft murmurs of people talking at other tables quieted. Megan, however, wasn't so quiet, words surprisingly taunting. "Only if my mistress approves."

Arrogance! Naðr's eyes shot to Megan's and he sat back. "Your mistress's permission means nothing when it comes to your king's desires."

A little grin curled up the corner of Meyla's lips as she looked from Megan to her father. But it seemed even his daughter was feeling above her station because of what she said next. "I suffer from my cycle. I need my top slave by my side."

Naðr didn't miss the way Raknar's lips twitched in repressed amusement. Two could play at this game. Eyes on his daughter, he said, "Then you will leave Valan for an eve and join Megan because I wish her company." He smirked at his daughter. "You, of course, can wait in the other room."

Meyla narrowed her eyes a fraction but said nothing more.

All might have gone well enough from there had Megan not spoken. "Maybe I don't want her to wait in the other room."

Naðr bit off a piece of bread and chewed slowly, considering her. Teetering on the edge of frustration, he decided it best to take this conversation outside so he grabbed his cup of mead and stood. "Megan, join me. Now."

When she started to shake her head, Raknar took her elbow and made her stand. "If the king says now, you listen."

Megan's eyes widened at Raknar before she tore her elbow from his grasp. Her gaze went from Valan to Meyla, something soft and indefinable in them. "Sure. Okay." Then her eyes flickered between Raknar and Naðr. "Brutes."

Naðr led her out the back before he steered her along a path that led into the mountains. While he did not intend to go far, they didn't stop walking for a while. Though he knew it was a bad idea to take her so far off, mainly because it allowed too much privacy, he couldn't help himself. He enjoyed watching the sway of her backside and her full, curly hair blowing in the wind. His hunger for her had only grown tenfold in the past few days and he licked his lips, still tasting her tongue wrapped with his. If the raven hadn't come he would have already been between her legs.

But it had.

"Stop," he said when they came along a waterfall not gushing but slicing smoothly down a rock face. Dragon blood sizzled beneath his skin so he tore off his tunic. After splashing cold water over his head, he nodded at a good sized stone. "Sit."

For a moment it seemed like she'd defy him until her eyes landed on his bare chest. Muted, she slowly sat, appreciative gaze raking over him. But though it seemed she liked his body, it didn't ultimately stop her from speaking.

"You like ordering people around, huh?"

Naðr scooped water into his mouth and eyed her. If nothing else could be said for his twenty-first century woman, she didn't fear him in the least. As he stalked toward her he wondered yet again...did he want her to? *Hel* no. He wanted her to give him a good fight. Better yet, he wanted her to give everyone a good fight.

Encased tight within the mountains, free from the raven, he didn't hesitate to act on what he'd wanted for the past three long nights. Cupping the back of her head, he pushed her shoulder back then swiftly used that same hand to yank her leg to the side so he could settle between her thighs. Wide eyed, caught off guard by his determination, she started to shake her head but he closed his lips over hers.

As it was the first time they kissed, her sweet lips fell apart beneath his. Soft, pliant, eager, she groaned as her tongue warred with his. So aroused it hurt, he started to push up her skirts while moving his hips against hers. The dragon eyes rose up in his vision, as needy as him. Breath harsh and staggered, he trailed his lips down her neck as he continued pushing up her dress.

Her hand met his and pushed it back down.

"No," she said between kisses, her tongue exploring his mouth before she pulled back and shook her head. "No."

He cupped and stroked her clothed breast, her words halfway infiltrating his conscience, his body determined to respond to hers. "*Yes.*"

When his lips tried to meet hers again, she cupped his cheeks, eyes both wild with desire and determined. "No. It's time to talk."

Naðr ground his jaw, his rock hard arousal pinned against her clothed center as he worked to reign in his lust. He'd yet to take a woman against her will and wouldn't start now. Still, he ground against her so slowly that Megan's eyes drifted for a moment before she again shook her head. "No. Talk."

"Loki's balls," he mumbled hoarsely as he pulled away.

Rolling onto the rock beside her, he kept one hand on her hip, fell back and stared at the sky. If he didn't release his seed soon he'd weaken to the point that Odin wouldn't want his ass in Valhalla to begin with. No warrior could ever fight and win if the stiffness between his legs kept him from warring to begin with.

Megan leaned forward, head in her hands, and breathed heavily.

Naðr closed his eyes to any hope of Valhalla, put the back of his hand to his forehead and muttered, "Talk then, woman."

Megan pushed aside his hand. Her voice might have been breathy with lust moments before but now she sounded clipped. "I'll talk but you'll look at me while I do, not act like you're humoring me."

Naðr opened his eyes to half-mast and watched her. "Will I now?"

Instead of getting angered at his indifference, she laid back on the rock as well, propped her hand beneath her head and stared at the sky, words soft. "You will if you want to know more about the raven."

Naðr ignored the extra thud of his heart, voice equally soft. "What raven?"

Megan ran her foot up along the rock, enough so that her dress tightened around her slim leg. "She visits me too."

While he could easily share thoughts with his brothers, it wasn't nearly the same with a woman he hadn't bonded with. So he was careful with his words. "Who is *she*?"

Megan didn't answer right away, her hand running along her thigh as if she subconsciously meant to tempt him. "I have no idea. But I'm fairly certain she tried to lead me to you." Her hand trailed up her stomach. "You both came when the box did."

The seers flashed in his vision.

"Box?"

"Yes," she whispered, her sensual demeanor shutting down as she continued to stare at the sky. "I found it on the shore in front of my house." She closed her eyes. "It contained three stones and had your name carved into the inner lid."

Interesting. "The stone you have has the Spirit Ship on one side, the Vegvisir on the other. What of the other two?"

Her eyes flickered to the tattoo of the Spirit Ship on his shoulder and the smaller Vegvisir tattoo faded over the lower right hand corner of it.

"The second stone has the Helm of Awe, or Aegishjalmur, on one side and the Hugin and Munin symbol on the other." She frowned. "So the Helm of Awe, a rune stave, is a protective symbol meant to instill fear in one's enemies and the Hugin and Munin, Odin's ravens, of thought and memory."

"Raknar's tattoo," he whispered, eyes to the sky again.

Naðr ground his teeth and swallowed. As they knew, this meant Raknar had a strong enemy on the horizon. One so vicious that he'd need magical protection. And one so poignant that Odin would be watching closely. Or at least that was a portion of what two such symbols together could mean. But his brother was more vicious than most so would likely manage through what the seers foresaw.

More worried about his youngest sibling, Kol and his inclination toward women and their easiness he wondered if the last stone would be a match, sealing his fate. "What of the third stone?"

When Megan remained silent his eyes turned to hers, unflinching and deadly serious. "Tell me."

Her gaze was stronger than he would have expected. "Valknut." Her eyes didn't waver. "Hrungnir's heart. Knot of the Slain. And the Web of Wyrd."

The Web of Wyrd served as a reminder that the actions of the past affect the present and that present actions affect the future; all timelines inextricably interconnected. He'd been uneasy when the interlocked tattoos appeared on Kol. That they were on this mystery stone confirmed his discomfort.

He frowned and sat up. "Certain death."

What sort of agreement was this that he and his sacrificed so much? But he knew. Naðr held his forehead and closed his eyes.

Megan's soft hand fell on his shoulder. "Please talk to me. I need to understand."

And she did. More than most. Head still braced in his hands he started to explain.

"I owed a Scotsman as well as both his gods and mine a great deal. So two things were given. The first, Meyla gave Adlin MacLomain a son. This child will lead to the births of many important MacLomains to come." Naðr hesitated, still wondering if he'd gone about all of this in the right way. "The second was less for him but his offspring, my descendant, Torra MacLomain. Still, it was always to repay Adlin a great debt. Regardless, I love Torra so I must take the second part of all this as my own."

Megan said nothing but waited.

So Naðr continued with a twist, possibly sneer, to his lips. "Torra feared her dragon blood, the dragon within her, would hurt her clan so I enlisted the seers' help to repress the beast for ten winters." He shook his head, frustrated. "But while she thought the seers' demands were minor they weren't."

Though she tried to hide her distress, Naðr heard it in the slightly higher octave of her voice. "I don't understand."

"Because I'd aided in such an agreement they wanted three souls in return."

Megan shook her head as she looked at him.

Naðr met her eyes. "Four women traveled back in time to Scotland where they found true love and helped Torra defeat evil. But Viking seers didn't help Torra for ten winters prior without more sacrifice than what my descendants gave. Because I'd enlisted their help they agreed that three souls would be sufficient payment instead of four. Souls from the future that would become Viking and perhaps someday travel to the kingdom of Valhalla and tell Odin that the *seers* had sent them. The fate of these three souls would rest with me and my brothers until that day came."

Megan sat up and matched his frown. "Torra." Her eyes met his. "Any chance she loved a highlander named Colin MacLeod?"

That was about the last thing he thought she'd say. "She did." Naðr narrowed his eyes slightly. "What know you of that?"

She stared at him in disbelief for a long moment before finally saying, "I have a manuscript back home that touches on a lot of this. Adlin MacLomain is in there as well as four women from the future. Even Meyla." Her voice grew softer. "And you."

He had no idea what to make of what she'd said save Adlin was likely still very much involved. Meddlesome wizard. Yet even with such revelation he was interested in one thing above the rest. "What of me in this *manuscript*?"

"You were in it." Megan offered a small shrug. "Better yet in a tapestry then on and off in Torra's mind."

Restless, he stood and looked out over the bay. "Who created this manuscript?"

"A woman from the twenty-first century wrote it. The cousin of a friend." Her voice was hesitant, almost incredulous. "It's all true, isn't it?"

Hesitating, he slowly nodded. "Yes. It is."

"Yet I didn't read anything about Valan or how he ended up here but then there *were* pages missing."

Naðr continued to stare out over the sea with heavy thoughts. "It's not important why he's here just that he is and won't be returning to his time." Then he muttered, "Unfortunately."

Megan joined him, her gaze less on the sea and more on the ships. "So you and your brothers each have a tattoo and are apparently obligated to women from another time." Her voice grew softer. "Is that why Raknar's been drilling me about my sisters?"

"Drilling?"

"Asking."

"Likely." He arched a brow at her. "How many do you have?"

"Two."

"Convenient."

Her lips curled down and she crossed her arms over her chest. "You mean to say that a deal was struck with seers that my siblings would be doomed to end up here…stuck in this time?"

"It was said that three women of the same bloodline would come. It was not said from where or what era." His eyes slanted toward her. "None have arrived before you."

"Assuming I'm even one of them," she said carefully, frown deepening.

Naðr didn't doubt for a moment that she was. "You knew me when you arrived. I know you read about me and found the box. But what of this raven." He purposefully brushed her arm with his knuckle. "And the desire on your face when you first saw me."

Her arms tightened and plumped up her breasts. And while he imagined her reply would be less than truthful it wasn't.

"You're pretty easy on the eyes, Naðr," she stated bluntly. "But that wasn't the only reason." She sighed, her eyes not shying from his in the least. "Around the time I found the box of stones, I began building a boat…a small version of a Viking ship actually."

He couldn't help but grin. "You know how to build a boat?"

"Don't sound so surprised," she said. "But yes, I have a passion for boat building. Anyways, since I started working on it, not only has the big raven visited but…"

When her words trailed off he said, "Go on."

"Well, I swear I heard your name on the wind. More so as time passed."

"Hmm." His amused gaze continued to pin her. "Yet you think you are not here for me."

"I don't know. Maybe." She shook her head. "Something happened beneath the water when I was with the ship. An unusual wave. But I get the impression if I traveled back in time it was because the ship led me here not you."

Naðr narrowed his eyes. "What ship?"

Megan swallowed, emotion in her gaze as she nodded at the harbor. "The one you sailed in on when we first met."

He looked from the harbor back to her. "But my ship is not *beneath* the water, woman."

"Not yet," she murmured.

Alarm grew. "Explain how you were beneath the water with such a ship to begin with."

94

"I was diving off," she cleared her throat, "off someone's boat. In my time we breathe through tanks so that we can stay underwater. The location was a few thousand feet off the coast, not far from my house. At first we only came across Viking weapons. Then, after that strange wave, I came across your ship...on the ocean floor."

The idea of his beloved ship sunk didn't appeal in the least. "You can see as clearly as I that my ship is afloat so you must be mistaken." But he wasn't done. "What made you go diving where you did to begin with and who was with you?"

Though she didn't show it, he sensed her discomfort.

"An acquaintance discovered treasure and wanted me to lead his team."

She was skirting around the truth. Naðr was about to pull it from her when Raknar's voice entered his mind.

"We've got problems at the docks. Bring Megan."

"Come," he said under his breath, aggravated by not only their conversation but by lust still unfulfilled. Despite her negative news, the latter hadn't abated in the least.

Megan almost seemed relieved that their conversation had halted. And while he thought to keep questioning her on their walk back down he decided the time would be better spent mulling over what she'd shared. He'd question her more later, once he'd had his fill of her beautiful little body.

Several minutes later, Naðr pulled on his tunic and attached not only his sword but a few daggers. He didn't miss the unmistakable gleam of desire in Megan's eyes as she watched him. Let her keep thinking she wasn't here for him. He knew better. Since the raven had visited her as well, there could be no doubt that the gods had ensured her safe arrival. And he'd be damned if she was meant for his brothers.

The crowd thickened the closer they got to the docks but all stepped aside to let him and Megan pass. He made a point of taking her elbow and steering her closer to him while he met the interested eyes of many men. They didn't mistake his silent message.

She is *mine.*

I have claimed her.

The last of the crowd separated as they approached. Kol, Raknar and Kjar stood with their arms crossed over their chest eying the oddly dressed filthy men who watched them warily.

Megan stopped short, eyes round. "Oh hell."

Naðr looked from her to them. "You know those men?"

But she only shook her head which apparently meant yes as she muttered one word. "Nathan."

Chapter Eight

Megan cringed. This *so* wasn't happening.

But it clearly was.

Nathan and one of the other divers she'd gone down with were standing at the edge of the dock. While the unknown man eyed Naðr's brothers and cousin with outright fear, her ex-husband didn't seem all that threatened. But then she'd never seen him frightened by anything.

His eyes flew to hers and widened as they approached. "Megan, thank God you're all right."

Then his gaze went to Naðr and she had the pleasure of seeing a flicker of both uncertainty and, oh look at that, *fear*. She didn't much blame him. The Viking king seemed entirely unimpressed. Ferocious almost. For a moment, she almost imagined it was because her name had come from a strange man's mouth.

Truly though, what fresh hell was this that her ex was *here*?

Naðr sauntered around the men, eyeing them up and down. Eventually, he stopped directly in front of Nathan. Her ex wasn't a small man at six foot three but the king had him by a good four or five inches. Not to mention everything else about the Viking was bigger and wider.

Eyes narrowed to dangerous slits, Naðr's voice was low and gravely. "How do you know my woman?"

His woman? Oh Lord.

When Megan went to step closer, Kol's hand wrapped around her upper arm and he shook his head.

But Nathan hadn't come as far as he had in life by letting other men intimidate him. Eyes just as narrowed as the kings he said, "I was married to her."

While she thought for sure Naðr would go all 'Conan the Barbarian' on Nathan, he surprised her when he turned his head and eyed her with an irritating smirk. "Is this true?"

Megan stood up a little straighter, offended. Then again, Nathan wasn't at his best, especially in a torn wetsuit with his scraggly hair standing up at odd angles. After an unavoidable sigh she took credit for the dirtbag. "Yeah, I guess."

Nathan frowned. "You *guess*?"

Her eyes narrowed on him. "Be grateful I said that much."

"Bitch," he said under his breath.

Naðr's hand shot out and wrapped around Nathan's neck in a heartbeat. Her ex's eyes bulged as he grasped at the king's forearm. Not fazed in the least, the Viking pulled him close and whispered something in his ear. Nathan tried to nod despite the death grip.

When Naðr loosened his grasp just enough, Nathan's eyes went to Megan and he croaked out, "Sorry. *Really* sorry."

Hmm. Maybe she'd enjoy this whole 'Viking for a boyfriend while time traveling' thing. Especially if it put Nathan in his place. When at last Naðr released him entirely, her ex held his throat and gasped for air.

"How are you here?" she asked. "And where are my sisters?"

Nathan shook his head, a wary eye on Naðr. "Me and Tony washed up on the shore three days ago. Lost the other guy. No sign of Veronica or Amber."

She hoped this time travel escapade only included those who had gone beneath the water. Yet Guardian was here.

"Where are we, Megan," Nathan asked slowly.

About to answer, she stopped when her eyes zoned in on what he was holding. The metal cylinder she'd found on the underwater ship! When she tried to step forward, Kol's grip tightened on her and he again shook his head.

"Big oaf," she muttered to him then nodded at the tube while speaking to Naðr. "*That* belongs to me. I lost it when I was searching for Guardian."

Better to say lost than willingly tossed aside.

Nathan held it back when the king reached for it. Yet the moment Naðr's eyes narrowed again, her ex reluctantly handed it over. Megan didn't miss the flicker of vague recognition when the Viking touched the sea treasure.

Naðr's eyes went to several men nearby. "They smell. See that they're bathed then keep guard over them until I return to the holding."

"Food and drink?" one asked.

Naðr's eyes shot to her and he arched a brow in question. She decided if they starved or not.

Oh, she *really* liked this 'Viking boyfriend' thing. Though tempted to say no she nodded. While they were dragged off toward the fortress, Naðr made a motion with his head that she follow. It seemed Kol and Raknar would be joining them.

So while she got to watch them all stride away from the massive longship a few days ago, now she strode alongside them toward it. Or at least she hoped that was where they were heading. The closer they drew to it, the wider her eyes. Black-bellied clouds rolled across a tepid blue sky as heavy drifts of snow white fog curled around the mountains. Though the sail remained down the pure scale of the great ship stood stark against the choppy gray water.

Naðr strode just ahead of them, his heavy booted gait rumbling over the dock as he closed in on a ship that well-complimented him. This was his element. Where he belonged. When they reached the ship he climbed the ladder smoothly then stopped on the boat's edge. Turning, he held down his hand. Speechless, she stared up at him, caught by his imposing stance and the brilliance of his fierce blue eyes as they met hers.

His long legs adjusted easily to the sway of the boat as his fingers curled slightly. "Come. Let us see if this is the ship you think it is."

Eager, she climbed up then gripped his hand. The moment she did it felt like a red hot poker seared the back of her right shoulder. A small cry broke from her lips as he pulled her up then into the ship.

His brows drew down, troubled eyes on her face. "What is it?"

"I don't know." Megan put a hand over her shoulder and blinked away the water in her eyes. "Pain. Here."

Raknar and Kol had just joined them as Naðr brushed aside her hair and lowered the material of her dress.

"*Hel*," Naðr murmured and she cringed as his finger dusted the delicate flesh.

Megan tried to peer over her shoulder. "What?"

The burn had sizzled down to a dull sting.

"The Vegvisir," Raknar said, surprise in his voice.

Megan frowned at Naðr. "What's he talking about?"

The king touched the bottom part of the interlocked tattoos on his shoulder. "You have been marked with that which is on your stone, the Vegvisir, a magical rune stave that aids in sea navigation."

"I know what a Vegvisir is," she said, frown in place lest the men see how scared she truly was that a tattoo had suddenly appeared on her shoulder. "Why the hell is it there?"

Kol nodded at the cylinder in Naðr's hand. "Look."

While they seemed almost nonplussed by her new tattoo, what was happening to the tube got more of a reaction. Megan's mouth fell open as two symbols glowed gold and blue up and down the sphere. Interlocked over and over were the two symbols marking both her and Naðr.

The same two on either side of her stone.

The Vegvisirs glowed gold.

The Spirit Ships, blue.

"Both are the exact colors of your eyes," Raknar murmured.

Naðr's brilliant blue eyes met hers, his words thick with promise and challenge. "Do you still doubt you are here for me, then?"

While she could retort that Raknar had blue eyes too, the color glowing wasn't pale blue in the least but a perfect match to the king's. Not to mention, she'd felt a certain transcendence the moment their eyes connected...as if the past and future merged in a powerful connection suddenly fluctuating between them.

Megan didn't answer Naðr but dragged her eyes to the cylinder when Kol mentioned that it had stopped glowing. And though she was scared about her new tat and the strange object in the king's hand, her eyes were unavoidably drawn to the ship she stood upon.

Unable to stop herself, she stepped away from the men and walked to the base of the great dragon prow. Staring up, she smiled, remembering how she had so recently floated down its great wooden neck. Turning her face into the cold wind, she stared down the entirety of the ship and murmured, "God, it's so *incredibly* gorgeous."

Her eyes went to the wrapped sail. What she wouldn't do to see it billowing. Better yet, billowing over the open sea. Only after staring in mesmerized adoration for a stretched moment did she realize how quiet the men had grown. When she glanced their way it was to find all three staring at her with an avid, almost feral appreciation. It seemed Viking men got turned on by a woman who truly loved a boat.

Naðr's narrowed eyes slid from his brothers to her before he growled under his breath "mine" and headed her way. Megan leaned back against the base of the prow as he approached. If she wasn't mistaken, the raw look in his eyes bespoke a man with only one thing on his mind.

And it wasn't joining her to appreciate his ship.

Though she made to dart away, she didn't move nearly fast enough. Naðr might be huge and on a rocking ship but he was faster than a striking snake when he snatched her wrist and yanked her against him. He didn't need the prow of the ship to support them but braced his legs and enfolded her in his arms. Sea salt rode the whipping wind as he tilted up her chin and closed his warm lips over hers.

The same exact feeling she'd had so close to this spot at the bottom of the ocean roared through her. Raging heat ignited beneath her skin as his eager tongue stroked into the needy recesses of her mouth. Moaning, eager, she wrapped her hands into his hair and took him deeper.

He grabbed her backside and squeezed. Rougher than anything she'd experienced before, Megan didn't groan in pain but unabashed pleasure. He took her to the edge of something fast, furious and dangerous and she *liked* it. There was a reckless abandon in the way he plundered and explored her mouth with his lips, tongue and even teeth.

"Going to share some of that," Kol drawled from nearby.

Though Naðr seemingly ignored him, Megan pulled her lips away, throw off by someone standing so close. The king's eyes slid to his brother. "Never."

Kol's lips quirked, eyes amused. "Guess I'm just asking to be punched again."

Megan frowned at Kol. "Who punched you?"

Kol just chuckled and nodded at the cylinder in Naðr's hand. "Plenty of time for you to have your woman, brother. For now, what's in that." Then his eyes went to Megan. "And who are Amber and Veronica?"

"Her sisters." Raknar leaned against the center mast, eyes intent on Megan. "Yes?"

Megan untangled from Naðr and offered no answer. Kol and Raknar weren't going anywhere near her sisters if she had anything to say about it. Especially not Amber. She couldn't even begin to imagine what her lustful sister would do with or *to* these men. And Veronica? She'd likely take one less-than-impressed look then stroll in the opposite direction, her infamous stilettos at the ready to whip if either made a move.

So she tried to deter any 'Viking meets modern day woman' interest and nodded at the cylinder. "Let's focus on what matters. What's in that?"

Naðr flipped the tube in his hand, eyes on hers. "It cannot be opened but I know what it holds." His eyes lingered, watching her reaction. "And I know why you have that tattoo on your shoulder."

Kol crossed his arms over his broad chest and rocked back on his heels. "Then by all means *share* brother."

Meanwhile, Raknar kept his steady eyes on Megan and she knew his thoughts hadn't for a second strayed from her sisters and the potential loot they might lead him to.

"Besides me, only Megan will ever know what's in this cylinder because it is hers alone." Naðr's surprisingly tender hand closed over her shoulder, his fingers dusting a now painless tattoo. "As to what she's been marked with, it is a claiming of the seers." His hand squeezed gently and sensual chills raced up her spine. "She is here for *me*."

"We gathered that," Raknar said dryly. "But what of the things you are not telling us, my *king*."

Naðr's eyes lingered on hers for another long moment before he stepped away and met Raknar's eyes. Though definitely close, it was clear the middle and oldest brother could easily butt heads. Their spirits were designed to challenge others.

"Somehow Megan coming in contact with me, this ship and the cylinder all at once ignited the bargain we struck with the seers. At least my part of it." Naðr strolled along the ship, his hand trailing its edge with affection much like hers had on the boat she'd built at home.

Though clearly relaxed and comfortable in this environment, his eyes were sharper and harder than usual when they met Raknar's. "Which means yours and Kol's is not far behind."

A hungry gleam filled Raknar's regard. "I look forward to it."

"The plunder anyways," Kol remarked. Then his suave eyes swung to Megan. "Me? I look forward to the lusher part of this commitment."

Megan knew all too well what the borderline debonair Viking with his smooth good looks referred to. And it wasn't her. Eyes narrowed to slits, she said through clenched teeth, "Don't even think about it."

Innocent, he shrugged as a dimple-ridden grin crawled onto his face. "Might have no choice in the matter, Sea Siren."

The blood in her veins grew sluggish and the wind almost seemed to slow down around her. Nobody had ever called her that but Sean. "What did you just say?"

Kol eyed her, interested. "Which part?"

Attention caught by the change in her voice, Naðr was slowly making his way back in their direction.

Eyes locked with Kol's, she frowned. "Sea Siren. Why'd you call me that?"

"Look at you," Kol said easily as his eyes went to her hair then raked down her front. "You were born to be on the water." His eyes roamed the boat then went back to her. "Born to scream over the sea louder than the siren's themselves."

Megan didn't know what to make of the moment. It was unusual, different in a way she couldn't quite explain. Though by no means arousing, there was familiarity…almost as if Sean himself could have said every word that had just come from Kol's mouth.

Startled, she jumped a little when Naðr came behind her and tucked his front against her back, warm words against her ear. "Who called you Sea Siren?"

Where she'd hesitated to speak of Nathan earlier, she had no such reservations when it came to Sean. "My best friend."

Kol's brow's arched and the corner of his lip pulled down a small fraction almost as if he sensed something in her words. Raknar moved closer as if he sensed something as well. Again, she felt that overwhelming mystical feeling with the three she'd had the first night she'd arrived.

The words *dragon blood* floated through her mind once more.

"What *are* you guys," she whispered, tilting her head back against Naðr's hard chest.

Though none touched her but the king, chilled wind heated around her as Kol and Raknar drifted just beyond her reach.

"*Yours*," whispered Naðr, his hot lips trailing down the side of her neck.

Megan inhaled sharply as his strong hand latched onto her hip and he nipped at her delicate flesh. It might have been simple intoxication caused by the feel of him but she swore Kol and Raknar's eyes glowed as they watched. One's light blue, one's nearly black, both were intense, pleased, welcoming.

Yet there remained a definite wall between her, Naðr and them. Something made of the king's possession as his other hand spanned her opposite hip, measuring her dimensions, before crawling across her stomach. Red-hot delicious shivers spanned out from his spread palm, crawling and licking, they slowly wrapped up over her breasts. Nipples tight and tingling, the heat spanned up her neck and down her arms.

Megan couldn't stop it if she tried.

Her eyes slid shut.

She almost felt drunk as she waited…anticipated.

While the top half of her felt enflamed and aroused, what happened to her bottom half made her eyelids flutter and mouth fall open. Megan's jaw trembled as fiery hot flames snaked downward from Naðr's hand and wrapped between her legs. An indescribable mix of pain and pleasure rolled over her as sharp arousal made her moan and squirm within his tight hold. Visions started to snap on and off behind her closed lids.

Huge wings against a dark, moonlit sky. Large, dominant bodies. Fierceness. Control.

Naðr held Megan more securely as the heat between her thighs seemed to curl up inside her. Eyes still closed, she gripped his hand, dug in her nails and arched as the muscles between her legs started to flutter.

God above this was too much.

Seconds away from what would likely be a crippling climax, the heat started to dissipate and his soft words slowly reeled her back from where she was heading. His raspy, thick words forced her away from sweet oblivion.

"Not yet, beautiful."

Startled and confused by the aching, hollow feeling between her legs and the icy wind whipping her face, her eyes shot open. Heart thudding into her throat, she blinked several times. Though Naðr was still at her back, arms wrapped around her, his brothers were gone.

Simply not there.

Confused, she tried to talk. Nothing came out but a strange, gasping sound. Swallowing hard, she licked her dry lips. What the *hell* had just happened? Naðr's mouth traced a delicate but pressured trail over her jaw as he turned her head. Helpless to do anything else, she opened her mouth to his and swallowed the taste of him as he devoured her.

But before she could drown in the crashing, hungry sea of his touch, he slowly pulled away, his growled words vibrating against her lips. "Not yet."

Not yet. As she slowly but surely unraveled from the bizarre spell she'd been cast under she straightened. Not yet? Of course, not yet! Jerking away, Megan frowned as she again surveyed her surroundings. Smoothing down her unruly curls, her eyes narrowed on the rather complacent Viking that'd been at her back. "Your brothers were *just* here and I didn't hear them leave. How is that possible? Where'd they go?"

A small grin ghosted Naðr's lips as he offered a loose shrug. "They left a bit ago but you were…" his lusty gaze raked her body, "busy."

Megan rolled back her shoulders, shook her head and refused to look away. Though ridiculously tempted to bend over and let him have his way with her, pride kept her halfway human. "Tell me what just happened because it wasn't normal."

A deep chuckle rumbled up from his chest but he gave no answer. Jumping up onto the dockside of the ship, he held down his hand. "Come on, beautiful. I'll take you sailing on this soon enough but for now," his lips curled into a rakish grin, "I'd rather get to know the man you loved before me."

Cocky! But she couldn't help but appreciate his smooth tactics. So as she took his hand and allowed him to pull her up she murmured, "You really enjoy being you, eh?"

In return, Naðr slapped her backside while simultaneously swinging her down so she could navigate the ladder. Still, as they walked down the dock, Megan wasn't ready to give up. "Seriously,

105

where did your brothers go? One second they were there, the next, gone."

Megan refused to over analyze the wings flapping when she closed her eyes, better yet what they symbolized. It also seemed that he wasn't going to further inquire whether this was the ship she found beneath the sea and she was just fine with that. It was a truly sad topic and hopefully just a weird non-existent twist to the time travel.

Instead of answering her question about his brothers vanishing, he said, "Tell me about *Nathan*."

The way he said her ex's name sounded like he'd licked rotten fish beforehand.

She knew he'd tell her nothing more about his brothers right now so she nodded at the cylinder in his hand as they walked. "Tell me about what's in that."

"Did he beat you?"

"No." She again nodded at the cylinder. "Is it something bad?"

"Depends on how you look at it." His gaze stayed on the shore. "Did he hurt you?"

"Depends on how you look at it."

Naðr's eyes cut to hers and narrowed before they once more focused on the village ahead. "Do you want me to kill him?"

"No," she replied instantly and honestly. "Will what's in that cylinder help me get home?"

"No." His voice roughened. "What do you want me to do with him?"

It was less of a question and more of a reluctant curiosity about where she stood emotionally.

"I need answers from him." Then you can kill him. But she'd never say it nor mean it. Cheating bastards didn't deserve death. They just didn't deserve love. At least not as deep as hers had run. "When are you going to let me see what's in the cylinder?"

"After."

"After what?"

"After you get your answers."

Fair enough. "Will I like what I find in that cylinder?"

"Depends."

"On what?"

They'd nearly reached the end of the dock and a crowd was, as always, waiting.

"On you," he muttered before several men fell alongside him and she fell back. It seemed to be a thing with these Viking men that they left you on a cliffhanger. But she couldn't entirely fault Naðr. He was in charge here and that meant spreading his time around. A nod, maybe a 'see you in a bit, okay?' wouldn't hurt. But no. Instead she was left in a sea of Vikings busy as ever in commerce.

Thank any god listening that Meyla happened to come along. But then would the king's daughter mysteriously just appear? She doubted it.

"Come." Meyla led Megan toward the vendors. "Let us shop."

When she nearly asked why, Meyla shook her head and looked skyward. "You were out on father's ship with him and my uncles. Trust me, clearing your head with simple things is the least I can do for you."

Did she understand what had happened then?

"What's going on, Meyla?"

But like her father, the Viking girl didn't seem up for giving answers. Instead, she stopped at the first cart and eyed the wares. She pointed at a few items. "Pale gold seashell earrings for the king's woman."

His woman. Here we go again. Megan did her best to shove aside memories of almost getting off in his arms not that long ago.

"I like green," she remarked.

Meyla eyed her as though she was clueless and took the offering without giving anything in return.

Megan shook her head when Meyla tried to steer her away. "Aren't you going to pay or trade something?"

"Not necessary. You belong to my father."

Frustrated, she stopped and shook her head. "I belong to no man." She eyed the peddler. "He either paid for what you just took or made it himself. *Give* him something for his efforts."

Astounded, Meyla's rounded eyes met hers and a harsh frown slashed her lips. "I will *not*."

Of all people, Raknar came alongside and pressed something into the peddler's hands. Steering the women into the crowd, his voice was stern as he looked at Meyla. "Back to the holding with you, little flower."

107

Megan strongly speculated he held back chastising his niece until listening ears weren't around and she gave him *some* credit for that. Yes, he spared her dignity but would she really learn a lesson? But then Meyla's actions with the vendor struck her somehow out of character so she had to wonder.

Raknar stopped them just beyond the outer gates of the fortress and nodded at a swath of fabric hanging from what appeared to be a fairly popular cart. He pointed at an extremely well-made pale tan sleeveless leather tunic. "That one." Then he looked at a gorgeous deep blue tunic with long sleeves and lots of coverage. "And that one for Meyla."

Meyla's frown turned into a wide smile as the vendor handed it over. Grinning, Raknar wrapped his niece under his arm. "If you cover yourself respectably and Valan keeps wearing trousers, your father might just come around." Then he winked. "And don't we all want that?"

Naðr's daughter dished out an even wider smile. "Yes we do."

Raknar looked from her to the vendor then back again. "And?"

Meyla dug into her pocket and handed over some coins. The vendor nodded and smiled even before Raknar gave him several more coins, took the material and ushered the women forward.

"Good girl," he murmured in Meyla's ear before pushing her along.

Then, as she figured would end up happening, her and Raknar were walking alone. He handed her the tan tunic. "For you."

Surprised by the kind gesture, she said, "Thank you." Megan hoped he wouldn't bring up what had happened on the ship...whatever that was. Best to keep the focus on Meyla. "You're a good uncle."

"She's sacrificed a lot for her father and deserves Odin's blessing." His hand touched her lower back as he steered her through the crowd.

Megan thought back on what Naðr had told her before Nathan arrived. "Did she really have a child with Adlin MacLomain...one that she had to leave behind?"

The girl was so young. It was hard to imagine.

Raknar's jaw clenched but his words were at odds with apparent frustration. "Meyla is Viking. She did what was asked of her."

Now that sounded like a boatload of crap.

"So she really had a child and left it," Megan shook her head, "wherever she left it?"

"*Him*," Raknar said.

Megan thought about how clear she'd been about gender with Raknar's son, Heidrek when it came to Guardian.

"Him," she said. "I'm so sorry. I didn't mean to sound insensitive."

Raknar said nothing more about Meyla's child but at least the strong set to his jaw softened. Yet still, she felt Naðr's brother close off as he escorted her. Megan had a million questions but couldn't seem to put them to words as she eyed him.

Something about Naðr's middle brother was offsetting while simultaneously drawing. Either you were on his good side or on a side that shut you out completely. And he didn't seem to want to meet you halfway if you ended up somewhere he didn't quite like.

Raknar followed his own path and either you were on it or not.

Better yet, he allowed it or not.

Nothing more was said as he at last handed her off to their family slaves, kind-hearted women who said little but seemed happy enough. Meyla, meanwhile, wasn't busy primping and pressing but laughing alongside Kol as they shot arrows into a target. If nothing else could be said about the society she'd landed in it was that family stuck by family and all were well loved. Almost as if he sensed she was passing, Kol cocked his arrow but still managed to look over his shoulder and wink at Megan.

And despite herself, she gave him a small smile.

What was it about Naðr and his brothers? Though determined to find them all barbaric and beneath the level of society hers had evolved to, it wasn't quite working out like that. Yes, she'd always loved Viking history but in truth, the real thing should have shown her how far humanity had come.

But it wasn't.

Okay, maybe as far as technology, modern day conveniences and a host of other things but when it came to people being decent and honest…well, she was starting to think the ninth century beat the twenty-first.

Or at least right here, right now.

Megan conveniently pushed aside all the weird voo-dooey stuff that'd happened on the ship.

In truth, it was downright easy to set aside all the oddities as she basked in being pampered for presentation. By the time the chatty women around her were finished, she felt like a princess.

A warrior princess.

They'd banded her hair back just enough that her wild, unruly curls didn't touch her face but twisted down her back. The sleeveless tan tunic Raknar picked out was fitted snuggly enough that it offered up a little extra cleavage and left her slender, toned arms and the new tattoo bared. Strapped by a thin leather belt, the tunic was shorter than most, highlighting the soft, supple, fairly tight leather trousers she convinced Meyla to let her wear. Add in the dangly earrings that matched her eyes and Megan wasn't feeling like herself in the least when she entered the main holding.

But then none of that mattered when she saw who sat next to the Viking king with a wide smile on his face as his determined eyes met hers.

"You've got to be kidding me," she whispered.

"Welcome to my world," Meyla said, coming alongside as she eyed the head table and offered a loose, 'see what you get' shrug as she strolled on, words lingering…

"Is that not your former husband sitting beside my father?"

Chapter Nine

One look at Megan and his cock about burst into flames.

Overheated and eager for battle, Naðr tore off his tunic, spread his legs and sat back.

Nathan, her former husband, went silent when his eyes locked on her. The man wouldn't shut up before she arrived and truth told, Naðr was interested in just about everything coming out of his mouth. Sea expeditions, Viking treasure, riches to be had.

Until *she* walked in.

Now it was time to have some fun.

Naðr didn't blame Nathan for going silent. Megan was dressed in something made of heat and passion and dark, mouth-watering nights. Typically women only wore leggings if they were going raiding but it seemed she was readying herself for another sort of battle altogether. He tore his gaze from her for a split second. Long enough for Raknar to wink at him. Lip curling up, Naðr inclined his head then redirected his attention back to Megan and patted his lap.

But it seemed his little twenty-first century woman wouldn't come to him so easily this time. Instead she tore her arm from the girl leading her and frowned. Maybe it was the alluring outfit she wore or a new sense of familiarly, but Megan strode right up to the head table, slammed her hands down, leaned forward and glared at him.

"In no world will I sit on your lap," she sneered, narrowed eyes flickering between Nathan and him. "Not with him there."

Naðr met her angry glare for a long moment, relishing the dare in her eyes. Because there *was* a dare. He leaned forward and grinned. "No?"

Her eyes widened then narrowed. "No."

"I think you *will*."

But it seemed she decided to punish him for thinking to force her onto his lap again because she proceeded to do the very *last* thing he expected. She didn't just saunter but swung her hips as she walked around the long table. The hall quieted as everyone watched

111

her. He imagined all of those in the great halls of Valhalla did as well.

Naðr could have supposed a great many things but never that she'd snuggle her perfect ass down on her former husband's lap. Nathan's eyes widened as she propped her chin in her hand on the table and narrowed eyes on Naðr, words soft. "No. I. Won't."

He'd never been so aroused in his life. Feisty wench.

"Sea Siren all right," Kol muttered from beside him.

While he knew she expected him to drag her over, Naðr was much more interested in letting her bask in her own ill-chosen tactic. With a relenting sigh, he took a long swig from his horn then raised his voice to the crowd waiting with baited breath. "Who am I not to share with such an esteemed guest?"

All roared with approval though many cried, "As long as you have 'er in the end."

Megan, however, seemed less than impressed when Nathan shrugged and pulled her back against him. Still, she kept an even expression no matter how hard she glared at Naðr.

Yet he found himself caught in his own trap as Nathan eased his eager hand onto Megan's thigh. Downing the last of his ale, Naðr received another and returned his attention to the futuristic man. "Tell me again why you wanted Megan to help lead your Viking treasure expedition."

Megan's narrowed eyes stayed on Naðr though her words were directed at Nathan. "Yeah, I'd like to know as well seeing how it was a whole lot more than what you said."

"It wasn't rea—"

Nathan's words stopped short when Megan's hand slammed down on his as it inched up her thigh. With a disgusted look on her face, she said, "Obviously it *was* something. What?"

Brave, presumptuous soul that he was, Nathan offered a small smile and loose shrug as his hand continued to inch up. "What? There was," he glanced around the hall before meeting her eyes again, "*this*."

Megan started to talk, incredulous, before she stopped and slowly shook her head, eyes widening. "You knew that we could travel through time. Somehow you *knew*."

Nathan huffed, condescending eyes on Megan as though she was of ill-mind. "Not my fault you were too slow to catch on."

Naðr had done a lot of Loki-ridden shitty things in life but he realized he'd never stooped so low as he had in this moment. A moment when he let a good woman sit on a bad man's lap. He knew on the docks that Nathan was hel's scum yet here he was allowing this display to corner Megan…to make her truly see her former husband for what he was.

Fire blazed through his vision so quickly that the next thing he knew his brothers were holding him back as his blade trembled against Nathan's neck. Naðr had no idea how they'd gotten on the floor. No idea when he'd managed to lock a death grip on the fool's neck. It was a rare day that berserker fury seized him so thoroughly.

In fact, his warriors had never seen it outside of battling.

As the dragon's blood haze slowly abated, Naðr clenched his teeth and pressed the blade tighter. Only one thing stopped him. His brothers.

"Don't," Megan murmured as she crouched alongside.

Then he realized. She'd been saying 'don't' over and over again for several moments. Eager for blood but more eager to heed her every desire, his eyes met hers, his word hoarse and the first of its kind. "*Please.*"

Naðr didn't care if it made him look weak. He'd give her this. A strength within his people. Because somehow he knew she deserved it.

And damned if she didn't take it.

Megan drew back and looked down her nose at Nathan. A long moment passed before she shook her head. "No, don't hurt him. Let him stay. I want answers."

High on Megan's well-seized power, Naðr cocked his head and grinned as he dug the blade in a bit deeper, a fraction from the man's death vein and leaned in close. "Count yourself lucky you've one of Freyja's warriors sparing you." He brought his lips close to the trembling man's ear, words heavy with promise. "Because I would *not*."

When she made to step away, Naðr came easily to his feet and grabbed her wrist. "Sit." Kol moved down one seat. "Beside me."

Appreciation that he wasn't asking her to sit on his lap flickered in her eyes and she nodded. Raknar shoved Nathan back into the chair Naðr had torn him from. This put the king between Megan and her former husband. The man's uncomfortable eyes flashed between

Naðr and Raknar who plunked down a little too closely on his other side.

Naðr pushed away the drink he'd given Nathan earlier, crossed his arms over his chest and sat back. Blade still in hand, he forced his body to relax as his eyes narrowed on the foreign man. "Tell us how you knew about this place." He clenched the hilt of his blade with promise. "This time without insulting Megan."

Nathan's eyes skimmed over the blade and Megan before he focused on Naðr. Considering he'd come so close to death, his words were fairly level. "Before I enlisted Megan's help, I'd already brought up Viking treasure from the waters in front of her house."

Megan frowned. "I *knew* it. What'd you bring up?"

"A cylinder similar to the one that was taken from me when I arrived here." Nathan had the nerve to scowl. "It contained a map within a map. Better yet, a map within a graphic design of the Nine Worlds. Etched within Midgard, Middle Earth, our planet, was a smaller map, one that clearly had a starting point coordinating from where we dove to *this* location."

"Strange," Megan murmured. "So obviously, despite how impossible the concept, you thought it somehow led from our century to this one. Why?"

When Nathan hesitated to answer, Raknar draped his arm on the back of the man's seat and pulled his dagger free.

Nathan got the point and continued. "Another sheet of paper was with the map. Written in Old Norse, I had it translated. It told of three stones with runic symbols. How they supposedly allowed certain people to travel through time. Something to do with Viking seers and of all things, Scottish magic."

Naðr narrowed his eyes and growled, "Keep talking."

"The goddess Freyja's name was mentioned, as well as the Celtic god, Fionn Mac Cumhail." Nathan shook his head. "Odd mix of information to say the least."

Was it ever. But it fed into everything he and his brothers had agreed to. Save Scottish magic being involved. That was never part of any agreement.

Adlin MacLomain was up to something.

Or had been.

"Why don't you get around to the part that led you to seek me out," Megan said. "Because as I suspected to begin with, it had nothing to do with showing me any sort of kindness."

"That's not entirely true." A smug smile curled Nathan's lips. "Are you not sitting in the midst of a society you've dreamt of nearly all your life?"

Kol stood, stretched then braced his hands on the back of Nathan's chair when Raknar removed his arm. Leaning forward, he murmured close to the swine's ear. "You want to be very careful with your tone, stranger."

Now Nathan was surrounded by Naðr and his brothers.

Not a place any man disliked so much by Megan wanted to be.

"Again, what made you seek out my woman," Naðr said.

Nathan's eyes went from Megan to Naðr and though he clearly wanted to comment on the king's claim, his brooding eyes focused on the table. "According to the scroll, the key to traveling through time was located in a box, one that held three stones. Through this stone my era and this era could harness the power of Bifrost, the Rainbow Bridge and allow for time travel."

"Hence the Nine Worlds being depicted around the original map." Megan's chin jut forward as her eyes stayed locked on Nathan. "Again, why me?"

"Your name was mentioned in the scroll," Nathan replied, his eyes on her not Naðr. "And the king's."

Naðr wondered just how much Megan would tell Nathan about what she'd found on her shore. As he suspected, little. "Odd as all this sounds it still doesn't explain why you would need me. I don't know anything about a box or stones."

Nathan suddenly seemed overly aware of the men surrounding him and Naðr tensed. He'd been around far too many people who kept secrets they were afraid to share. And while tempted to simply let his inner dragon rip the information from the coward's mind, he'd not take this moment from Megan. So he shot his brothers a look and shook his head a fraction. They were not to attack.

Megan was no fool though. She sensed Nathan was about to say something that would anger her. "Tell me."

For all the healthy fear a man should have in his current position, Nathan was quick to smooth his features and look her dead in the eye. "You're lying about the box and stones. You've got them. I had your house tapped."

Megan simply ground her jaw and stared at him for a long moment. Unable to help himself, Naðr rested her hand on his thigh and covered it with his own. The next move was hers. If she gave him permission to kill her former husband, it would be done before she finished speaking.

"All so well planned," she finally murmured and took a healthy swallow from her mug as she admirably repressed all emotion and contemplated Nathan. "You needed at least one stone to help you travel through time. You've always been a deceptive bastard who didn't play by the rules. Why not just hire thugs to steal it from me. Why bank on me bringing it when we dove."

"The scroll spoke of a connection across time between you and Naðr Véurr." Nathan couldn't quite seem to keep a sneer out of his voice. "And based on how you spoke of him to Sean and seemed unable to part with the stone, it seemed like a sure bet that you'd bring it with you diving."

Raknar wrapped his hand around the back of Nathan's neck and squeezed, eyes narrowed. "I'm pretty sure Kol mentioned something about your tone."

Meanwhile, Naðr slowly flipped the dagger over and over as he watched Nathan. Yet beneath the simmering need to run the blade across the man's throat, he felt an unexpected sense of triumph. So that look of desire he'd seen on Megan's face when they first met had been cultivating for some time.

"What else did the scroll say," Megan said, voice stern, eyes unrelenting. "And why did the ship and wreckage look as though it'd only been beneath the sea for mere days."

"Neither the ship or wreckage were there when I retrieved the scroll and map." Nathan's eyes stayed on her. "They appeared for you. As to the scroll, it said little else."

"Every little bit matters," Kol rumbled, his fists tight on the chair.

Though he hesitated, Nathan at last continued, voice low. "Dragons were mentioned. Beasts that struggled against bargains struck."

"Beasts." Raknar chuckled, eyes dangerous. "Says a man with a corrupt soul and no respect for women. I think you know nothing of what makes a *beast*."

Naðr kept a grin hidden when Megan stood then slid onto his lap. Propping her hand within inches of his interested groin, she trailed a finger up Naðr's chest though she eyed Nathan. "I don't think dragons exist, do you?"

Nathan shook his head and started to speak but she cut him off. "But then I didn't think time travel existed either so what do I know."

Some might think she was goading her former husband not only with actions but words. But Naðr knew better. Megan was exercising freedom and likely revenge on Nathan. And while some men might find it offensive to be used in such a way, Naðr wasn't one of them. He understood the aftershocks of heartache. He also knew she wasn't in love with this man anymore. Which was too bad for Nathan. He'd only met Megan a few days ago but already knew she was irreplaceable. Strong, beautiful, courageous, any man would be privileged to call her theirs.

When Nathan leaned forward to grab the mug Naðr had moved away, Raknar put a hand on the table and shook his head. "You are no longer a guest but a prisoner."

Kol stepped away as several warriors came forward. One yanked Nathan's chair back and the other pulled him to his feet before they led him away.

Naðr nodded at the chair Megan had abandoned then at her. "Return to it if you like."

It was a chair that gave her great honor. Not only that, it gave her freedom from his lap.

She eyed the chair then Meyla in the one next to it, angling her backside over his arousal as she contemplated, voice raised a fraction. "It's a good seat. Is it truly mine?"

It was important that she knew it was but he suspected she had a reason for asking. Still, he'd not take from her a sense of belonging. "Yes. It is. As long as you would like it."

Megan nodded, a lovely, far too innocent smile on her face when her eyes met his. "Then I'd like Valan Hamilton to take it for tonight."

Raknar snorted.

Kol chuckled.

A sunbeam of pure joy covered Meyla's face.

"Of course you would," Naðr muttered but appreciated the way she'd outmaneuvered him. His people had heard him give her the chair, one that openly declared her as his. That meant she could do with it what she wished. Cornered, he nodded his consent.

And damn if the Scotsman wasted any time plunking down next to them.

When Megan made to stand, Naðr wrapped his arm securely around her waist, offered her a devious grin and shook his head. "The only place for you besides that chair is right here."

Her eyes didn't shy from his in the least as the corners of her lips twitched, fighting a grin. "And here I thought you were working at being a gentleman."

"Gentleman?" Kol asked as he sat next to Raknar.

"It means civilized and polite," Megan offered.

Raknar snorted again and shook his head. "Civilized, barely. Polite? Never."

But the way he said it encompassed him and his brothers with pride.

"I don't know." Megan stopped Naðr's hand before it wandered to her breast. "I've seen you all be polite one way or another since arriving." She paused. "Sort of."

Naðr pulled Megan so that her back rested against his chest and her thighs neatly straddled one leg. This not only gave him the benefit of feeling her backside against his arousal but allowed him to keep a close eye on Valan. So far the Scotsman was being respectable enough and both hands were where he could see them.

Though the crowd was less boisterous than the past few nights, many danced and ate, enjoying what time they had with loved ones before more ships went out. There was constant traffic in and out of his ports and more lives lost than usual lately.

He knew King Rennir was behind the added violence. Though his patience was wearing thin, Naðr had yet to act on it. So his men grew restless. They wanted revenge. Not only that, they wanted to raid new territory. The Kingdom of Northumbria for the most part was fine but its uppermost point, Lothian, was off limits. That area was too connected to Adlin MacLomain and he wouldn't have it.

"He didn't tell us everything he knew," Raknar said softly.

Torn from thought, Naðr received a horn of ale and drank deeply. No, Nathan had not told them everything but he would. In time. "He's somehow connected with Rennir."

Not only his brother's but his daughter's troubled gaze landed on him.

"Who's Rennir?" Megan asked.

"A rival king." Kol frowned as he looked at Naðr. "What makes you think such?"

"My gut." But it was more than that. It was in the questions not asked and answers not given. "We'll question him more effectively on the morrow."

"What of the Scottish magic that was written of in the scroll." Valan's eyes met Naðr's. "Did it have to do with Adlin MacLomain?"

That the man sat next to him was enough. He had no desire to converse with him. Instead, he decided to focus on more pleasant things so ran his hand along Megan's slim shoulder and collarbone. And though she might have shivered at the touch, she still tilted her head and cocked a brow. "You gonna answer Valan's question?"

"No."

"Because you don't know the answer or you're just determined to make life hard for Meyla?"

If anyone else said such he'd be aggravated. Instead he was amused. "I'm determined to make life better for Meyla."

"So is Adlin at work here then?" Valan said, jaw set, clearly trying to keep frustration from his voice.

Naðr knew the Scotsman was a warlock. Little good it did him when faced with a dragon though. But that wasn't what truly ate at him when it came to Valan. Though the man was ultimately here to keep Torra MacLomain safe, he'd done things before so dishonorable that it was hard to see genuine decency in him.

If that wasn't enough, Meyla had to go and fall in love with the traitor.

The king was not daft. He knew the difference between simple infatuation and true love. And what his daughter felt for the Scotsman was the latter. And, though it irritated him to no end, he knew Valan felt the same. Which only proved love like that could happen twice in one lifetime. After all, the only reason Valan was here was because he'd loved Torra MacLomain so completely.

But that didn't help Naðr any when trying to push past the man Valan had once been.

Still, he knew Adlin would want Valan to have an answer to the question he'd asked. "Yes, Adlin is at work here. Not sure how yet but because there is such a connection between me and Megan I'd say the MacLomain wizard spoke with the seers or perhaps even the gods and somehow shifted the tide of all that's happening."

Megan seemed cautiously relaxed as she studied the horn of ale in her hand. "I wish I'd taken the time to read the manuscript more thoroughly."

"Not part of your story, I'd say," Meyla murmured and while she leaned closer to Valan they didn't touch or hold hands. A far cry from how they'd acted before Megan arrived. A change, Naðr admitted, he rather liked.

But even as he kept an eye on his daughter and Valan, Naðr grew tired of analyzing them so focused on Megan. Burying his nose in her soft hair, he inhaled deeply. Though she'd been bathed her hair still held the faint hint of sea salt. Caught on the wind when she stood upon his ship, it was a scent that belonged to her. A scent that no soap would ever wash away.

Megan was of the ocean and wind, of adventure and ceaseless craving. He wondered if she truly realized how restless her soul was. How freeing a woman like her was to *his* soul. His brothers had sensed her essence as thoroughly as he did on the ship earlier. While they'd certainly lusted, there was more. Somehow Megan belonged to them all. As did those closest to her.

Viking men had no issues sharing their willing women any more than male dragons did. Their society was far different than the one she came from. One nurtured by hundreds upon hundreds of generations who worshiped the Christian God. Even so, there were several in their Viking society that preferred one partner and none took issue with it.

This would be such a time.

Because he would not share Megan with his brothers.

Unless she wanted such.

Naðr gritted his teeth. He wasn't such a fool that he'd say no if she decided she wanted Kol or Raknar. Not only his Viking but his dragon blood wouldn't allow him to. But hel if he'd ever deal well with it.

Still lounging against his chest, Megan turned her head and whispered in his ear. "The whole 'smoldering' look on your face doesn't really translate that you're at least trying when it comes to Valan."

"You assume he was on my mind at all," he said softly, enjoying the warmth left on his ear by her words.

"I could only hope. That would mean you were paying attention to how good they're being." Her lips stayed close, tempting. "What else could you be thinking about?"

Naðr adjusted his hips to remind her of his ceaseless arousal. Then, to see if he could make her squirm, he said, "I was considering sharing you with my brothers."

Megan stilled but didn't jolt away as she would have even a day ago. "I made it clear how I felt about that sort of thing."

"When first you met us." He trailed a lazy finger up the soft skin of her arm. "Much can change as you get to know people."

"Not that." Gooseflesh rose from the tips of her fingers up to the edge of her tunic. "I'm into monogamy."

Familiar with the word, relieved, he pressed his lips to her temple but gave no response.

But it seemed his lack of verbal response didn't sit so well because she leaned forward, robbing his chest of warmth. Megan said nothing at first until she turned the conversation to Valan and Meyla. Naðr finished his ale and grinned. Let her be defiant. He was good at that. Though he spoke to Raknar, he gripped the top of her thigh and swiped his thumb over the top of her center, dusting the knob he knew she wouldn't be able to ignore.

Mid-sentence, Megan snapped her mouth shut abruptly.

Kol, with a rakish twinkle in his eyes, looked at Megan. "What was that? You didn't quite finish your thought."

"She didn't, did she?" Raknar said, out of form but likely ready for some light-heartedness regardless of his brooding nature.

Meyla shook her head and pulled Valan's conversation her way.

Obviously referring to his restless hands, Megan lowered her brows and frowned at Naðr. "Getting bored?"

He grinned. "Almost."

Again, she surprised him when she got up, pushed aside the plates and cups then sat on the table in front of him, legs not quite spread. "Okay, then let's talk about dragons."

Chapter Ten

Megan would be the first to admit it. The warm, strong ale was going straight to her head.

But then so was Naðr Véurr.

The man was an intoxicating blend of hot dominant male meets honor gone wild. Careful not to show her arousal, she didn't squirm. Careful not to show how nervous she was sitting in front of the king with her legs too spread to be considered anything but a challenge, she white-knuckled her hands over the edge of the table. "Well then?"

Meyla cocked her head in what might almost be pride.

Valan buried his head in a long draw of ale.

Raknar and Kol gave her their undivided attention.

The king? He lounged back, muscular leather-strewn legs spread, horn braced in a loose fist as his eyes did a slow, appreciative crawl from the tips of her toes to the defiance in her eyes. After making a thorough visual project of everything she had to offer, he drawled, "I thought you didn't believe in dragons."

"I don't." Her brows slowly pulled up. "Yet."

Arrogance smoothly draped over his words, Naðr's gaze stayed with hers before his eyes lazily went from Kol to Raknar. "What say you, brothers? Do dragons exist?"

Raknar gave a small shrug, eyes never leaving Megan. "Hard to say."

Megan wasn't shy in the least as she met Raknar's eyes. "I would expect nothing less than honesty from *you*."

Then, poker face intact, she swung her gaze to Kol. "But you?" She twisted her lips. "Are another story."

Kol wasn't offended in the least. Nope. A wide smile split his face. "I love you, woman. Turn from Naðr and I'll keep you satisfied." He shrugged loosely and winked. "Until I get around to lying again."

This earned a few laughs from nearby men.

Naðr offered one of those deep chested chuckles he was so good at and directed his question at his middle brother. "And what of you, Raknar. How truthful are you really?"

Raknar sat on the table next to Megan and eyed her up and down. "Truthful enough."

If she was learning one thing quickly it was that these brothers weren't quite as predictable as they seemed. But then again, she surmised there was always an ongoing game being played between them. While she'd like to say it was the Viking mentality, it was really just brothers being brothers. This behavior wasn't all that different than what she saw between close friends, family and fellow seamen back home. They protected one another because their life was always one made of unpredictability.

The sea was friend to no man and didn't always send you home in one piece. Add the whole warrior, raider thing into the package and the possible death sentence was all that much more likely.

But eye on the ball.

And that ball was dragons and the unbelievable possibility that they existed.

Better yet that these brothers *were* such.

Megan's eyes flickered between Raknar and Kol before landing squarely on Naðr. Fun aside, she wanted a solid answer. So she ignored her trepidation and handled this situation as she had so many others when in real estate. *Directly.* "Do dragons exist? Are you one?"

Interesting that though the world narrowed down to Naðr's singular answer, those around her continued to drink and party despite how loud and clear she'd addressed him. The king, too comfortable in his skin for his own good, remained relaxed, curious eyes studying hers. "And what would you say if I said no? Better yet, what would you say if I said yes?"

Megan wasn't slowing down. Spreading her legs a bit further, she braced her hands between her thighs and leaned forward. "If you said no I'd say I thought as much." She licked her lips, determined to disarm him. "If you said yes..."

One black brow slowly raised and the cobalt in his eyes magnified as she left her words hanging. Eyes drifting down to the erection between Naðr's legs, she twitched her shoulder, almost as if she meant to shrug but couldn't quite do it. Lips pursed, she considered, before at last saying, tempting, inciting with her next statement. "If such a mighty creature existed I can't imagine a man like you," she dragged her eyes languidly between his brothers then back to him, "being one."

Though Naðr and his brothers didn't seem amused in the least, Kjar, the mega Viking and boat builder she'd met the first night, offered a full, throaty laugh. Then he plunked onto the table next to her, facing away from the brothers. After a hearty rip into a bone of meat, he tossed a glance over his shoulder at the king. "I *like* this one."

Megan drank deeply from her horn and nodded at Kjar's meat. "Is there more where that came from?"

Kjar's lips curved up. "There is. But how 'bout a dance first?"

She'd been watching everything the past few days. Kjar was not only Naðr's cousin and master boat builder but someone the king cared deeply for. If she could safely dance with anyone, it was him. Grinning, she nodded. "Yeah, I'd like that."

Kjar tossed aside his meat, grabbed her hand, whipped her around and pulled her off the opposite side of the table so fast that Naðr and his brothers spun away in a blur. The shipwright Viking released a heady burst of laughter and moved with surprising agility as he brought her close.

He was young, maybe mid-twenties, but he had the bearings of a man much older. As though he'd been watching the world through hard eyes since he was old enough to stand. Yet somehow the hardness in his eyes didn't translate to his skin. Where Sean already bore the lines of a man who spent far too much time on the water, Kjar's was surprisingly smooth.

Tattoos wrapped everywhere on his strong body, including a few on his bare head. Thin tendrils made of Norse markings. They almost reminded her of the vast symbols she'd seen carved into her longship on the bottom of the ocean. Startled, Megan realized those *same* symbols had not been carved into Naðr's ship sitting in port.

Her eyes shot to Kjar but his gaze was averted.

Was this just some warped coincidence?

No. Not at all. And she didn't know *why* she thought that.

"You protect him somehow," she whispered.

Kjar's strong, silent gaze met hers moments before heat came against her back. This time Naðr wasn't letting her play the field.

This time he meant to claim his territory. Unlike the first night, she wasn't sandwiched between two men long.

The shipwright brushed his lips across her temple then moved away.

Naðr kept her back against his front, wrapped an arm around her waist and the other across her chest. Though her arms were pinned to her side, his body swayed slowly, gently, as though he wanted to let her know there was no anger...only passion.

Caught in the protective, possessive embrace, her eyes slid shut.

While she'd flirted with the idea that he and his brothers might actually be dragons, she didn't believe it. Not really. Yet as she sunk into the blackness behind her eyelids, she recalled all too well the flashes she'd seen on the ship and the otherworldly sensations she'd felt.

Could such a thing really exist?

Had someone asked her a week ago if time travel existed, she would have said 'hell no' yet here she was. Immersed in an era so unlike her own.

Still.

Dragons?

When nothing but flesh and blood men stood before her?

Naðr's lips nuzzled past her hair and warmed against the sensitive skin above her collarbone. Just like that, thoughts of dragons and 'what if's' went flying out the window. Groaning, she pushed back against him. Not caring in the least that they stood within a thin crowd, his hand left her stomach and his long fingers grazed just above the area between her legs.

Though she hadn't known him long it already felt like eons.

The whispers on the wind, his name in her mind and on her longing tongue for so long. He'd done impressive things today, mostly putting Nathan in his place. But even more, he'd shown her that she had a place in this, *his* world, if she wanted it. All she had to do was sit by his side and say yes. And she had...until she didn't.

Megan wanted the truth no matter how scary.

And she'd get it.

Until then...her lips fell apart when one strong hand cupped the side of her breast and the other curled lower. It might have been a dance floor throbbing with flashing strobe lights and hundreds of swaying people for all anybody paid attention to his near lewd groping. And, though she supposed for a second she should push him away, Megan drowned in a moment she never allowed herself.

Lust. Pleasure. Need.

Back home, she'd watched people behave like she did now from the sidelines. Her and Nathan took their potential clients out, wined and dined them. All the while, Megan had stayed stoic by his side. Neither of them, or so she thought, had any desire to dance as well, certainly not put on a lewd display. No, they'd only help finance what it took to loosen people up. Anything to land the next big deal…and it always paid off.

Now she was the one on the dance floor. She was the unabashed exhibitionist. But even as she tensed, caught in memory, Naðr's hand left her breast and cupped her jaw, turning it until his lips folded over hers. The gesture wasn't violent but welcoming, as if he'd been waiting to do it for decades.

Though his fingers stilled, blood rushed to her lips as she swirled her tongue around his. There was nothing but pure temptation here, from the burn of his lips to his moan into her mouth. He was hungry for everything she was willing to give.

This was the moment.

The one that she could pull away *or not*. The one that kept distance between them.

Whether back home or here in the ninth century, it didn't matter. They'd arrived at the tipping point. Either she could step back from the edge or dive head first. Three days. Three months. Three years. It didn't matter how long they'd known one another. Everyone had their moment.

Theirs was *now*.

Megan knew it like she knew how to breathe.

She turned and looked into his eyes. Naðr looked right back, eyes dark with primal heat. But it was clear. She *still* had a choice. The king cupped her cheek, face expressionless as he kept his gaze locked with hers. Caught in the tumultuous blue depths of his silent inquisition, she almost faltered.

But didn't.

Instead, she stood on her toes, drew his lips down and closed her mouth over his. He offered no response save the tilt of his body so that their lips could more easily find one another's. Time seemed to stretch as he allowed her lips to play over his. And, *oh*, did they ever.

She didn't just press and lap, but used her teeth to clamp onto his lower lip as she released a low, feminine snarl.

Violence came soon after.

Not because she'd bit down too hard. No, if anything her bite had inflamed the beast. Naðr pulled back, eyes round before he released a sharp burst of laughter then scooped her up and swiftly flung her over his shoulder. The world flipped fast then all she could do was watch the ground pass beneath his long legs.

Megan knew better than to fight.

"Are you really doing it like this?" she asked, heat flaming her cheeks.

Naðr said nothing as he tromped along, the cheering crowd, and they *were* cheering the king's departure, were soon left behind. They left the main building and entered another. Megan thought for sure he'd fling her down, spread her legs, and have his way with her.

But she was wrong.

Instead he set her on her feet and nodded toward the mammoth fur covered bed with an intricately carved dragon headboard. "*This* is where you sleep now."

Bewildered, she watched as he poured ale into two mugs then turned; face rather bland considering the passion he'd just shown in the hall. "Well." He nodded toward the bed. "You best get there as that's where you need to be."

Absolutely clueless, she looked from him to the bed then back. "Weren't you supposed to toss me onto that and have your way with me?"

Amused, Naðr's lips curved slowly as heat gathered in his eyes. "Yes, I was supposed to."

The way he said it, his voice so low and sexy, made her knees weak and she lowered to the edge of the bed.

"And would you have wanted it?" he murmured.

Heck yes. But he was supposed to take that from her so she didn't think too hard on the fact she was sleeping with a guy she'd known less than a week. That would have…who knows, made it somehow more acceptable. Modern day girl gets taken by the brutish, uncivilized Viking sort of thing. That washed. Right?

"Let's just suppose," he said softly as he sat next to her, eyes direct. "That I *am* part dragon. What would you say?"

To begin with, Naðr was being far too passive. Eyes narrowed, she set aside her drink, gaze never leaving his. If any of this was true then she'd give a like response. "If." She eyed him. "And not to sound cliché but *if* that were true…" Megan paused, not sure where she wanted this to go. But then she did. All or nothing. "I'd want honesty about it. I'd want proof."

Naðr cupped her cheek, eyes intense, searching, before he at last nodded. Though she still waited for him to shove her onto the bed and have his way with her, he didn't. Instead, he stood and held out his hand. "Come then, I want to show you something."

Unsure, Megan eyed his hand. Naðr was no beast. He was human and sincere, or so said his steady gaze. Slipping her hand into his, she stood. Naðr brought her against him and whispered, "Close your eyes, beautiful and *look*."

Trusting him, she rested her cheek against his hard chest and closed her eyes.

Images flared and reality shifted. Or so it seemed.

This time she wasn't seeing leathery wings flap against the horizon but on either side of her as she flew over sharp mountains then a raging sea. Icy wind rushed by her face but didn't seem to touch her warm, powerful body.

"This is what it feels like to fly with me."

Megan kept her eyes closed. Unafraid, she somehow knew it was Naðr's voice within her mind. Rich and deep with his essence, it burned a blazing path through her as thorough as the feel of the great beast she surely possessed. His massive wings flapped and they sailed over several longships speckling the open sea. Though in awe, she soon became aware of two more creatures flying on either side. Both immense, she could barely process what she looked at they were so magnificent.

One was shades of pale gold with intense searing light blue eyes…

Raknar.

The other, multi-layered shades of mahogany and flecks of burnished gold with lethal obsidian eyes…

Kol.

For a split second it almost seemed she could see her own reflection in the sharp white clouds ahead. Slightly larger than the other two, jet black scales with blazing cobalt blue eyes…

Naðr Véurr.

Shocked, her eyes flew open.

Everything fell away and she once more stood in the king's arms.

"Holy Christ," she cried and tried to pull away.

But Naðr kept his arm around her and his calm eyes level on her face. "So now you have the answer to your question."

Though completely stunned, she was surprised to realize that she wasn't all that frightened. Shouldn't she be? But being inside Naðr, flying in what he became, was more jolting than terrifying. While the creature he became contained a silent fury, it also seemed to have a deep-seated, unwavering strength of...*character*? There was no other way to describe its noble bearing other than that it was deeply engrained and part of a legacy that kept the creature kindred both to humanity and a higher power.

"I am both human and dragon," Naðr said. "Born to protect what few of us there are left."

"Naðr Véurr," she whispered. "Serpent protector. Does that mean Meyla and Heidrek are also part dragon?"

He shook his head, troubled, voice soft. "No. As the centuries pass, our dragon blood transfers to our descendants less and less. That's why there are so few of us. Me and my brothers all being part dragon is truly rare."

"I'm so sorry," she murmured. "No wonder you sacrificed so much for Torra MacLomain."

"We would've done just about anything to help her," Naðr said. "Or for our descendants without dragon blood."

She didn't doubt it for a second. Anything for family.

That aside, Megan realized there was no repulsion in her newfound knowledge about him being part dragon. But then he was all handsome human male right now and her mind was more wrapped up in that than anything else.

Naðr tilted up her chin, his eyes softer than she'd ever seen them. "I showed you a glimpse of the dragon when we were on the ship. It was because of my dragon magic that you never heard my brothers leave. It was part of the reason you became so," a small grin tugged at his lips, "lost within my touch."

Ah, well that certainly made sense. But she suspected she'd responded as much to the man as she did to the dragon within.

"Now you know the truth yet you do not fear." He brushed his thumb over her lower lip. "It is a rare woman that isn't afraid of the dragon."

"I'd imagine," she murmured, startled to realize he was right. But she had no time to work toward *why* that was as his gaze took on a hungry edge. Deftly, with far too much talent, he untied the strings of her tunic with a few quick flicks of his fingers.

Megan's heartbeat kicked up a few thousand notches and breathing became impossible as he made quick work of removing the leather material altogether. Then, ensnared by her breasts struggling beneath the thin white tunic, he trailed a slow, purposeful finger down her upper chest.

She might not have run in fear from the dragon, but Naðr Véurr like this, tall and gorgeous, with his near feral eyes and wicked intent, had her whole body trembling. Shaking in something close to fear but not quite, she could barely swallow.

Unrecognizable emotions churned beneath the surface. She perched motionless as his finger hooked over the top of the thin material between her breasts. His eyes locked on hers and she knew he warred between how much she could handle versus how much he was about to take. Yet they both knew he'd end up tearing down any defenses she might have erected after Nathan.

But Megan wasn't the sort of woman to back down from a challenge either.

So when he tore away the material and his ravenous, appreciative eyes lingered on her nudity, she stood proudly and redirected her attention to his too-ripped-for-his-own-good body. Licking her lips, she admired his broad shoulders as she lightly trailed her fingers down the thin layer of hair on his muscled chest. Then she continued down his six-pack abs until she hooked her finger over the top of his pants, mimicking what he'd done to her.

His lips curled ever so slightly and humor mixed with desire as his slow and thorough appraisal of her shifted to one of increasing challenge. Rigid, eager, his thick erection leapt a little, pushing forward slightly beneath the tight strain of leather. In direct response, her nipples tightened almost painfully.

God, there was a whole lot of man here, in more ways than one.

Muscles strained as he kept his hands fisted by his side and allowed her all the power. She supposed this was his way of letting her know he could hold back both the man *and* the beast within.

But she wondered for how long.

Finger still hooked, she moved forward just enough that the base of her palm pressed against his arousal while she traced the curling tat that snaked down his rock-hard bicep. She'd never been overly drawn to men with ink but Naðr wore it so well that a fresh burst of moisture pooled between her thighs.

His nostrils flared and a small, knowing grin slithered onto his face.

Yet he waited and watched, a hard set to his jaw as his hooded eyes continued to make a slow walk over her exposed skin until he fixated on her throbbing lips. Suddenly drawn to the heavy sweep of his ebony lashes and the unrelenting slashes above, she ran her finger along his eyebrow then followed down over the strong cheekbone. All the while she rubbed her palm back and forth slowly over the steel length below. Eager to tempt, maybe even toy with him, she pressed her thumb between his lips while firmly grabbing below.

Naðr thrust his hips forward a scant fraction as he pulled her thumb into his mouth. His tongue wrapped around her vulnerable digit once before his teeth clasped gently, reminding her exactly who was in control. His pupils flared half a heartbeat before he chuckled low in his chest.

Then his large hands grabbed her backside and lifted her in such a way, she had no choice but to wrap her legs around his waist. With her thumb still held hostage in his hot mouth, Naðr hopped onto the bed and locked her into position against the wall just above the headboard. With one hand, he kept her braced inches above the long sweeping body of the dragon carved into the wood beneath.

He held her that way for a long moment, red hot desire flaring within his unwavering regard. Sweet, drawn out anticipation made her heart hammer. Thump, thump, it pounded blood through her veins and had her gasping for breath.

The small fire in the corner kept his face hidden in shadows as wind started to batter the roof. The crackling flames mixed with the sound of distant drums.

Cupping his hand around the back of her head, he released her thumb and nibbled his way along her lower lip instead. A shudder rippled through her when he dug his hand into her hair and only allowed her close enough that her overly sensitized nipples brushed his hard chest. Yet even as she tried to squirm closer, he kept her at bay, tongue licking the seam between her lips as if sampling a rare delicacy.

This particular brand of torture was the dominance she'd felt not only in the Viking but in the dragon. Though it seemed far away, she knew the sound that fell from her lips was half growl. Digging her nails into his back, she grabbed his lips with hers and utilized every sensual weapon known to woman when *she* kissed *him*.

And, if she didn't know better, Megan got him.

Though it seemed for a moment he'd take back control and continue his slow, sensual assault, he instead groaned, yanked her tightly against him and kissed the world right out from under her. Harsh, brutal, but oh-so-talented, his tongue and lips made quick work of twisting her entire soul into unparalleled oblivion.

Kissing him with equal zeal, she clawed her nails down his back and ground her pelvis against him, so damn needy it hurt. Lips still working their magic against hers, he pulled back just enough to reach between them and yank hard, ripping her trousers down the center. Cool air slipped between her legs briefly before he ground his hot, leather-clad length between her thighs.

Megan whimpered, tightened her arms over his shoulders and pulled up as she moved against him. Sweat slicked their skin and a raspy mewling sound broke from her chest as she ground and rolled her hips. When she gasped for air and her head fell back, he lowered her until she perched on the headboard while he nipped and sucked his way down her neck.

Now he was moving against her. One hand kept her backside protected from the wood while the other fed her breast to his starved mouth. Though aching to fill the emptiness between her legs, a whole new flood of fire raced through her veins when his teeth clamped over her pebbled nipple. Crying out, Megan was stunned when her body locked up in an arch and an orgasm ripped through her.

And this was no average climax.

On and on, it curled her toes and made her lips quiver as blood pounded in heavy throbs from her core through every limb. Even her fingernails tingled so strong were the waves of release.

Ruthlessly taking advantage of her untendered vulnerability, he held her in place. Then he thrust harshly against her while suckling deep before cinching his teeth just hard enough. She understood in that pleasure-defining moment that teasing then thinking to control her Viking king would only ever be rewarded with an unthinkable, walk-the-edge dangerous blend of both pain and pleasure.

Another sharp release tore up her spine then zig-zagged everywhere. Sharp, non-stop flutters fanned out from the epicenter between her thighs. Completely at his mercy, her muscles shook and quaked. Hand again wrapped in her hair, he held her just close enough that he could view the vulnerability of release reflected in her eyes. Fascinated, pleased, he watched her so avidly that she felt exposed.

Yet somehow there was an unexpected level of intimacy fluctuating between them she'd never felt with another. It stretched and elongated the endless aftershocks thrumming through her. So when he pulled her off the headboard and braced back on his heels, she could barely focus never mind keep her arms over his shoulders.

Though her legs still straddled him, Naðr tucked her head against him, cheek against his chest. As her muscles jerked and fluttered uncontrollably, he stroked her hair gingerly. But Megan had to wonder through her thin grip on reality, was this just more teasing? Because there could be no ignoring the heavy throb of blood pounding within the thick erection pressed between her legs.

The king was far from finished with her.

But again he proved he was no brute as he rested his chin on the top of her head and continued stroking her hair. Only after her body finally went slack did he grasp the back of her neck and pull away until his lust-ridden gaze once more connected with hers. Their eyes held for several long moments before his lips whispered over hers far more tenderly than she expected.

Even as Megan thought he would kiss her, he didn't. Instead, he cupped her cheek and ran the rough pad of his thumb casually back and forth over her lower lip. All the while, he held her backside firmly while rocking his hips just enough that the sensual release moments before slowly but surely rekindled. Not only the gentle motion of his body but the way his eyes never for a second left hers made clear his intentions.

His lips again curled up slightly and he moved her forward. Megan felt like melting wax in his arms as he swung her so that she kneeled on the bed. He yanked away the remnants of her pants and paused. Even without the strength to look back at him, she sensed his blatant admiration.

"*Hel* woman, you are beautiful," he whispered. Then, curling over her prone, bare body he braced her hands over the headboard and pushed her knees together. Brushing aside her hair, he pressed his warm lips against the vulnerable area at the base of her neck. When she arched her chest forward, he gripped her hips firmly and trailed his tongue down her spine.

Jaw quivering, she pressed her forehead against the headboard and pushed up with her backside, wanting, no needing, far more. Then, as if determined to drive her lusty anguish through the roof, he nipped at her backside while wrapping his hand down between her thighs. When she yelped, he growled. One hand clamped over hers on the headboard while the other wrapped into her hair tightly.

A warning.

One that had saliva pooling on her tongue.

Then he pulled away for a brief moment and she heard swooshing. The next thing she knew his body again curled over hers.

This time the leather was gone and skin met skin.

Megan whimpered in what sounded precariously like relief as his rampant arousal rested against her backside. And though his hand moved back and only rested suggestively on her hip, fast fire unraveled through her blood and her skin burned with heat.

Even so, something deep inside alerted her to how far she'd really come and that she wasn't on birth control and that unprotected sex wasn't safe regardless. But it seemed he followed her every thought because his murmured words came close and soft against her ear. "I am part dragon. There is no sickness in me nor will anything come of this union you do not want."

Well, what the heck did he mean by that?

But it didn't much matter when he turned her lips to his and wrapped his tongue into her mouth. Just like that, she was once more possessed. Tucking back against him, she again arched as his hand swept over her stomach and firmly cupped her breast. Lips never leaving hers, he kneed her legs apart and once more closed a hand over hers, his fingers caressing the back of hers whisper soft.

Then he hovered, almost as if he cherished the moments he kept her in exquisite agony, wondering if he'd give her what she so needed. Waiting, waiting, waiting even as his tongue wrapped with hers, carving out her mouth as though he meant to own it.

Thud. Thud. Thud. Her poor heart slammed frantically.

Slow, so slow she clenched her teeth and groaned, he ever-so-slightly dragged his hand along her belly until he brushed his finger over her clit. She inhaled sharply as he worked his fingers so deftly that flesh swelled as quickly as blind need.

Then, suddenly, he drove into her.

Megan cried out, vision dimming as his nimble, talented fingers kept at her center and he thrust inside her completely. So long, thick and filling, her throat clogged with emotion.

Unable to process the sensations rolling over her body in heavy waves, she pressed her cheek to the headboard and dug her nails into the wood. While some men might have slowed and let her ease into the intrusion of his body, Naðr wasn't one of them. Keeping one hand between her legs, his other again clamped hard over one of her hands as he thrust. Every less-than-gentle push of his hips wrestled a new sound of pleasure from her lips.

When his mouth came close to her ear and murmured several tempting, dirty words she thrust back against him. This, it seemed, was just what he was looking for because he yanked her back and pulled free. With a quick thrust, he flipped her onto her back. The next thing she knew, he scooped his arms beneath her knees, and once more filled her.

Megan didn't recognize the look in his eyes any more than the long, low steady moan breaking from her chest as his sweat-coated muscular body raped her of coherency.

In. Out.

In. Out.

Over and over.

Though fast and furious, his movements now were languid compared to what came next. Sharp, near-violent, he thrust so hard they dragged fur across the bed beneath the weight of his tireless pursuit. Megan tried to grip him, the bed, anything, but his movements were so intense, the weight of his body on hers so thorough, that nothing was going to save her…from him.

She wasn't sure her body could handle another intense climax but it didn't much matter when she made the fatal mistake of looking into his eyes. Those surreal, otherworldly eyes of his. Except now they didn't look at her with blatant need but something she couldn't put words to. As though she'd been looking into their perfectness her whole damn life and was only just remembering.

They not only made a meal out of her physically but emotionally. Swamped in unanticipated emotion, she tried to press her lips together but they only fell apart, quivering with unchecked desire. Again taking advantage of her vulnerability, he hooded his gaze and brought his lips closer, while grinding and thrusting even deeper.

Ripped from the oblivion she'd nearly drowned in when with his gaze, he forced her down another path entirely. One made of his hot breath against hers and the unyielding strength of his body as it slid over hers, faster and faster. Enthralled, lost, she dug her nails into his forearms and tried to ground herself even as everything fell away.

Almost as if he was angered though she somehow knew he wasn't, he pushed his arms higher, pulling her legs further up, and locked his lips against the side of her neck. Tears leaked from her eyes as he rolled and ground his hips. The room tilted and swayed as powerful sensations battered and whiplashed against her. Lost, drowned, done, her stomach clenched so painfully that she arched into a rainbow, thrust back her head and screamed.

Naðr dug his hands into her hair and locked his teeth onto the side of her lower neck.

The unbearable pain in her stomach grew into a tiny pinch as though a foot long needle stabbed her. Pause. The planet stopped spinning. The world went quiet. Every part of her being, physical and no doubt emotional, recoiled into a tight little ball. Then ba-*boom*. She released another long scream when sinews attached to tendons attached to muscles tried to detach from far too many bones as her body almost seemed to blow apart.

Truly scared but wholly swept away in the sharp release it brought, her eyes popped open even as the room grew dark. She heard Naðr's deep masculine roar as he locked up against her but she was too far gone, transported to another place, one made of weightlessness and drifting on thin air. Bursts of honeyed pleasure continued to wash over her as she stared aimlessly.

Lost.

Found.

It was hard to tell.

But then it didn't much matter as everything went hazy then all dimmed before ultimately snapping away into darkness.

The next thing she knew there was a heavy spat, spat, spat.

Then a lick across her face.

She slowly opened her eyes. Not to Naðr over her or even *in* her but gone entirely. Instead, Guardian was curled up by her side. Eyes shining, her dog smiled. Tucked beneath thick furs on Naðr's bed, Megan wasn't far from where they'd last…

Another lick across her face.

Patting Guardian, she sat up, disoriented. What the *hell* had happened? But she knew all too well based on the pleasant sting between her legs.

She'd slept with her Viking king.

Flopping back, she stared at the high thatched ceiling above and stretched. Not just slept but had the most amazing sex of her life. *How* had he pulled that kind of ecstasy from her? Then she remembered…

He wasn't just human but *dragon*.

But could that alone atone for all he'd made her *feel*?

Megan couldn't help but grin. No, what had happened between them had been all human, all them…*him*.

"Mistress," a girl murmured as she entered.

Uncomfortable being addressed by a stranger, she pulled the fur closer around her and nodded at the girl who had entered. When Guardian released a low, unusual growl, Megan put a hand on her dog's neck and shook her head.

But she paid attention.

Guardian rarely growled.

Why now?

"The king sent me to care for you." The girl poured water into a cup and held it out to Megan, words soft. "Please. Drink."

Guardian growled again, the sound low in her chest as she eyed the servant. While some people might be inclined to shake their head, even say 'enough' to their pet, she wasn't one of them. Rather, she decided to pay attention to the warning. So Megan simply nodded at the girl. "Thanks. Leave the water and go."

Yet even as she said it the girl squeezed her fist and tossed what looked to be powder into the air. The next thing Megan knew her head was spinning as Guardian stood over her, hackles raised and ears alert, low growl increasing.

Then as she tried to raise her weak hands, everything erupted. Her dog barked and launched. A knife sliced. Guardian fell across her chest whimpering. Terrified, she tried to lift her arms to protect herself but couldn't. Then her dog was pushed aside and she was yanked forward.

A blurry face filled her vision, her words sharp before all faded away...

"You now belong to King Rennir."

Chapter Eleven

Naðr sat back on his haunches and eyed the peach strewn sunrise with a small smile on his face. It had been a long time since he last truly appreciated the glory and silent patience of a new sun as she crested the horizon. The way it tossed fresh light over the sea and skimmed like an eager caress over the lines of his ships.

"She's pretty enough," Kjar grunted and spit out a nut.

Rocking back on his heels, the king draped his arms over his knees and kept on grinning.

Kjar popped another nut in his mouth, eyes never leaving the long length of the ship. "So you'll be keeping her then."

Past Valhalla then back to Middle Earth he would. Megan was like no other. But it would do him no good to seem eager. "She is here as long as she wishes."

Back against the center mast, his shipwright snorted and spit out another bit of shell. "Said so loosely. Then might she wish to try me out before leaving." He chuckled. "Maybe then she will not wish to leave at all."

Not offended in the least by his man's honesty, Naðr murmured, "Maybe not."

Foot suddenly braced on the bench by his side, Kjar rested an elbow on his knee and eyed his king. "It is my greatest hope you only speak from Loki's ass when you say such, cousin." He arched a brow. "Or else more than just me will see past your 'claim' and try to take her."

Naðr stood, stretched and slid a sly grin Kjar's way. "Could be I will have to marry her."

Kjar huffed his words away with a loose wrist. "You've known her a few short days and though more foolish than most, even you are not so stupid."

Grin widening, Naðr spread his arms and turned to the sea, more alive than he'd been since his Aesa passed on to Valhalla. "Even Odin knows how stupid I might be right now, my friend."

Kjar jumped from the boat, his tender gaze never leaving the ship's fine lines as he muttered, "Bless the gods that even Aesa would forgive your foolish words right now."

Disturbed by the change in tone, by his cousin's insinuation, he kept his voice low and dropped his arms. "Aesa is long gone. Megan is not."

"Not long you've known this one," Kjar rumbled, not shying away from Naðr in the least as their eyes locked. "Yet so soon you say goodbye to your wife."

It didn't matter if Aesa had been gone five long years. With Kjar's sharp, reminding words she once more stood alongside them, skirts blowing, shield held strong in hand as she looked at him with fierce pride. Pained by the memory, he turned his face to the wind.

Kjar joined him, munching a nut as he eyed the sea. "I mean no harm, my king."

Though he meant to retaliate, his cousin's opinion held sway if for no other reason than his own flare of guilt. But he couldn't temper what he felt for Megan. No matter how hard he tried. That he'd known her for such a short time didn't matter. His dragon blood and the beating heart within his chest made it clear she could be his mate. She possessed strength, passion, intelligence. And something more he couldn't quite figure out. Whatever it *was*, Naðr wanted it.

Badly.

And though he'd taken of her lovely, responsive flesh the eve before and found unspeakable passion, it wasn't nearly enough. Yet still, he'd not made a show of claiming a woman since Aesa was taken from him.

"Did you not suggest I make Megan my own just yesterday morn," Naðr grunted.

Kjar simply stared at the sea for a long stretch before he eventually nodded. "I did." Then his eyes cut to Naðr. "But I never meant that you would give her a chair beside yours."

When Naðr ground his jaw, his cousin continued. "That chair was Aesa's. Cherished. It is meant for she who you claim to remain yours. Not she who you will allow to leave if she *wishes*. No, she who sits in that chair stays, in this life then in the chair by your side in the great halls of Valhalla as you toast a horn of ale to Odin."

Naðr frowned.

He knew damned well what it meant.

"When you gave the chair to *Megan* that meant there was no longer room for Aesa, *here* nor *there*," Kjar growled.

What, was he supposed to never have another woman sit by his side? Yet he knew how protective his kin were of Aesa's memory.

"Maybe," Naðr said softly, dangerously, between his teeth, as his eyes met Kjar's. "I believe Odin would allow *two* women to share such a seat. That my god is capable of such mercy. Because would it not be such if I found myself lonely for so long here on Middle Earth then, despite how I fought it, eventually found love again?"

Though blasphemous righteousness flashed in Kjar's eyes, he didn't miss a flicker of something else. A softening. "I like Megan but cannot help but defend Aesa."

And he understood that. He suspected more than anything, especially based on Kjar's show of support to Megan the eve before, that his main concern simply lay in not wanting Naðr to let her go so easily.

Naðr clasped him on the shoulder, words soft. "I know."

As if he'd been reluctant to bring it up but figured it needed saying, Kjar eyed him. "Aesa's raven came the first night Megan was here. What did it tell you?"

"That change has come," Naðr murmured. "That me and Raknar must let her go."

Kjar's expression hardened and he inhaled deeply. "Yet you kept your distance from Megan for days after."

"Do not think it was easy for me to hear such a message." He started walking down the dock and his shipwright kept pace. Though he knew his cousin had more to say he remained silent as Meyla headed their way. Kjar nodded and strode ahead when she stopped before Naðr.

"Father."

"Daughter." Naðr slowly steered them back the way she'd come. "You're up early."

"I am." Meyla seemed to consider her words carefully and rather than address the issue he knew she was here for, she instead said, "So is Megan to your liking?"

"Yes." He eyed her, curious. "And is she to yours?"

"Does it much matter what I think?" she murmured.

Naðr frowned, took her hand and stopped them. "It always matters what you think."

Meyla notched her chin and didn't shy away from his gaze. "Really? It doesn't seem so lately. Since Valan's arrived you've been impossible."

When his frown deepened, she continued. "I know he did some less than admirable things in his life but by coming here so that Torra might remain safe, he rose above his previous actions. Why can you not see that?"

"Might it be said that he ultimately came here because he'd laid eyes on you in Scotland?" Naðr countered. "So although his actions seemed noble they were likely done out of selfishness."

"Is loving me so selfish then?" She stood up straighter. "Do I not deserve it after what I left behind in Scotland with Adlin MacLomain? Do I not deserve it after leaving a child I loved, not to mention a man I'd come to care for a great deal?"

Perhaps that was half of his frustration right there. That she *did* deserve to be loved after what she'd sacrificed. And despite how he tried, Naðr found it difficult to believe that a man like Valan could love so deeply twice.

Still, things couldn't continue as they were between him and Meyla. His daughter was his world and until King Rennir started causing so many problems, they'd been very close. Maybe Megan was right. Maybe he should start trying to push past his dislike of Valan if for no other reason than to ease the tension between him and his daughter.

So, though it took a great deal, he spoke the words she needed to hear, grateful they didn't sound strained. "If Valan makes you happy then you have my blessing."

Though her eyes narrowed slightly, there was a new light in them. "*Truly?*"

Naðr nodded, voice firm, eager to see her happy. "Truly."

He couldn't hold back a smile when she flung her arms around his waist and pressed her cheek against his chest. If nothing else could be said for the Scotsman, he'd treated Meyla well since arriving here and stared at her often with tenderness. Not to mention, he'd saved Megan from drowning. So he supposed the man had *some* decency rattling around inside him.

Naðr wrapped his arms around his daughter and held her tightly. It'd been far too long since he felt this. She might be a woman grown but Meyla would always be his little girl. A piece of him and Aesa that would live on.

But despite speaking of his deceased wife with Kjar and reconnecting with his daughter, Naðr's thoughts continued to wander back to Megan. Since leaving her in his bed this morning, he'd felt like a new man.

Meyla pulled back and slipped her arm into the crook of his elbow as they continued walking. Contented it seemed by their discussion, she remained silent for some time before speaking, a touch of humor in her voice. "So I take it Megan is no longer my slave."

Naðr quirked his lip. "I think we both know she never was to begin with."

"Mmm." Meyla pursed her lips, considering. "I like her."

"Do you?" Because nothing would mean more.

Meyla nodded. "She has fire in her." Then his daughter eyed him with a smirk. "Not many women stand up to you. In truth, none do." Then her voice softened but wasn't as sad as he thought it would be. "Not like mother did."

Naðr pressed his lips together, caught in rare emotion.

"Mother would like her too," Meyla said, sounding quite sure and pushing aside heavy emotions for them both. "She'd want you to teach Megan how to fight because something tells me she'd do well with a weapon."

No doubt she would.

The idea of Megan with a sword in hand aroused him to no end. She'd been a wild little thing in bed with her golden eyes soft and simmering as she tempted him then blazing pure fire when she fought against him. Then there was the dewy, well-sated look after…

He cleared his throat and set aside thoughts of her before his groin tightened.

Meyla was about to speak but stopped when Megan's dog, Guardian trotted slowly out of the front gates. Naðr tensed as the dog lumbered toward them; fur bloodied, barking and growling all at once as her weak, vague words hit his mind.

My person. Gone. Taken. Bad.

Chest tight, furious, refusing to panic, Naðr picked up the dog and strode quickly into the compound, all the while flinging words over his shoulder to Meyla. "Find the healer. *Now*."

Meanwhile, he shoved words into his brother's minds. *"Megan's been taken. Gather twenty of our best men, provisions and weapons then meet me out back."*

Past repressed panic, Naðr was now nothing less than infuriated as he made quick work of soothing Guardian. Soon enough, he left her with Raknar's son, Heidrek and gathered up as many weapons as he could strap to his body and comfortably travel with. If he could shift into the dragon right now he would. But agreements had been struck and for now, he would not.

Kol, Raknar, Kjar and twenty of their best fighters met him on the path leading up into the mountains. All looked grim and said nothing when met with Naðr's heavy scowl. Receiving a satchel, he wrapped a fur cloak over his shoulders and ground out, "How the *hel* did Rennir's men get her? I sensed *nothing*."

Because he knew it'd been the enemy king. And being the strongest with dragon magic, Naðr should have at least sensed it. That's what irked and worried him the most.

"Better bring your prisoner if you want to make a trade."

Naðr froze when the foreign voice entered his mind. *Loki's hel and cock.*

"Rennir's bitch has her," he bit out. So as he suspected all along, Rennir was somehow involved with Nathan.

Kol and Raknar cursed but awaited his orders.

Jaw grinding, his frown deepened. Nothing good would come of Rennir getting his hands on Nathan. A man like the rival king shouldn't have access to the future any more than the queen who now sat by his side.

While Naðr normally wouldn't do anything to put his people in harm's way, he vaguely wondered if he wasn't getting ready to do just that when he barked at several warriors. "Go get the prisoner who sat by my side last eve."

His brothers, even Kjar, knew better than to contradict his order but he didn't miss the firm set to their jaws or their wary glances. He knew what went through their minds. *You're thinking with your cock.*

Maybe he was.

But he'd be damned if Rennir got ahold of Megan.

Because the tyrant didn't have her yet. Led by his *queen*, his witch, he'd sent in a small band to kidnap her. One that knew these mountains better than most and would be moving fast…maybe. Naðr didn't wait for the men retrieving Nathan but strode on. They knew how to track despite snowfall and would catch up.

His brothers fell in on either side and said nothing at first. As Naðr knew would be the case, Kjar kept the men far enough behind them that they could speak in private. And it didn't take them long.

"You're quick to give up a prisoner who could cause us great harm," Raknar said.

"Especially considering we can't shift to the dragon," Kol reminded.

"Maybe," Naðr gave. "But more harm will come from Rennir getting his hands on Megan."

Raknar's eyes narrowed. "Because of the agreement with the seers?"

"At the very least." Naðr shook his head and gave them logic. "Only Megan knows where the three stones are. And those stones are directly connected to our power…to us. If he gets his hands on them real trouble will come. One that will likely destroy us all."

"Why bother bargaining for Nathan then?" Kol said.

"Because the man's arrogance knows no bounds," Raknar spat. "Within Nathan's mind lays all the information about the scrolls and what they contained. Then, when ready, Rennir assumes he'll so easily again take Megan." His brother's eyes went to Naðr. "Which leads me to believe he knows something we do not."

And though it was likely the last thing Raknar would want to hear he said, "Or his queen, Yrsa does."

Raknar clenched his jaw and Kol cursed beneath his breath.

Done with the conversation, Naðr said, "After we get Megan back, we will visit the seers."

Hearing the finality in his tone, his brothers said nothing more. He'd tucked Megan's stone in his pocket that morning and nobody save her would get it from him lest off his dead carcass. And that wouldn't be happening any time soon. He might have agreed not to shift into a dragon for now but fighting in human form had always been his passion above all others.

So, though his worry over Megan grew, he focused on rage as they climbed higher into the mountains. Naðr thought of the various ways he intended to kill the men they'd eventually catch up with. And they would. Sooner rather than later. As the hours passed he kept nothing but vengeance in his heart and prayed to the gods.

When snow and ice started to spit from the sky while sunlight sliced across the clouds whirling up through the peaks above, he grinned. When Thor's hammer fell and thunder rumbled and belched overhead, his lips spread into a wicked smile.

His prayers had been answered.

Chapter Twelve

My dog better not be dead. But though she'd worried endlessly, now was not the time for further speculation. Megan spit snow off her lip and glared into the charcoal lined eyes of her captor.

Pale-faced but remarkably beautiful, the woman stared back, her red lips full and uncompromising. Like smoke from a pipe, her breath met the icy air in thin tendrils of steamy fog. Somehow this far-too-worldly creature had been the timid mouse of a servant who'd lured her from Naðr's bed to begin with.

A heavy white hood intensified the woman's biting blue-green eyes as her penetrating gaze never left Megan's face. There was no need to guess at *why* a woman leading so many men held her captive. She craved power. Having dealt with a lot of power hungry people in her life, she recognized one who wanted more than most.

At last, the woman spoke, her voice a soft, sultry purr. "I see the draw the dragon king has to you." Then she paused, speculative. "Even how you might tempt his brothers as well."

Megan had no idea how she understood the woman's words without her stone but speculated the new tattoo might have something to do with it. All her old business instincts kicked in and she kept quiet, eyes unwavering from the woman's. Best to let her talk so that things could be learned. People always had a weakness and she guessed based on those few words that Naðr and his brothers were at the top of this chick's list.

Grin small, the woman released a breathy sigh and leaned back. "What think you of Naðr Véurr? Ferocious bit of man him. Did you find his cock satisfying?" A low chuckle simmered within her chest. "I always did prefer Raknar's." She shrugged. "But then again…"

Her words trailed off as she watched Megan, sly grin unwavering. Refusing to be baited, Megan kept a level glare and said nothing.

"I like you," the Viking woman said, voice once more a soft purr. "Strong, unbending…at least for *now*."

The way she said 'now' sent chills up Megan's spine. There was something entirely not only wrong but corrupt about the woman, something that somehow took away from what would normally be stunning beauty.

"*Oh.*" A little grin hitched the woman's lips. "Here they come."

What was she talking about? Megan couldn't hear a thing but wind whistling through the mountains. Even the fifty or so warriors she'd been traveling with all day were utterly silent. But all gripped their swords and axes, eyes to their surroundings. Suddenly the air felt heavy and oppressive despite the cold.

Then, as if he didn't have a care in the world, Naðr strode out of nowhere, axe swinging back and forth loosely by his hip. He wore a devilish grin even as too many of the enemy surrounded him.

Thank God.

Crazed but calm at the same time, his eyes remained locked on the woman sitting opposite her. While one part of her wanted to run to him like the silly girl in a bad horror movie, she'd never be so foolish. Instead, Megan waited and tried to figure out how the heck to help.

"Yrsa," Naðr's deep voice rumbled as he stopped, shook his head and rested the handle of his axe casually on his shoulder as though contemplating which tree to cut down. "Why does this not surprise me?"

"Naðr Véurr *'the bold'*", she drawled as though she didn't think him bold in the least. Standing, she pushed back her hood, inclined her head and offered an equally unaffected grin. "Where are your brothers then? It's been far too long."

Kol and Raknar stepped forward, just as casual, flanking their brother.

None said a word but eyed each other for a long moment.

Unleashed tension snapped between them and her captor.

Finally, as though she'd been waiting centuries to say such, Yrsa's eyes landed on Raknar. "There you are, love." She tilted back her head and slowly licked her lips. "Still tempting as ever."

Face stoic and unreadable, Raknar remained silent as Naðr spoke. "Give us Megan and I'll kill your men fast rather than," he eyes slid languidly over several of Yrsa's warriors, "*Far* too slowly."

Megan held her breath as tension crackled. Though only Naðr and his brothers had appeared, she sensed the enemy's palpable fear.

"Yes. Right. Them." Yrsa made a loose gesture with her hand that brushed away her men as though blood didn't still pump through their veins. "Replaceable."

Then she swept a stern yet somehow cunningly lusty look over those defending her. "Is that not right?" Before any could make a move or give a response she shrugged and locked eyes with Naðr. "But of course I'm right and *my* men know it. They love me as I love them."

Naðr let her words sink in as his grin dropped and his eyes hardened. "Love aside you've one of two options now."

When he paused, she arched a brow in question.

The king seemed to enjoy the game as he let his axe swing back and forth, lazy eyes crawling over his opponents. The corner of Naðr's lips jerked up as though he'd rather not talk but dig his blade into the nearest man. His eyes snapped back to Yrsa. "Why don't you tell me what you think those options are."

Her eyes stayed steady on the king. Instead of reciting Naðr's possible options she gave but one of her own. "Give me *Nathan*, take *Megan*, then leave or," and she seemed to cherish the challenge, "We war here and now."

The corner of Naðr's lip inched higher and his eyebrows arched. "But of course."

Then he made a motion with his hand.

Nathan was dragged forward, bedraggled, the opposite of the smooth businessman she remembered. For a moment, a scant second, she almost felt bad for him. Then the feeling passed. He'd brought this on himself.

"So we will exchange prisoners?" Yrsa said.

Naðr didn't look Megan's way once but kept his eyes pinned on the Viking woman. "We will."

"Good." Yrsa swiftly lifted a bow and arrow, looked Megan's way and offered a loose shrug. "Men, what good *are* they?"

Megan had a split second to understand her meaning before Yrsa released the arrow and *whiz*, it thumped into Nathan's heart. Time froze. Holy *hell*. She didn't recognize the strange strangled sound that broke from her chest when Nathan's eyes met hers and he fell to his knees.

Still caught in her ex-husband's dying gaze, she barely processed what blew up around her. Daggers, swords, arrows, everything was unleashed. Because for whatever reason, the enemy killing Nathan, who was surely the enemy as well, meant a mini-war here and now.

Calm under pressure despite how frightening the unfolding scene, Megan swallowed but didn't panic when one of Yrsa's men fell dead at her feet. Survival mode in high gear, she quickly wrangled both his blade and shield from him then ducked behind a nearby rock.

She kept the shield up, stayed put and peered out at the battling. Well, to be honest, mostly Naðr Véurr. *Christ*, was he impressive. She laid eyes on him seconds before he tossed aside his shield, ran forward, whipping not only his axe but dagger. The axe thunked into a man's forehead. The dagger, straight through another's throat.

Then, eyes crazed, a wicked grin still on his face, he yanked another dagger from his boot and unsheathed a sword. With a solid, impressive round-house kick, he slammed an oncoming man in the chest with his foot while simultaneously slicing another across the chest with his dagger. Laughing, he started sparring with his sword even as he punched yet another.

The man was completely insane.

But damn, did it work for her.

One thing she started to notice however, no matter how many Naðr fought and killed, his brothers and his men stayed close, protecting him the best they could. Even so, Naðr seemed equally determined to defend his brothers as he cut down several who got too close.

All the while, Yrsa watched, patient arms crossed over her chest and dagger in hand. Should Megan confront her? See if she could manage at least with this sword? Probably not the brightest idea because she got the distinct impression the woman could fight well.

The king and his brothers fought their way closer and closer. Naðr had just dug his dagger into the gut of one man while thrusting his sword across the throat of another, all the while roaring, "Come then Yrsa, don't be a coward. Fight!"

Naðr was within a dozen or so feet and still parrying with several warriors. The fighting was nearly on top of her so Megan figured she'd make her way around the backside of the rock. Maybe she'd get a better opportunity to help if she caught one of the enemy warriors unaware. Hindered by the heavy material, she lost the cloak and stumbled through a thin, icy layer of snow beside the rock face. She'd just rounded the corner when a strong hand clamped over her mouth from behind.

Though she executed about every self-defense move she could think of, the brute of a man still managed to wrap an arm around her stomach and drag her backwards. Most of the day she'd endured lewd glances from these men but because of Yrsa none touched her. Guess that'd changed despite the nearby battle. Refusing to panic, Megan remained calm and waited for the first opportunity to retaliate.

Breath whooshed from her lungs as he slammed her down onto her back. Furious, she tried to knee him but he deflected. She drove a fist into his side. He chuckled. So she dug her nails deep into his arms. Eyes cruel, the swine laughed harder.

Well this wasn't good.

The next thing she knew he'd pinned her wrists above her head with one hand and locked another meaty palm tightly around her throat. Sneering, she spit in his face even as she gasped for air. That didn't faze him in the least. When her body started to grow weaker he took advantage and settled between her legs. Oh crap. Tunnel vision twisted up between her and the madman holding her down.

Suddenly, he was yanked back. Hand to her neck, struggling for breath, Megan blinked as Naðr tossed aside her assailant. Growling, enraged, he leapt onto the enemy and started punching.

Over and over, the men tagged one another as they rolled through the snow. Yet soon enough the king managed to wrap his hands around the other guy's throat and squeezed hard. The enemy struggled for a few long moments before he finally went slack.

Naðr wasted no more time on the man but rushed over to her. Though outrage simmered in his regard, tenderness and concern softened his voice when he cupped the side of Megan's neck and gently ran his thumb over her throat. "Are you all right?"

There was likely already bruising from being strangled. Megan nodded, still a bit shaky. "I'm fine. It's okay."

She gripped his arms, almost afraid to ask. "How is Guardian?"

"Your dog will be fine. She is strong," he assured.

"She's not dead?"

"No." He shook his head. "She's alive, so you need not worry."

Sharp relief flooded her.

151

The rest of the fighting died away and she didn't have to wonder who won as Raknar, speckled in blood, shook his head when he joined them. "Yrsa was never even here to begin with. Damn seer."

Seer?

But she had no time to ask more as Naðr led them back to where Yrsa had been. It appeared all who had fought for the woman met a brutal death. Sobered by the carnage, Megan kept silent.

Then her eyes fell on Nathan.

Sprawled out, he lay in blood stained snow, eyes wide to the sky.

"Jesus," she whispered and went to his side. The moment felt surreal as she crouched and swept her fingers over his eyelids, closing them. It was hard to believe he was gone. Most of her adult life revolved around this man. Or at least it had. He did a lot of rotten things but he didn't deserve this. Did he? What exactly had he been up to? And why, when Yrsa seemed to want to trade for him did she then decide to kill him? But then Raknar had said she wasn't here to begin with.

Megan came to her feet when Naðr wrapped a cloak over her shoulders.

"We need to leave soon." Naðr glanced at Nathan before his concerned eyes went to Megan. "I know he was your mate. We will give him a short but proper burial."

She was touched by the gesture.

"Thank you," she whispered before her voice grew stronger. "But only if it won't put you and your men at further risk."

Naðr gestured at Kjar and nodded toward Nathan. His cousin seemed to understand. Nothing was said as the men, including the king and his brothers, covered the body with rocks. Megan understood that this was their way of showing respect not to Nathan but to her.

In little time they finished and gave Megan a few moments alone. Never could she have imagined closing such a large chapter of her life on a mountain in ninth century Scandinavia. But though she searched for anguish she found none. If anything, she realized she felt not sad but numb.

Eventually, Naðr came alongside and took her hand, his touch soothing. "We must go."

Megan trailed her eyes over the burial site one last time and joined him. Naðr said nothing as they headed downward. She knew he was giving her time to mourn. But the truth was she'd lost Nathan a long time ago and though some might think she should feel more, she simply did not.

The sky was darkening and snow fell heavier when she at last broke the silence. "It was a pretty steep climb coming up in daylight with no snow. How will it be going down?"

"We will not be making it back to the holding today. We'll spend the night on the mountain."

That made sense she supposed. Hard to imagine where they'd make camp though. Megan nodded and eyed him. His tousled black hair and fur cloak were a startling contrast to the white snow. And when those blue eyes turned her way, it took about everything she had to keep thoughts of last night out of her mind.

But it seemed he'd seen what he was looking for because he stopped short, pulled her close and wrapped his hand around the back of her neck. His voice was gruff, noticeably impassioned. "I'm sorry Yrsa managed to get you. I've never worried over a woman like I did you today. *Hel*, it was no good."

He brushed his thumb slowly back and forth over her jaw line, eyes locked with hers. And while some men might say a great many tender things at that moment, Naðr's idea of romancing her was entirely different. "You will learn how to fight and defend yourself. Then I will know you're safe when I am not with you."

"Well, while I'm here I hope to stick around you and your family as much as possible."

"*While* you are here," he mumbled but then something shifted in his gaze and he gave a brief nod. "Because you intend to find a way home."

"Naturally," she responded, voice guarded and softer than intended. Megan swallowed hard, stunned to realize the idea of going home, of leaving *him*, made her stomach flip and chest tighten. She bit her lower lip. Heck, she'd technically only known him mere days. But her heart apparently didn't care in the slightest.

While she sensed he wasn't pleased in the least with her desire to find her way home, he wasn't the sort to try to convince her otherwise. At least not with words. Instead, his eyes fell to her mouth; intrigued it seemed by her top teeth nibbling at her lower lip.

153

In direct response, she rubbed her lips together, wetting them. Though a purely subconscious action, heat gathered in his gaze. With a low, hungry growl, he cupped her cheeks and closed his mouth over hers.

Holding on for dear life, she wrapped her arms under his cloak and around his waist. Anything to anchor herself within the swiftly rising tide of sensations. There was a new urgency, one she suspected had a lot to do with releasing the pent up trauma from the day's events. Already, she matched his aggressiveness and wrapped her tongue around his, twisting and searching in a matched rhythm. Hard, fast, desperate, their mouths explored, searched, and needed more.

"Plenty of time for that once we make camp," Kol said in passing, humor in his muttered words.

But Naðr took his time ending the kiss, lips warm and thorough. Even as he reluctantly pulled back, his lips brushed over hers several more times. Yet still he cupped her cheeks, his thumbs dusting over the top of her cheekbones as he looked into her eyes. Megan's breath caught at not only the desire she saw there but the blatant yearning for something else altogether. She realized in that moment that his feelings toward her had grown as quickly as hers had toward him.

When he took her hand and they started walking, she felt considerably less heavy of heart than before. Though snow fell harder, towering trees kept the bulk of it away. Naðr's expression and demeanor had shifted once more to being a leader as he ordered a few men ahead to scout for any lingering trouble. Honestly, she'd been surprised by the caring, almost gentle man he'd been minutes before.

Unlike just about everybody else she'd met in life, it seemed that Naðr Véurr was unlikely ever going to be someone she could easily figure out. Sure, she hadn't known him long but Megan got the impression the king preferred being unpredictable. Anticipating his words and actions was tricky and she expected that wouldn't change.

And she wouldn't want it to.

Megan inhaled deeply and shook her head. Why was she thinking as if she'd be staying? Eager to move away from her misconstrued thoughts, she steered into safer waters. Or fairly safe. "So why did Raknar call Yrsa a seer and say she wasn't actually here? Because she definitely seemed like she was here as we traveled today."

Interestingly enough, asking questions like this didn't seem all that far-fetched anymore.

Naðr didn't answer right away, as if debating what to say. When he did speak, his tone was tepid. "Yrsa is one of five sisters, all of who are seers. All were very beautiful."

Though it seemed the last thing he wanted to do, he continued. "Born at the peak of our highest mountain range, Galdhøpiggen, the sisters were revered from the moment they first drew breath. But as they grew, three became restless, wanted more. Two, braver than the third, left a few years earlier. One of those two was dark souled. She raised an army and helped Rennir's brother who was then king."

"Yrsa?"

"No." Naðr shook his head, lips wry. "This happened several years ago. And even then, she was not as evil as Yrsa has become. But she was harmful enough that when the gods sent me Adlin MacLomain to help, I welcomed him openly. Even my brothers and I couldn't fight Yrsa's sister alone. With Adlin's help we could."

Naðr's eyes grew distant as he remembered something only he could see. "And there can be no doubt that Odin and Freyja favored us as well when we won."

Though she knew just about everything there was to know about the Norse gods it still seemed strange to hear them talked about so reverently, as though they were right here, right now, listening.

"Adlin MacLomain." She frowned. "This is the debt you owed him then? Why Meyla left a child behind? The reason Valan Hamilton is here?"

"Partly, yes." Naðr pulled her hood over her head as they walked. "But Meyla and Valan weren't connected through the child. Valan is here because of my agreement with the seers."

"Right. The seers. One you defeated with help from Adlin MacLomain, one was Yrsa. But you said three grew restless and fled the mountain. What happened to the third?"

Naðr said nothing at first, his strong jaw hitched with emotion until he at last said, "Actually, one seer was married to Raknar. I married the other."

Chapter Thirteen

Naðr wanted to broach this topic about as much as he wanted to share a horn of ale with Loki. Yet he'd led the conversation down this path so would see it through. Besides, he wasn't such a fool that he thought he'd be able to keep this knowledge from Megan. Regardless. It didn't make the moment chafe his rhetorical ass any less. Some things you just hoped to hel you wouldn't have to share. But now he had no choice. After all, he'd walked himself right into it.

So as the path thinned and they made their way down through the mountains, he kept talking even though her eyes rounded and lips fell open a fraction. "Though a seer, my wife, Aesa, was wild and restless. She couldn't live her life on Galdhøpiggen so left the circle of sisters. Strong, a warrior above all others, I loved the woman fiercely."

Megan nodded, her answer simple and supportive. "I get that."

She *got* that?

He barely did. Even to this day. Their love, even their desire for one another, had always been a battle. But that was Aesa. Fierce. Consuming. Mostly loyal.

"But which one married Raknar?" Megan didn't allow him to help her down a gradually slanting rock face but slid until she had sure footing. "Oh wait a second…" her words trailed as she clearly put the pieces together.

Naðr leapt down and caught her around the waist before she so boldly made her way down the next rock face. "I think you already figured that out."

"Shoot." She frowned, golden eyes meeting his beneath lowered brows. "Yrsa?" Megan shook her head, disbelieving, lips in a thin line before she ground out, "*She* was married to Raknar?"

Naðr wasn't about drawing out the moment so nodded and helped her down the next mini decline, muttering, "In another life."

"Really? Another life?" He was about to respond when she rolled her eyes and quirked her lips. "You've got to be kidding. But I guess asking about Raknar having a wife in another life isn't such an 'out there' or crazy question, considering all this, now is it?"

Only because of his dragon blood did he understand her dialect but when she spoke words like this, he was lost. 'Out there?' 'Crazy?' But Naðr was human enough to follow her meaning. "Yes, they were married."

"Well, that explains her lusting after him then."

Naðr flinched and pulled her after him. He could only imagine what Yrsa might have said before he and his brothers arrived.

Megan's voice grew soft. "Is Yrsa Heidrek's mother then?"

"Yes." Naðr frowned. "Raknar's boy has had the affliction with his speech since her departure."

"That's awful," she whispered. Though it seemed Megan would ask more about it she didn't, but fell silent, as if lost in thought. Her stoic gaze proof of the pain she felt for Raknar's son.

"So Yrsa is a seer and wasn't actually here today. How exactly did she manage that?" Megan asked.

"Through the power of interactive illusion."

"I see…I guess." Even as he helped her down a sharper ledge, Megan stayed focused. "I get what happened to three of the sisters. What about the other two who stayed on the mountain?"

When she slid down the ledge, he caught her slim waist in his hands and met her eyes. "They are why you are here. *They* are the seers who I owed a debt for helping Torra MacLomain."

Megan blinked and frowned. "But what do they *do* up there all by themselves?"

"Besides keeping life very interesting for me, I'd say busy making more bargains with unsuspecting souls."

"Ah, so I'm interesting, am I?"

Naðr grinned. "More so by the moment."

He steered her down a side path into a wide clearing of pines completely surrounded by sheer, towering mountain faces. His men were already gathering wood for a fire and several had gone off to hunt.

Megan's eyes rounded a little as she took in their location. "Wow, it's gorgeous here."

"And well-protected." He put his hand against the small of her back and nodded at the fire being lit. "Go warm yourself while I build a shelter."

Though trembling from the chill and no doubt shock from all that had happened today, she said, "I don't mind helping you."

Naðr leaned close and murmured in her ear. "Go to the fire. Sit. Find some peace after a difficult day." Then he nipped her earlobe lightly, words heavy with insinuation. "You can help me later this eve."

Her eyes shot to his.

He winked.

"Of course I'll help keep you warm," she murmured and headed toward the fire. "Damn cold out."

Oh, she'd warm him all right. Naðr pulled skins from his satchel and made quick work of tying them off to a few select trees. Then, drawing on very little dragon magic, he dried the ground on the inside, plumped it up with pine needles then tossed down a few thin blankets before calling Megan over. He pulled her into the tent and handed her a dry dress. "Here. You're wet and need to change."

"Thanks." Her brow swept up when his eyes roamed down her body. "I was under the impression I was going to be warming up by the fire *before* warming up in here."

"And you will be," he promised, hauling her close. "For the most part."

There was something irresistible about her. While he could admit he favored Aesa's wild streak, his wife had never needed protecting. And, though he might deny it, he realized he rather liked the mix of strength and vulnerability within Megan.

She murmured something incoherent, a tremor rippling through her body, as he yanked away the cloak and enfolded her in his arms. He liked how responsive she was. How her body melted against his as if it recognized its counterpart, as if they'd embraced many, many times before.

While tempted to take her as he had the previous eve, he wouldn't now. Because whether or not she realized it, Nathan's death hadn't quite sunk in yet. Though Naðr had no use for the man and Megan obviously had a rough history with him, she'd lost an old love today. While he didn't think it would bring her to tears, it was a loss.

So for now, Naðr was determined to make her feel…loved? Or at least more comfortable than he'd made her feel since she'd arrived from the future. That thought in mind, he kept his lust at bay and helped her remove the damp dress. But the gods knew there were all sorts of creative and pleasurable things he wanted to do to her. Things she'd never see coming.

"Do you realize you're smirking?" she said under her breath as he tossed aside the garment.

"Smirking? Am I?" he replied innocently as he moved behind her and rubbed her shoulders.

"You are," she breathed, muscles relaxing bit by bit as her head fell back.

Which gave him a perfect view of her tightened nipples. Naðr bit the inside of his lip, determined to be affectionate rather than seduce. But it was damn hard. Just like his cock. He closed his eyes and focused on easing the tension from her body. He could do this.

It didn't help in the least when she pressed her backside against him. *Hel*. When her body fluctuated against his, he inhaled sharply, pulled away and grabbed the dry dress.

"Arms up," he murmured, eyes shooting to hers when she complied, her movements slow and if he didn't know better, sultry.

"Like this?" Her brows perked and her lips curled up as his gaze dropped to her uplifted breasts. Heaving beneath her unsteady breath, they were a delicious beacon in the smooth sailing waters opening up between them.

Sea Siren to say the least. This one belonged to Freyja.

He met her grin with one of his own before he slid the dress over her head. "Perfect."

When the material deprived him of all her smooth, taut skin, he pulled free her unruly curls and licked his lips. All he wanted to do was dig his hands into its rich thickness and bite every last inch of skin left available to him.

"You're surprising me," she whispered, coy eyes never leaving his face.

"And you're tempting me," he countered.

"Tough not to."

"Is it?"

"You know it is."

"Good."

Pleased, he wrapped the fur cloak over her shoulders, brushed his lips across hers then pulled her out of the tent. It was nearly dark and though the snow had lessened some it still fell heavy enough to drift lightly through the thick pine cover overhead. The majority of his men had returned and either sat on logs or stood around the campfire. Hare and squirrel roasted on pits.

"Holy testosterone," Megan muttered. "Wish Meyla was here."

Testosterone? But he understood enough her meaning. The opposite gender. Though he sensed she was being truthful about wanting Meyla here, he didn't think she was bothered in the least by so many men. If anything, he suspected she got along better with men than she did with women.

"So they join us again." Kol grinned as he tossed Naðr a skin of mead then handed Megan the same. "Who would've guessed?"

Naðr gave his brother no response, nodded at his men then drank deeply.

Despite his strong opinions that morn, Kjar, not surprisingly, positioned himself next to Megan. While none of his men would dare go near her since the king had laid claim, his cousin tended to lean toward precaution. Battling and killing made for an extra lusty lot and she was the only woman to be had.

Raknar was especially somber as he sat on a log, skin of mead hanging loosely between his legs as he stared into the fire. Like Naðr, his brother had hoped Yrsa wasn't involved with Rennir, so today's revelation cut deep. To see his former wife could be no easy thing and his dark thoughts reflected on his face. Though caught off guard by her actions, Naðr made no move when Megan sat next to Raknar. His brother didn't seem to notice in the least. Yet she was offering comfort without saying a word.

As he knew would be the case, Raknar remained silent.

So Naðr turned the conversation to the future, no matter how much his brothers wouldn't want to hear it. "Today was nothing but a ruse, testing our boundaries to see if we'd keep our dragons repressed."

"And we did," Kol said, irritated. "Not sure I am willing to do it again, brother."

"We stayed true to our promise and that will count for something," Naðr said carefully. "Beyond the dragon within, we're warring men." He nodded at many of his warriors with pride. "That alone means much."

His men nodded, raised their skins, rumbling their approval.

Even Kol knew enough not to press the issue with so many listening, so he grunted and drank. Yet he shared his brother's distress. It was unnatural to keep the beast within tamed, to only embrace the human half.

"Rennir has the information he needs and will come by ship soon." Naðr looked at his brothers then to the rest of his men. "When he does, there will be many and it will be war."

"So we will wait for him ashore," Kjar said.

"Half of us will." Naðr looked in the direction of the sea. "The other half will battle on the water."

This news introduced another rumble of pleasure as men nodded and drank. When too many eyes continued to fall on Megan, Kol plunked down on her other side. If nothing else, he and his brothers protected their own.

Kjar's expression remained devoid of emotion even as he kept a close eye on both Naðr and Megan. There was much to be said but not here. Not with so many listening. For now it was best that all wind down from the battling and rest. So, knowing Megan was well protected by his kin, Naðr went about visiting with his men. Most were pleased with the death dealt and a battle well fought. But a few had unrest in their eyes even as they grinned.

They'd wanted more raiding before this and now combined with Rennir closing in, discontent grew. What nobody save his brothers and Kjar knew was that the raids had slowed down because of the enemy king himself. Rennir was set on intercepting their raids and fighting to the death. Naðr took good care of his people. They did not lack in wealth. So for now, until he settled things with his enemy, he saw no point in putting them at risk. Not over old grievances that had nothing to do with them.

But greed was greed and he didn't fault his men for it. They were part of a clan that was amongst the strongest and most fierce in the land. Not only that, like him, they were adventurers and seafaring men. To hunker down, even half of them, at port and wait like cowards for the enemy to come to them went against their very grain. Yes, they wanted their family protected but at heart they likely wondered why they were in a position that their kin needed defending to begin with.

The sun had long set and most of the mead drunk by the time he made his way back to Megan. Meanwhile she'd made good use of the time and had not only his brothers but Kjar sitting alongside her. While they undoubtedly were there to protect her, all seemed quite content with their mission.

Even Raknar.

While he wasn't exactly smiling, there was a much needed light in his eyes as he didn't chat but watched her. Kjar had a casual grin on his face as he conversed. Kol was downright flirting as he bumped her shoulder and chuckled. And Naðr's approach didn't throw him in the least. Shoulder resting comfortably against hers, his youngest brother grinned. "I kept her well entertained for you, brother."

Setting aside his discontent over his men's worries not to mention his own with what lay ahead, Naðr mustered up an easy smile. Megan was dealing with enough. She didn't need him to add to it. "Did these fools feed you?"

"Yeah, thanks."

When she smiled a few knots in his shoulders and neck unlocked. The genuine warmth of her regard felt like a much needed safe haven from the heaviness of his thoughts.

Kol eyed Naðr's skin. "It's still full. Drink."

"I will if you give up your seat."

"It would never happen." But a wide smile soon followed as Kol stood. "If I didn't love the hel out of you."

Naðr clapped his brother on the shoulder then sat between Megan and Kjar, wearier than he'd ever let on.

"What about you?" Megan said softly, nudging him a little. "Have you eaten?"

"Some time ago," he assured. But he hadn't. It was the least of his priorities.

Within moments, Kol was pressing meat into his hands, voice low. "Eat."

Naðr nodded his thanks and ate, eyes to the fire.

"And drink," Megan murmured.

When his eyes turned to her, she grinned. Raknar leaned forward, nodded at him and echoed her words. "And drink."

So he drank as he ate, ears still to the conversations happening around him. While especially tuned into the beauty by his side, nothing would ever stop him from listening…hearing. It was a fine-honed skill he'd learned long ago. One that gave him a feel for the energy, the very life force of the men around him. If they were happy, he needed to know. If they were discontented, he needed to know.

Meanwhile, Kol squeezed himself between Kjar and Naðr as he swigged from his skin. It gave the king the fire at his face while those who mattered most surrounded him. Megan, seeming to understand that though he was by her side he still needed to pay attention to his men, turned her conversation Raknar's way. Yet despite his determination to listen to others, Naðr was drawn not only to her warm body but to her gentle words.

"So we'll go fishing. I used to go back home. A long time ago." She nodded. "I'd like to do it again."

"We will," Raknar agreed, a sense of purpose in his voice. "There is klippfisk aplenty."

Megan shook her head. "I'm not familiar with that type of fish. What does it look like?"

Raknar looked for words but couldn't find them so scooped up a handful of snow. "A bit darker than this color. Flaky, dry meat. Very good."

"So like cod or haddock?"

Confused, he shook his head. "I don't know. Could be."

"No matter." Megan nodded, eyes alive. "We'll plan on going fishing then."

Naðr kept emotion buried but knew Kol was having more difficulty keeping silent as he took another long swig from his skin. It was a rare day that Raknar spoke not of conquest but of their baser roots. That of being sons of a fisherman.

Yet despite the pleasant turn of conversation, he remained weary.

Kjar's calm eyes met Naðr's and he lowered his head. "Sleep for you and Megan then."

"Sleep," Naðr agreed and stood. Though Kjar had implied Megan would go when he did, it would not happen like that. His woman had offered solace to his brothers this eve and he'd not haul her off if she did not want to go. No, if she desired to join him it would be of her own free will for all to see. Leaving her alone now was not a concern. Many had gone off to sleep but even so, his men had watched her this eve and if anything, respected the camaraderie she'd formed with his kin.

Megan was a good woman.

She deserved to make her own decision on when she wished to sleep. As to who she would sleep with, that was decided. But even then, on such a night that she'd lost a love, he would not pressure her.

But Naðr would not leave without saying goodnight. Crouching in front of her, he cupped her cheek. "You did well today." Even though he meant the exchange to be formal, his fingers drifted over her soft skin before he kissed her cheek, voice loud enough for all remaining by the fire to hear. "Visit with my brothers then come rest when you are ready."

Her eyes locked with his and she nodded. "I will."

He nodded as well and left.

Kjar grabbed his wrist in passing. He removed the half full skin from his hand and replaced it with a full one. "Sleep well, cousin."

Naðr clasped his wrist in return, nodded, then made his way into the tent. Yet his steps were heavy and the air in his lungs heavier. As he had the previous night, the urge to toss Megan over his shoulder and slam her down beneath him was strong. But like then, he wanted her to move forward with knowledge and a sense of self-security. Last eve, it had been sharing that he was half dragon. This eve? That he would not force her to do anything she did not want to do. Unless it risked her safety. But they'd deal with that possibility when and if it came.

So upon entering the tent he sat, elbows rested casually over bent knees and did his best to wait patiently. Thankfully, she didn't make him wait long. The fire was still crackling when she ducked into the tent. Kneeling, she paused and allowed her eyes to adjust. When they did, her hooded gaze locked on his.

Naðr's dragon blood had never sizzled so sharply around a woman. Free, untamed, her blond curls were back-dropped by warm, orange light and the outline of her body was so tempting he hungered...

For her.

Them.

Everything.

Megan crawled forward until she knelt in front of him. Eyes partially masked in darkness, she said nothing, just stared. It seemed like the moon grew full five times in the sky before she at last spoke, tone husky, throaty. "This is happening so fast. What are we doing? What are *you* doing?"

What *was* he doing? But he already knew. In all honesty, he was fairly certain he'd known since the moment he laid eyes on her.

"I am choosing my mate," he said bluntly, watching her reaction closely. From her small hitch of breath to the flutter of her eyelashes. "The amount of time I've known you does not matter. I want you…us."

"Mate?" she whispered, unsure. But his words had increased her heartbeat and the scent of her desire. Whatever she might say, Megan liked his declaration, which aroused him all that much more.

"Yes, the dragon within wants you."

She considered that, cheeks flush. "And what of the man?"

Naðr called on the great strength of Odin to help him ignore the increasing scent of her arousal as his eyes remained locked with hers. "You already know the answer to that."

"I can't stay here," she murmured but the pain in her eyes was unmistakable. "I *won't* stay here."

Though her words rankled, he understood her reasoning, her very defiance. Would he not feel the same way if he was in her era and his family was still here? But that didn't lessen his desire to keep her. Yet it had to be on her terms…because she chose to. So though not necessarily his strong point, Naðr decided right then and there that he'd do everything in his power to persuade her, no matter how much finesse and charm might be required.

And then there were other ways as well.

Ones that he intended to use as a persuasive weapon against her.

"You understand, right?" she said softly. "Because you have a very devious look on your face right now."

"I do not know this word 'devious'," he lied and slowly removed the cloak, exposing her to the chilled air. When a shiver rippled through her, he spread his own cloak in invitation that she join him.

"Pfft. Yeah right." But it seemed his potential warmth was too tempting when she boldly lifted her dress enough so that she could straddle him. "You understand every word coming out of my mouth thanks to seer magic or the dragon within or whatever's at work here."

Naðr wrapped his cloak around her and cocooned them as he pressed his rigid length against her heated core. Fire flared over his skin at the look in her eyes. He wanted her squirming helplessly against him.

But not quite yet.

Though difficult to give control to another, Naðr did. Where he had taken her ruthlessly before, now he wanted to see what she'd do about her own desire. Better yet, he wanted to see just how much she was willing to take. But then the moment she'd spread her legs and pressed against him, she was well on her way to taking a great deal.

Chapter Fourteen

Megan sensed the power shift between them the moment she ran her tongue up his neck, nibbling the whole way, until her lips hovered centimeters from his. The man released all her sexual inhibitions. While she'd always liked the act itself, something about Naðr introduced a whole new world of possibilities.

Ones made of wrenching lust and unabashed, driving need.

Maybe some wouldn't have hopped back in the sack so fast. But then she supposed those same women wouldn't have slept with him so soon to begin with. Hard to imagine looking at him. And though she knew his looks and killer body were part of the driving force behind her covetousness, there was also a sense of time dwindling away. It was impossible to know how exactly she'd traveled back in time to begin with. So the more she got to know Naðr the more edgy she became about their time together being brief. Because she'd meant what she said about going home.

Home. A place she seriously didn't want to think about right now.

No, she'd much rather focus on her Viking king.

She loved his aggressiveness but something about him allowing her to take control was heady. And not an opportunity she'd let go to waste. That in mind, she flicked her tongue over his lips and ground then rolled her hips. A low groan rumbled in his chest and though he grabbed her backside, he didn't take control. Yet a tremor rippled through him as though it took a great deal of effort.

Slow, languid, she continued to roll her hips and put her lips next to his ear whispering, "Let's see how long you last."

Then she nibbled his earlobe before grazing her teeth back down his neck. While she might have been chilled moments before, she wasn't anymore. Instead, a fevered heat was breaking out over her skin…one driven and ignited by the steaming body against hers. As she continued a low, grinding roll with her hips, she removed the cloak from around them both.

But even then she wanted more skin.

His skin.

Against hers.

Now.

She twisted her hands in his tunic, near growling, "Get this off."

"No."

"No?"

"Not unless you take it off."

Megan grinned at the challenge and decided it might be more fun to torture him instead. So she peeled off her dress and slowly kept up the grind that was bringing forth an even more dangerous, primal glint to his eyes.

Taking one of his hands in hers, she traced the tip of a finger down his palm, making small circles to match the pattern of her hips. Soaked between her thighs but determined to see how far she could push him, she brought his forefinger to her lips and drew it back and forth so slowly his breathing increased even more. Then, as she feathered her hand over the swell of her breasts, she pulled his finger into her mouth.

A match for what he'd done to her the night before.

The purposeful way she wrapped her tongue around it, groaned then sucked, hollowing her cheeks as her eyes held his, was done so with one intention. That he envision something altogether different in her willing mouth. His eyes narrowed a fraction and he pulsed heavily between her thighs. Her tight nipples strained almost painfully.

When she blew on his finger then sucked hard, he jerked against her, eyes widening.

She gave him the hint of a grin, eyes taunting.

It wouldn't be long now.

Depriving his finger from the hot heat of her mouth, she closed her eyes, leaned her head back and steered his finger down her neck inch by very slow inch. Honing in on the sensation of his wet, rough touch blazing down her bare flesh, she squeezed her thighs as sensation built.

A haunting, intense wind blew and created a low, bass-like moan through the mountains as if it echoed the cavernous ache growing within. Megan might've set out to drive him crazy with desire but was revving up her own engine just as swiftly.

Head still thrust back, eyes slit open just enough that she could hide behind her lashes and watch him, Megan curled his finger so that his nail scraped lightly up over the swell of her breast and around her nipple. Then she started to roll her hips in the opposite direction.

He clenched her backside tighter and flexed his hips with a groan. His previous words flashed through her mind, except now she heard them as low and demanding.

I am claiming you as my mate. I want you…us.

Blown away by the renewed impact of his words, her body blazed and the muscles between her legs started to ripple and clench. Either he sensed what was happening to her or he'd just had enough of the slow agony because Naðr suddenly ripped his tunic over his head and yanked her against him.

Skin to skin.

At last.

Her body exploded. A climax pounding through her so viciously that her jaw quivered and she screamed against the hard, hot skin of his neck, digging her nails into his chest. Christ, what the hell was this? They hadn't even had sex yet.

But they soon would.

Though he might've waited for her to come down from her cloud the night before, Naðr didn't seem so inclined now as he wrenched back control. Delirious, too far gone in pleasure, she could barely process his actions.

Until he clenched her backside and pushed into her.

Trapped between his strong arms, she whimpered in shock and oh so much rekindled pleasure as his guttural groan vibrated against her body. Pressing deep, he pushed past the pulsing remnants of her clenching orgasm.

"Too," she moaned, "much."

"Never enough," he said, voice low and deep and promising. Yet he stilled and ran his fingers up her backside, taking pleasure it seemed in the feeling of her innards grasping at him.

Drifting down, down, down, her body finally went even limper than before as threads of acute pleasure lingered. Full of him, locked within the powerful, muscled, comforting cage of his body, she floated, drifted…lost.

Until he once more found her.

Better yet, made her find him as he gave her a dose of her own medicine when he thrust and rolled his hips. Megan seized up and frantically twisted her hands up his body. But he was far too strong and didn't let her get far. Just enough that she clasped his cheeks, met his eyes, and pleaded for mercy.

But she should have known better.

None would be given.

Pants pulled down just enough, he braced his booted feet on the ground, legs spread, in effect pulling her thighs wider apart. Hell, the man meant to kill her slow and easy. Despite the inevitability of incomparable pleasure, as he began to move, her heart thundered louder, her lips drifted closer to his.

There was a tangible unspoken thrill in the method they provoked one another. Yet it was in such a sweet but unstoppable way as they pushed each other toward their breaking points. Give. Take. Give. Take. A flow and ebb that had her once more climbing toward another peak as their lips hovered a breath away from one another's.

"Megan," he whispered, eager, desperate.

Blood pounded in her ears and she rested her forehead against his as their hips worked together. Sweat slicked their skin despite the cold air and puffs of fog bursting from their lips as both became wrapped up in getting closer, deeper.

Then, in a motion that impaled her even more, he gave her arms freedom, kept a firm grasp on her backside, and fell to his back. Sitting upright, hands braced against his chest, she met his thrusts with pure, unadulterated fury. Engulfed in sensation, lost in his eyes, she rode him with enthusiastic vigor.

Now neither controlled.

Now, like the eerie howl of the wind, their souls cried out for the other as they tested new boundaries, ones made of challenge and consent, made of how far the other was willing to go. Then, as if it'd been there all along but she only now saw it, fire flared in his eyes.

Actual fire.

The dragon.

Controlled. Repressed. But there.

Somehow she knew it though her mind barely processed. He was baring himself to her... or at least a small portion. But it seemed so important and soulful that she choked not from fear but stark, vibrant need. She wasn't afraid. Not in the least.

Black. Long. Powerful. Scales.

Searing, pinning, surreal blue eyes.

All rose up in her vision before everything snapped shut and he rolled her beneath him. Though she had no idea how he'd managed it, his soft, supple leather pants and boots were gone. Now there was nothing but hot, slick, Viking male against her…

And dragon.

Somehow the beast within was here every bit as much as his human form. Brash, crazed, rough, yet remarkably tender, everything Naðr Véurr was made of engulfed her as he thrust again and again.

Rip-roaring and potent, the throbbing pleasure between her thighs didn't simply migrate but blasted through every tiny sinew in her body. Though it was an orgasm, it was so much more, something predatory and leading. Something that held her suspended and strung out. Like a too-stretched rubber band, taut and straining as he moved with her in a mutual, untouchable rhythm that was wicked, unstoppable.

"Naðr," she gasped, out of air but already blasphemously addicted to where he was taking her.

Then, as though her saying his name triggered it, he swelled within her and then thrust hard with a strangled roar. Megan arched, head flung back and cried out moments before her throat closed and a remarkably strong climax seized her in a vise grip. Again, as if ushering her straight into the afterlife to somewhere more beautiful than she could imagine, his words tumbled through her mind again.

I am claiming you as my mate.

Lost in pure, never-before-felt bliss, she grabbed onto the words to anchor herself. For a split second she felt like she was under the Atlantic again and standing on the Viking longship, desperate for something she could not see, could not touch.

Until she could.

Her Viking king.

Naðr Véurr.

Then, rippling and wholly lost, she found her way back into his arms, not beneath the dark sea or even beneath him anymore. Confused, she panicked for a moment. Then she realized she was cuddled against him beneath a blanket. Though the lapse in time mildly alarmed her, she was so sated that she instantly relaxed as his arm wrapped tighter around her.

"Shh," he whispered. "You're safe."

Her eyes drifted then slid shut. When next she opened them, dim light flooded the tent and he was watching her. Before she could say a word, he put a finger to her lips and shook his head. Trusting, she let him roll her until he came against her back and nestled her head in his arm.

Flooded by his spicy, spruce, outdoorsy scent, she curled back against him as he lifted her leg and slid into her. He didn't need to ready her at all. No, her desperately wanton body welcomed his thickness as though it had been lost without it. Megan pressed her mouth, teeth even, against his forearm, as it flexed with his movements.

Firm hand pressed against her stomach, he thrust slow and easy. Grasping his arm, she shuttered, drowning in waves of sensation. His lips met the side of her neck as his hand covered hers and dragged it down until she had no choice but to touch her clit.

Wind howled so strongly that it whipped down out of the mountains and blasted beneath the tent, chilling her lips and teeth. Yet it was a delicious countermeasure against the roaring fire he was creating beneath her skin.

"Noooo," she moaned as pleasure skittered through her veins, determined to eat her alive.

"*Yes*," he whispered in her ear as he moved not faster but slower, his movements so excruciatingly measured that sweat broke out and her vision blurred. Naðr dealt in pure torment and she was his very willing victim.

When the scruff of his facial hair brushed against her too-vulnerable cheek and the corner of his mouth hovered against hers, she groaned. As she licked her lips, so too did he. Then his tongue flicked against her lips as they both grunted and groaned with his next thrust.

Desperate to taste him, she tilted her head enough to capture his lips. Like an avalanche, his mouth closed over hers and he clenched her hip in a vice grip. His tongue swooped as deep as his next thrust and she cried into his mouth. Pressing her forward a fraction, he didn't need to move his hand down for friction but used her own compressed thigh to achieve his goal.

Pure bliss.

Everything catapulted through the roof as her body jerked once, twice. When she flailed and tried to escape, he pressed tighter, thrust deeper and sent her sailing clear over the edge. A sob broke from her chest as the pleasure ripped so sharply through her it felt like sweet, sinful pain. Then his hand slammed down beside her and he pressed unbelievably deep, releasing a ragged, deep-throated sound of intense gratification.

"*Mine*," he half growled, half groaned. His release seemed never-ending as he curled around her protectively, his hold on her body secure.

Muscles not her own, jerking, she held on tight and squeezed her eyes shut. *Mine.* His declaration fueled and elongated her climax, drawing it out until the world dimmed and she closed her eyes.

Time slipped away.

Contentment filled her.

Until it did not.

Megan suddenly stood on her deck at home. The raven perched nearby and watched her.

"What?" She shook her head as a sense of foreboding filled her. Black clouds rolled across a blue sky and time seemed to speed up. Within moments, Frenchman Bay was swamped in hurricane like weather. A Nor'easter. Rain fell in heavy sheets and gale-force winds gusted.

The raven stared at her for another long moment before launching into the air.

Dread filled her as she watched it fly toward where she'd gone diving. Megan blinked and shielded her eyes from the rain, stunned when what she viewed was so much like the picture Amber had drawn. Minus the raging weather.

Naðr's longship, the one she'd found beneath the sea, was turning toward shore, toward her.

Except this time it listed wildly and several oars broke free. Why was the sail still up? It should be down! Huge waves crested over the side. It should be steering into the waves but even she could see heavy swells came from too many directions. And the ship was far too close to shore.

Yet she sensed Naðr's need to get to her. His desperation. Then, to her horror, a mammoth wave combined with a severe wind gust and the ship teetered dangerously…then rolled. Her heart fell into her stomach and though she screamed, the sound was drowned out by a crash of thunder.

Then, as quickly as the ship slipped beneath the sea, her surroundings faded away.

"Megan, wake up, woman."

Confused, gasping, she blinked and stared into Naðr's concerned eyes. Once more in their tent, he crouched in front of her and held her upper arms firmly. She must have been having a nightmare. But it had seemed *so* real. Though shaking and still frightened, she was never so glad to see him. Alive.

Naðr waited and watched her closely before he whispered, "The raven came to you."

A chill ran through her and she nodded vaguely. Naðr pulled her onto his lap then wrapped a fur around her. He pressed her cheek to his chest and held her that way, warming her, for several long minutes. When at last her heartbeat settled, she pulled back and frowned. "How did you know the raven came?"

Steady eyes held hers for a few moments before he said, "The raven is a Valkyrie. It was she who often visited Aesa and it was she who chose her to go to Valhalla. I always sense when she is near."

Megan swallowed hard. So odd to have it confirmed that not only was her raven a Valkyrie but connected with Naðr's deceased wife. "Why does it sound as if you actually believe the raven was near and not just part of my nightmare?"

"Because it was." His eyes remained on her, unflinching. "While it might have felt like a dream, what just happened to you was more like a glimpse at a possible reality. When the raven took your mind there, my dragon was able to follow your thoughts and see what you saw."

"Impossible," she whispered then sighed. If she'd learned nothing else since this all began it was that anything was possible. Heck, dragons existed. And…she'd slept with one…several times. That pretty much cleared a path for a whole new reality. She pinched the bridge of her nose and frowned. "I really don't want to imagine any of what I just witnessed happening."

Naðr stroked her hair gently. "A god showed us this for a reason and we will pay attention to the message." Then he pointed out the obvious. "I have spent the majority of my life on the sea. I know what I'm doing. My sail would have been down in such weather and I would have handled the ship much differently."

"Even if…"

When her words trailed off, he tilted up her chin and met her eyes. "Even if?"

Though a little embarrassed it seemed like the logical thing to ask. "Even if you desperately needed to get to the shore?"

The intense flare of his eyes, the absolute strength of what he'd be capable of when it came to her, crashed into Megan's senses.

"If you were in danger, I would shift into the dragon before I'd attempt to bring a ship into port in that kind of weather. And if I couldn't shift into the dragon, I'd swim."

Warmth burned through her at his impassioned words. Still. "Did you see those waters? You have no idea what Maine's coast can be like during a storm."

"I swim better than I sail. And no one can captain better than me." He cupped the side of her neck. "I will *always* be there if you're in danger."

Megan decided not to point out the obvious. That he would be *here* and she would be *there*. And she thought he wasn't supposed to shift. "Why was not shifting into the dragon part of your agreement with the seers?"

"We were given no precise answer other than that the power of the dragons could disrupt whatever magic is at work now."

"Now?"

"The magic of the gods and even the seers. The same magic that brought you back in time, that which will see through the bargain struck to help our descendant, Torra MacLomain."

"You and your brothers sacrificed an awful lot."

"As I said before, there is nothing we would not do to help kin."

"I know," she whispered. Needing to touch him, offer comfort, she brushed the back of her hand down his cheek. "It must take a great deal of strength not to embrace what you are. I can't imagine."

"It will not be forever," he murmured. "The day will come when we have fulfilled our promise."

Megan contemplated that and couldn't help but wonder exactly what that meant for her and her sisters.

Their conversation was cut short when Kol stuck his head in and grinned. "I can't remember the last time the king slept longer than the rest of us."

Naðr perked a brow. "Do I look like I'm sleeping?"

Kol's eyes swept over them, his grin turning into a full blown smile, crinkling the corners of his eyes. "No, but then you're not doing what I'd be doing if I had her on my lap."

This earned Kol a scowl from his brother. "We leave soon. Make sure the men are ready."

Kol nodded. He was about to pull his head out but paused and kept on grinning at her, dimples erupting. "You're a fine sight this morn, Megan."

Shameless flirt. Megan rolled her eyes and waved him away.

"I think my brother is half in love with you." Naðr pulled her to her feet and a grin much like Kol's crawled onto his face. "He has good taste in women."

Not one to dwell on flattery, she blew an errant lock of frazzled hair out of her face and shrugged. "Oh, I'm sure I look like a million bucks."

With a raffish gleam in his eyes, Naðr let the fur drop and enclosed her in his arms, mumbling, "You are so very beautiful," before his lips closed over hers in a hot, rough, ravenous kiss. The sweet sting left between her thighs from the night before raged into a throbbing demand. Megan clasped his tight backside, groaning with desire at the feel of the muscled curvature.

Naðr tore his lips away and groused, "Don't even think about it, Kol."

Megan rounded her eyes when she realized his brother was moments away from sticking his head in again.

Kol chuckled. "I'll keep my dragon at bay for you, brother but don't ask me not to think about what I'd see if I stuck my head in now."

Megan snorted and though it was about the last thing she wanted to do, she pulled away. "I'd say it's time to get dressed."

Naðr seemed less than impressed with the idea as he reluctantly yanked on his pants, muttering, "I look forward to getting you back to the holding and into my bed."

In complete agreement, she pulled on a pair of trousers, a tunic and boots he handed her, all the while frustratingly aroused. It seemed her body couldn't get enough of what he had to offer. When she stepped out of the tent, Kol was waiting with a shit-eating grin on his face. He held out a piece of meat. "Hungry?"

When her stomach rumbled, he chuckled. "Thought so. Busy night."

"Thanks," she murmured and took the food. Megan could only hope the wind howled louder than she had. But based on the amused glances Kjar and Raknar shot her when she joined them, she guessed she'd been noisier than a banshee. Even so, she was hard pressed to feel embarrassed. Their society was so completely different than hers, far more open and not so much in a depraved way. If anything, they seemed to take pride in her for a night well spent. And the truth was it had been one amazingly awesome night despite the nightmare.

Kjar handed her a skin. "I got you some mountain water."

Something had shifted with Naðr's cousin. While she sensed he liked her since they met, there was a new fondness in his eyes.

Megan smiled. "Thank you."

Nothing ever tasted as good as the icy water as it slid down her throat. She'd bet just about anything that she was running dehydrated from her overnight activities.

Even Raknar seemed a little less intense this morning as he pulled on her hood. "The winds are strong today."

They certainly were. Though it had stopped snowing, heavy gusts swung the pines back and forth overhead and twisted snow into heavy bouts of near white-out conditions. She nodded thanks and cinched the strings.

In record time, Naðr had the tent skins down and joined them. Megan handed him the water and pulled her eyes from the sight of him drinking it. So sexy. And too handsome for his own good. When he handed the skin back, that unmistakable twinkle had returned to his eyes. He knew he got her going in a *really* good way.

"The remainder of the journey down is not as steep but can be just as dangerous because of the weather," he informed and leaned close. "So let me help you today."

"I thought I did yesterday." But she knew she hadn't. Depending on men for anything wasn't her strong point. "At least most of the time."

Naðr twisted his lip and put his hand to the small of her back. "Let's go."

Half the men led the way, the other half fell in behind, cushioning their king in between. Naðr hadn't been kidding about the perilous conditions. She'd guessed the gusts were upwards of thirty to forty miles-per-hour and the snow damn near blinding.

But she wasn't a hearty New Englander for no good reason.

Head down, skin as protected as she could manage, she followed Naðr's every instruction without complaint and paid attention to everything around her. With a strong respect for Mother Nature, Megan knew how dangerous weather like this could be.

Hours passed before the temperature started to rise and the winds lessened. It was then, as the billowing snow fell away and the sharp, blue sky unraveled, that she was truly able to appreciate the stark, mouth-dropping beauty around her. Majestic, proud mountains curved down, silent sentinels over an endless swath of sparkling ocean. She still wondered which modern day Scandinavian country this was. Norway hopefully. With her own ancestry having roots here, it suddenly seemed…inevitable that she'd return.

Though he'd asked her several times during the descent, it appeared Naðr liked consistency when his eyes met hers. "How do you fare?"

"Good," she reassured and nodded at the view. "Your home is truly beautiful."

"Yes," he agreed, pride in his eyes as they swept over the mountains and down into the valley. "I have a deep love for her."

Caught not by the untouchable landscape but by the heartfelt expression on his face, she was blown away not only by the romanticism simmering beneath the surface but by how well-suited he was to this land. As though they were made for one another. Tall, strong, impregnable, impossibly striking.

Then his eyes met hers and her breath caught. Though she knew full well he'd been talking about the land, something in his rich, unwavering gaze bespoke a deeper meaning. That the words were said not only for his homeland but…for her, about her. Unexpectedly nervous, she tore her eyes from his and focused once more on the ocean.

They hadn't known one another nearly long enough to be thinking about love. Megan shook her head. She'd given her heart away once and swore she never would again. Nope, she'd buried the remnants of that smeared fairytale on top of this mountain.

"We must continue," he said softly and pulled her after him.

Yet the way he'd said 'continue' made it sound as if they were heading down an unavoidable path that didn't include just incredible chemistry in bed but much more. And if she didn't know better, she'd say he was looking forward to the journey.

By the time they made it back to the holding, the sun sat low in the sky, a warm welcoming orb that cast long, glittering spikes of whitewashed light over the peaceful sea. Megan laughed and crouched when Guardian limped rather joyfully into her waiting arms.

"I'm so glad you're okay, sweet girl," she murmured into her fur.

"S..she's just f…fine," Heidrek said moments before Raknar hoisted him onto his hip, grinning as he ruffled his son's hair with affection.

"Thank you for taking such good care of her, Heidrek," Megan said.

The boy smiled and nodded, immensely pleased.

The village was excited, happy faces abound as they welcomed back their kin. Kol wasted no time sweeping some random woman into his arms and kissing her soundly. Kjar waved to all and headed toward the docks, likely to check on the boats. Meyla flung her arms around Naðr and kissed him on the cheek. Megan grinned, glad to see father and daughter getting along so well.

Which brought her eyes to Valan. The corner of his lips hitched up and he nodded. "Good to see you back safe, lass. I would have come had I known."

She patted his shoulder. "Don't worry. Sounds like you'll get your chance to fight soon enough."

"Aye?"

"Yep, lots going on apparently."

Before she could share more, Naðr was by her side, whispering in her ear. "Go with Meyla. Get ready. Tonight will be a celebration made of readying for war with a little something else to keep spirits high."

When she looked at him in question, he only grinned. Then, before she knew it, he strode away, throwing over his shoulder. "Valan Hamilton, come with me. I wish to speak with you."

Valan looked as surprised as her when he nodded and wasted no time following.

Meyla wrapped elbows with Megan, smiling. "Good to have you back." Then she peered down at Guardian. "Come on then. Time to go get ready."

Her dog followed as they made their way into Meyla's building. Basins of hot water were already steaming in invitation and it wasn't long before they were both submerged. Eyes closed, head thrown back, Megan relished the water as it soothed sore muscles. It was no small thing climbing a mountain and coming back down within two days.

"You make my father very happy," Meyla murmured.

Her eyes met Meyla's. How to answer? Honestly she supposed. Well, at least as honest as she was willing to get right now. "I'm glad to hear it."

Naðr's daughter contemplated her for several long moments. "But you intend to try to go home."

Meyla was the closest thing to a female friend she had here yet she found her blatant statement unsettling. Probably because going home was something she was in no mood to talk about. "Yes. I need to try to get home. My sisters will be worried. And Sean."

"Who's Sean?"

"My best friend."

"Ah. Valan is my closest friend now." Meyla continued to study her in that offsetting way. A trait, Megan realized, that she'd inherited from Naðr. "I know you're already lovers but assuming you stay on longer than intended, do you think it likely you could ever consider my father a friend?"

It was an astute question and one that deserved a ready answer. But what was that exactly? Megan enjoyed Naðr's company...immensely actually. Yet would they make good companions? Could they become friends?

"Yes," she said. *Why,* she wasn't sure but knew it was entirely possible. Perhaps because of their love for boats and the sea or maybe because of their shared sense of dry humor. Whatever it was, she was drawn to what she sensed could develop between them beyond lust. There was a definite desire to know and understand him better, to learn about all he'd done in life to get where he was now.

Meyla gave a soft smile. "Well just look at what's hidden in your eyes. Friendship is inevitable. After all, you're already in love."

"In love?" Megan responded, a smidge too breathlessly for her taste. "Heck no. Sorry. I haven't known him nearly long enough."

And again Meyla sounded like her father. "Time means nothing. A day, a year, it varies for everyone how fast it happens but when it does." She gave Megan a knowing smile. "It's unstoppable."

Desperate to change the subject, Megan said, "Speaking of love, Naðr appears to have softened a bit toward Valan. Not to mention you and your father seem to be getting on well. I'm glad to see it."

"Yes, all is going much better and I'm fairly certain Valan and I have you to thank for that."

"Me? How so?"

"Besides cheering him up in general?" Meyla chuckled. "You offered us good advice and we took it. Though we didn't do it to upset father, we'd flaunted our desire for one another at every opportunity. Call it defiance I guess. On my part anyways. Valan isn't to blame. He couldn't help responding to my advances." She winked. "I'm very good at it."

No doubt she was.

Megan eyed her for a long moment and though she knew better, she wanted to better understand the complicated weave that had led her here. Because no matter what Naðr said, she knew Meyla and his involvement with the MacLomain clan not only involved her but may soon draw her sisters into this time-travel fold. "You don't have to answer if it makes you uncomfortable but I'd like…no, I *need* to better understand what happened between you and the Scotsman named Adlin MacLomain."

"Adlin," Meyla said softly. Though there was nostalgia in her eyes, there was also a great deal of fondness and strength when she said his name. "I loved Adlin. Not as I do Valan but certainly a type of love that I will never forget." Wisdom lit her eyes. "But that's not really what you want to know, is it? You want to know more about the child I left behind."

"Both," Megan murmured. "I want to know about both."

Meyla considered her words a moment before continuing. "Rennir's brother, the former king, had been a problem for many years. Not only did he want my father dead but he wanted me as his trophy. It was because of his strength combined with the seers' that father had to call on the gods. He and my uncles were younger and not nearly as powerful as they are now."

"You make it sound like years ago," Megan said. "How *old* were you when you had this child?"

"This happened two winters ago. I was seventeen." But she soon gave clarity as she seemed to understand Megan didn't have all her facts. "My father and his brothers are as one with their dragon blood. As such, they didn't come into their full strength and power until all three had entered into their third decade of life."

Ah. "So Kol turned thirty."

Meyla nodded, somewhat sad. "Yes. They're all getting so old."

Megan kept amusement at bay. Old indeed. "So that explains why they don't need Adlin's help this time to fight Rennir and Yrsa."

"Yrsa?" Meyla's frown grew heavy. "She's involved? Loki's balls. Poor Unkle Raknar."

"But what of you and Adlin and…" she trailed off.

"Adlin and I named our son, Darach," Meyla said softly, reverently. "It means 'oak' in Gaelic and we felt it suited the strength we saw in him." A calm pride lit her eyes. "And though I can visit him whenever I like I've already had the pleasure of meeting the men who descend from him. Good, strong, noble men who were of the next generation of MacLomains."

Again, Megan was in true awe of all this. "Yes, I read about them…even you."

"Good," Meyla whispered. "It's nice to know they live on even if in scripture."

Such an odd thing knowing that all of those people save Leslie and her Scot in New Hampshire were technically already passed away…including her friend Cadence. A chill went through her. If one *really* wanted to get technical, none of them had even been born yet and Megan herself was but a ghost of the distant future.

As everything truly sunk in, Megan looked at the other woman, concerned. "I'm so sorry you had to leave your son behind. Are you all right?"

"I wasn't at first," Meyla admitted, eyes suddenly staring at something only she could see. "But my father helped me through it. When he wasn't a shoulder to cry on, he was strength, telling me as Adlin had again and again that I could go back to Scotland and raise my son. But even I knew that if I did it would skew the pre-destined fate of the MacLomain clan and that what was destined to happen might be affected. So many might not have come together and found true love. I couldn't risk it."

Hell. Megan couldn't stop the tear that rolled down her cheek. Such strength. Such sacrifice. She was speechless. Not sure what else to say, she murmured. "I love that Naðr was there for you but *shame* on him for giving you such strife over Valan after you've gone through so much."

Meyla blinked a few times, tearing herself from the past. Then, as if dark clouds lifted and only sunshine lit her face, she shook her head. "You haven't heard the good news yet then?" A smile blossomed. "My father has requested that Valan and I be married this eve."

Chapter Fifteen

Megan supposed the timing for a wedding was just right in that it was what the Viking's called Frigg's day, which as she soon learned from Naðr, meant Friday in her era. Frigg being the god of marriage. Thank the god's then, possibly even Frigg, for the king's dragon blood, or she might have remained clueless.

Nonetheless, Meyla and Valan's wedding was by far the most unusual she'd ever attended. As it was for Valan, so it seemed, as his eyes widened more and more by the moment.

All poetry and forms of endearments had been officially banned at the beginning of the process. And wow, was it a process. Or at least that's the word she used for the bargaining and bantering going on.

Poems of love were an extra big no, no. After all, they were interpreted as a disreputable slur toward a woman and taken as a grave matter to her family. It seemed if a man hadn't actually slept with a woman yet, how could he possibly be passionate enough to recite a love poem to her? No wonder Naðr had been edgy when Meyla and Valan were so open with their displays of affection.

Megan could only suppose the rules when it came to the king's daughter certainly didn't apply to his futuristic woman.

All aside, Meyla looked beautiful with braids wrapped around her head and Valan was dashing as ever in what Megan assumed was full highland regalia, plaid in place, shiny brooch at his shoulder.

The smallest Viking she'd seen yet, standing perhaps five feet tall, held a scroll studiously and bargained back and forth loudly with Naðr. As his brothers were by the king's side, Kjar, thankfully, filled her in on what was happening.

Since Valan had no family backing him, this was solely for show. Basically it came down to how much Naðr would give to the dowry and how much Valan would repay him. And, though he was doing pretty well with everything, Megan didn't miss the hint of smug satisfaction in the king's eyes as he reminded his new son-in-law that his daughter was a grand prize indeed.

And if she wasn't mistaken there was a little something lethal in the look Naðr gave Valan as he blessed the union. Modern day translation…hurt her and you're dead.

Then there was the exchanging of swords. The husband entrusted his bride with his ancestral sword which in Valan's case it was hard to know what that was. Perhaps he'd brought one with him or one had been provided here in Scandinavia? Either way, Meyla would retain the sword until their first-born son grew of age then pass it down.

In return, she gave her husband the sword bearing the crest of her family. After that came the rings presented on the tips of those swords. This act emphasized the sacredness of their union. Then they joined hands upon the groom's sword to recite their vows. They were touching and profound, love so obvious in their eyes. The kiss that sealed their vows even had Megan averting her eyes.

Then it was time to feast.

As it turned out, feasting at a Viking wedding was a grand affair by anyone's standards.

Kjar, bless him, never left her side, filling her in on anything she didn't understand about their customs. The more she got to know him, the more she found the shipwright's actions at odds with his appearance. Although he looked fiercer than most, he had a way of maneuvering words and descriptions as surely as he must his hands when building those magnificent ships. Even then, there was much more to this man than met the eye. A mysticism she couldn't explain.

Where Naðr and his brothers typically sat at a table equal with all, tonight it was raised slightly to honor the bride and groom who sat on one side of the king. On his other side sat an empty chair then Raknar and Kol. Megan stopped and stared as the king's words two nights past echoed in her mind. 'Return to it if you like.' A chair that gave her great honor.

And there it was, empty, waiting…for her.

"You do not have to sit in it if you don't want to," Kjar said, words soft as he looked with pride at both the king and the empty chair next to him.

"Oh, I want to." She shook her head, shocked when a rush of sadness filled her. "But I'm pretty sure I don't deserve it."

Kjar's deep smoky green eyes never left her face. "Why not?"

Megan's mouth went dry as the truth stared her in the face. "Because I can't give him forever, because I need to go home to my sisters and let them know I'm okay."

"And if you were able to do that then come back to my king, would you?"

Lost in watching Naðr adore his daughter and trying his best to welcome Valan into the family, she whispered, "Yes. No. Maybe." She closed her eyes as pain squeezed her chest but her voice grew stronger as her eyes once more met Kjar's. "How could I ever leave my sisters? They *need* me."

He squeezed her hand, the gesture soothing, the usual devilish yet subdued demon gone from his serious gaze. "But what do *you* need?"

Him.

Naðr Véurr.

But even she wasn't such a fool that she didn't recognize she spoke not only from feelings of lust but the beginnings of something that made her feel so incredibly alive. Regardless, leaving her sisters behind wasn't an option. "I need to stay true to my family."

"You are as true to your kin as he is to his." Kjar nodded at the seat beside Naðr. "Go sit. It is your rightful place."

Why would he say that? She really had no right to that seat. But as he pressed his hand against her lower back and urged her toward the dais, Megan's feet wouldn't say no. The last time she'd approached Naðr like this it'd been with defiance in her heart. She'd slammed her hands down on the table in front of him and demanded respect. Now, it was the complete opposite. He wasn't determined that she come to his side but instead chatted with his daughter, genuine contentment on his face.

When she at last slid into the chair next to him, Raknar nodded, a small smile on his face as he handed her a horn of ale. Kol, two women on his lap, winked.

While it was nice to have their acceptance, what Naðr did meant more.

Though in conversation with Meyla and even Valan, he took her hand and threaded their fingers together on the table for all to see. Lightning bolts shot through her. Desire. But also a feeling of completion she hadn't expected. Music was lively, people were dancing, many were singing, but all she could see was their hands.

Every second that passed between that moment and when he turned toward her was made up of something she'd never felt before. A powerful, magnetic feeling that told her he was as eager to politely end his conversation and turn his attention her way as she was to have him do it.

So when at last Meyla and Valan became lost in one another's eyes, Naðr's gaze swung her way. Eyes hungry, devouring, he seemed to visually eat her alive from the thin braids of hair trailing down over the modest, almost matronly dress she wore for the wedding. Yet, when his pupil's flared she knew he was vividly remembering what lay beneath the material.

"I missed you, beautiful," he murmured, dropping their joined hands onto her lap then snaking his hand between her thighs.

If Raknar wasn't so close she would have yanked up her skirts and given him easier access. But a girl had to have some scruples. Or so she always heard. But that didn't keep her from sliding her hand over his waiting and willing erection.

"I missed you too," she whispered.

Naðr raised his horn to her. "Then let's drink to…love found?"

Sure, if that's what he wanted to call how horribly aroused they were. She tapped her horn against his. "To love found."

Then they drank. Too fast and no doubt too much. Several hours of wicked flirting later he at last stood, tapping his newfound horn of ale on the table to get everyone's attention. The music quieted, as did all in the hall.

Connecting remarkably sober eyes with many before he spoke, Naðr finally continued. "Thank you for joining us to celebrate my daughter's marriage to Valan, a man who will fight bravely alongside us."

Though the crowd roared with approval, Megan didn't miss the huffs and puffs of some as they eyed Valan's kilt.

Naðr, confrontational, quirked a lip and cast a sidelong glance at the Scotsman. "Yes, he wears a skirt but have you not all seen him wield a sword?" Then he snorted and winked. "And I'm not talking about the one he's been waving at my daughter."

This gained another roar of approval. One that the king utilized. "So you know how good he is to have come so far. But wait until you see him when he defends our people against King Rennir."

Megan sobered up real fast when Naðr pulled a dagger out of nowhere and buried it in the table, eyes sweeping over the crowd. A hush fell.

"You know our enemy comes." He met the eyes of several men. "Do you know what they want to do to us?"

"Kill us," someone cried.

"Let 'em try," another boomed.

Raknar leaned forward, eyes narrowed and challenging, voice loud, "And do you think they can?"

"Never," someone yelled.

"That's right," Kol declared and slammed his mug down. "Because nothing stands between us and certain victory."

Men nodded far and wide, eager for battle.

"Are you ready to go to Valhalla to protect our people?" Naðr roared.

The deafening approval that met his invitation made Megan's eyes widen. Only as the sound died down did she hear more voices ring out.

"I'll kill Rennir where he stands."

"I welcome a drink at Odin's table."

"Shove Loki's balls right down Rennir's throat I say."

Naðr raised a hand in the air, silencing the crowd while he held up his horn of ale. "The enemy comes. We *will* meet him and we *will* win. Just look at how the gods are at work, look at what they already sent me. Do I not have a woman from the future standing by my side? Nothing can stop us!"

A roar broke from the crowd.

Likely to fuel the fire he'd started; Naðr pulled her into his arms and kissed her soundly.

But something about what he'd done miffed her. Why did she suddenly feel used? He'd definitely used her to rev up the crowd. Was she some sort of pawn in a game to further his own ambitions? Was this the reason she'd been given the chair next to him? The crowd had heard and seen what they'd needed and soon turned back to being rambunctious.

Megan tore her lips away. Not overly fazed, he sat, bringing her with him. Though she squirmed, she was trapped in a cage of pure muscle.

Naðr eyed her for several long moments then said brief goodbyes to his daughter, Valan and his brothers before he swung her up into his arms and started walking. "What's got your blood fired, woman?"

"Put me down. I can walk," she muttered.

But he didn't until they reached his bed, and only then did he set her on her feet, eyes studying hers. "You didn't answer my question."

Fine, she'd answer him. "I wasn't crazy about that display you just put on."

His warm hands skimmed the sides of her neck gently. "Display?"

"I suppose I shouldn't care because I am leaving but I'm not a huge fan of being used like that."

Naðr's brows drew together and he frowned. "It wasn't my intention to make you feel used." One hand cupped her face, the other wrapped into her hair. "You are special to my people because the gods sent you. I wanted them to know that you are special to me as well."

She tried to ignore his distracting touch and heartfelt words. "What you said all but implied you only had me by your side because, as you seem to think, the gods sent me."

Awe heck. Megan bit the corner of her lip as the truth behind her irritation became blatantly obvious not only to her but to him. She wanted him to want her by his side not because the gods had sent her but because he genuinely cared for her.

A small smile came to his lips as he fanned his fingers over her jaw. "You're by my side because there is love between us. And because I want to show you respect. Not because I think you can further aide my cause. What is between us is strong and I do not want to lose it. I do not want to lose you."

Her throat closed at the desire in his voice, at the passion in his eyes.

He was being absolutely truthful.

Megan worked hard to keep emotion at bay but it was difficult as he gazed at her. Any aggravation she'd felt fizzled away and she blinked away the wetness in her eyes. Way too many intense feelings were blazing through her, frightening ones that gave her a good idea what to expect when she left because she *had* to leave. Reiterating that, she whispered, "You're going to lose me…this." She swallowed. "Don't you understand?"

A flicker of gut-wrenching sadness touched his eyes before he inhaled deeply and nodded. "I understand your need to get back to your sisters. I would feel the same about my brothers. And though I cannot say with absolute certainty that your family will become involved with our pact with the seers, it is very likely. Even so," he said softly. "I can offer you the comfort of knowing you *will* be returning to your own time."

Megan's heart thudded into her throat. "I am? How do you know?"

Naðr brushed his fingers over her cheek one last time before he crossed the room and pulled the cylinder she'd found beneath the sea out of a chest. "Because of this."

"I don't understand."

"Again, I cannot tell you save that it is a means to help you return here if you wish. You will understand when you open it." He touched her shoulder over the tattoo. "The Vegvisir, compass, will then help you find me."

Megan was blown away. "So because of these items you know with certainty I'll be going home?"

"Yes. The stone that helped bring you here and the tattoos me and my brothers were marked with were of the seers." He seemed to struggle with his next words. "The cylinder is of the gods. A means to give you the free-will to come back to me or not."

"Oh," she whispered, baffled as she met his eyes. "Why not tell me this sooner? Why not give me the peace of mind?"

"Because they were not easy words to say." He frowned at the cylinder before his eyes went to hers. "I didn't keep such to myself to cause you further distress. I suppose I'd hoped you wouldn't want to go and I'd figure out a way to keep you. But since this cylinder is here, I will have no choice in the matter. I'm sorry for not telling you sooner."

Megan sat down slowly as he continued speaking while putting the cylinder away. "I've had a case fashioned for you to strap to your back. It's just big enough to hold the cylinder and stone. From now on, you must keep it with you."

A chill raced through her as the weight of his words settled in.

"Hell, Naðr," she murmured. "You took a pretty big chance not making sure I had it with me up to this point, didn't you?"

While she should have been elated that she'd somehow be going home, what she found so incredibly daunting was that she might have had no way to get back. And *that* irrefutable revelation sucked the air from her lungs. The idea of returning to him was by no means off the table.

"God," she whispered and shook her head. "What's happened to me."

Naðr turned and eyed her. If she wasn't mistaken, relief softened his eyes as he strode over and pulled her into his arms. Done with words, his lips met hers. Different than his previous kisses, this one bespoke deep emotions, ones that came from his heart, even his soul. Drawn, magnetized, she met him halfway, submerged then drowning in an unfamiliar, fervent joy.

He only pulled his lips away long enough to yank off her dress and his tunic. Talk of inevitable separation drove them together, their need desperate, eager. A small gasp left her lips when he cupped her backside and ripped the ground out from beneath her. The next thing she knew, her back was on his bed, her rear end right at the edge.

Megan's surroundings grew hazy with anticipation when he knelt between her legs and kissed and licked every bit of flesh he could find from her ankles up. By the time he braced her knees on his broad shoulders she was outright swooning. Primal, uncensored lust flared in his eyes as he grasped her hips and dragged his hot, determined tongue up her inner thigh then flicked it across her center. She inhaled sharply, back arching.

After that, everything became moments made of her frantically grasping at the fur beneath, groaning as he went on a very thorough quest, working her hypersensitive flesh into a pulsing frenzy.

Building, building, building, the peak he drove her toward came fast and furious.

"Naðr," she cried out as the explosion hit. Pure, blazing white light flashed in her vision before a hundred more colors. Her eyes rolled back in her head and her body seized. All the while, his strong hands locked her in place and his hot breath fanned the pulsating origin of her endless pleasure.

Once more cupping her backside, he brought her further onto the bed and laid her down. Pliant, still basking in the afterglow of climax, she watched him from beneath lowered lashes as he removed his pants and came over her. Lost in his tender gaze, she opened not just her body but so much more to him.

His nimble fingers started to unweave her braids as he ran his lips along her jaw, neck then softly over her collarbone. The way he touched her now was painstaking. It was so excruciatingly profound, she felt cherished, worshiped. By the time he made it back to her lips, tears were leaking from the corners of her eyes.

"Megan," he whispered between kisses.

This time when he moved into her it was different than before. This time they were making love in every sense of the word. She could feel it in each move he made, every move she made. Something deep down inside was swimming to the surface as she trailed her finger up his spine, lost in every detail. From the fluctuation of skin over muscle as he eased in and out to the weight of his hips as they moved against hers.

Heat and touch rolled together, fusing them in twisted limbs, as if they couldn't get close enough. Meant to never burn out, a low blaze was quickly growing into a raging firestorm. Sweet, passionate kisses turned frantic. Teasing touches became grasping and insatiable. When their hands clasped tightly on either side of her head, she wrapped her legs around him and dug her heels into his lower back.

Though he'd taken her to the moon and back with his loving side, this ravenous passion that raged around them now suited Naðr like no other. Uncivil. Raw. Bold. Conquering. Those were words that applied to her Viking king when it came to taking a woman…when it came to taking her. A throaty, pleased chuckle made of pure need bubbled low in her chest as he slammed against her and she raked nails up his back.

There was something freeing in the way he took her now. The way she took him. Expression feral, rabid, he was every long, hard, thick inch, Naðr Véurr. King. Viking. Dragon.

Hers.

There was no slowing down. Both needed this too much. They rolled once, then again, before his movements became so aggressive she had no choice but to hold on tight. The unstoppable force behind his plunges increased and she latched onto his arms as he braced his hands by her head.

The look in his eyes was ten thousand types of unleashed drive. Reveling in the devouring way he watched her, Megan kept her eyes with his, daring him to take all.

And he didn't let her down.

With one hand cupping her backside and one protecting her shoulders, he lifted and slammed her against the headboard. This plunged him so deep that she had no opportunity to challenge him any further because both let go and fell apart in furious, heart-pounding, ceaseless release.

She cried out.

He roared.

Then everything blurred and drifted away into a place made of liquid muscles and incoherent thoughts. Ecstasy. Paradise. Harmony. A place where misery went to die and transcendence encompassed and transformed, where the mutual satisfaction of their bodies trembling incessantly against one another was what lovemaking *should* be.

Time drifted by as he pulled her into his arms and lay on the bed. Though she floated in that surreal place he was an ace at taking her, Megan remained aware of his eyes on her face. The gentle stroke of his fingers on the side and back of her neck. Naðr was allowing her to see everything in his open gaze, from his appreciation of how she'd just made him feel to the care he felt for her. Megan had no idea whether or not he saw the same in her eyes.

But it was certainly there.

Though a fire crackled, her skin was slick with sweat and chilling fast. Apparently sensing as much, he pulled a fur over them. Warm and drowsy yet wanting to know him better she said, "The first night I was here you spoke of your father, how he'd gone from boat building to leading raids. What happened after that?"

Naðr stilled for a moment and she didn't think he'd share…but he did. "My father was a different sort of man than me and my brothers. More like the king who eventually killed him, he tended to thrust aside good sense for ruthlessness."

Megan's chest clenched at the flash of pain that quickly fled Naðr's face as she waited for him to continue.

"But then most would say it was his sense of adventure and ruthlessness that earned him the position of king." Naðr frowned. "I'm inclined to say it was cold-blooded murder."

"What happened?" she murmured.

"He won over most, yet instead of trying to work with his own king; he boasted of his accomplishments and didn't respect but mocked he who was above him."

Megan squeezed Naðr's hand but said nothing.

After a few moments he went on. "My brothers and I came from humble beginnings. Before my mother ruined my father he was a different sort of man. One that loved his family and spent hours not only fishing but sailing and teaching us how to fight." Naðr's expression was grim. "He *was* a good father."

Megan almost didn't want to ask but she pushed her reluctant thoughts past her lips. "Why did your mother ruin him?"

"She left him…and us, for another," he said, as if he needed to rid himself of the words.

So where her father had betrayed, so too had his mother. And as sexually open as Naðr's society, it was obvious that some were devoted and monogamous. Or so her king had clearly hoped.

Even so, had his mother really left her sons? "Did you see her afterwards?"

"It was said that she tried to see us but father wouldn't allow it. He was of dragon blood. Those such as us are especially poor at dealing with betrayal." His eyes grew cold. "But it didn't matter. Our lives were set with our father's new goals. Done with women, he pursued power. And he used his dragon to get it, killing the king of this region unfairly."

Megan wasn't quite sure what to say to that. But as she met Naðr's eyes, she kept talking, determined to draw him out. "What did the people think of that? Of him becoming king?"

"The warriors loved him for it, but then warring men in my culture appreciate strength above all else. The other men, fishermen and tradesmen, as well as their families, had fear in their hearts. And they make up a greater part of my people, the very root of them."

It occurred to her how torn Naðr actually was.

"Though a warrior and king, you still relate more with those who come from humbler beginnings, don't you?" Megan asked softly, all ready knowing the answer.

"Yes, very much so," he murmured. "My father could have gone about it differently but the pain of what my mother did made him act foolishly." Naðr clenched his jaw. "No male of dragon blood takes what is not his by force, by using the creature that lives within, we earn it because the people respect, love and want us to rule."

Understanding that delving deeper into the details behind his father's murder of the prior patriarch would only discourage him, she said, "Tell me how you became king."

"Nothing so extreme as how my father did." Naðr's lips pulled down, as though becoming king was more of a burden than anything. "He died at sea. I was next in line."

The monotone way he said it saddened her because despite his dislike of the man, he'd obviously loved his father. "How long ago?"

"A year before Meyla was born."

Twenty years? "Seriously? You were fourteen?"

The corner of his lip twitched as he stepped away from the past and met her eyes. "Yes, on the cusp of entering my prime."

Though she tried hard not to, she chuckled.

"What?" The mental weight he'd been under vanished as her small smile brought one to his lips.

She shook her head. "Sorry sweetie, but where I'm from you're hitting your prime right now and will likely do so for a great many years." But she didn't want to lose this conversation so continued. "What did the people think of you becoming king so young?"

Naðr wrapped his hand around hers, clearly pleased by her response. "It was not good at first. I was challenged constantly. In battle, sailing, fishing, everything." Smugness met his words. "But I didn't inherent the family name, or my role as serpent protector for no good reason. I paid attention to what my people needed, all of them, from the warriors to the fishermen to the merchants and all else. I worked hard to bring everyone together, to make our people feel like family no matter their trade. And though my people know the dragon will always protect them, I prefer to give them my human side above all else."

So he was everything his father should have been.

But she wouldn't say as much.

Instead, she leaned over and kissed him. "I'm glad it all worked out."

Naðr nodded but said nothing as he eyed her. When at last he spoke, it redirected things her way. "So your father built a boat in your yard and called it Viking after a woman who wasn't your mother. Then he launched the boat and it sunk." He brushed her cheek, eyes so curious and warm she just about melted. "What happened to you after that save a continued love for Vikings."

Of course he remembered everything she'd said and owed him more of her own history. And though tempted to sigh, she wouldn't, because her history wasn't nearly as tragic as his. "I did the opposite of what every other kid on Earth would have done and spent more time with Dad. Mom was hurting but her pain was too much for me so I lived at the docks, on the boats and out at sea helping the guys fish."

"So you surrounded yourself with what was easy," he murmured, "And stayed away from the pain."

Thrown by his response, she said, "Believe it or not, Mom's choices put her in a worse position than Dad's. At least he was pulling in a little bit of cash, enough that I could skim off the top and set some aside for my sisters. The deadbeat my Mom ended up with was good for nothing and she wasn't much better in the earning department."

Naðr stroked her arm softly and though his words were non-confrontational they set her on edge. "What made you end up loving a life you forced yourself into. What truly made you love boat building, sailing, the ocean?"

Megan didn't need to give her response a second thought. "The freedom it gave me. There's nothing like the solidarity of open water. How it listens to you and only speaks back what you need to hear. Being on the ocean afforded me a sense of peace I couldn't find on land." She pressed her lips together. "And it gave me a sense of strength, one I needed to stay strong for my sisters."

Naðr remained silent as she sifted through thoughts before speaking. "Once my youngest sister was old enough to stand on her own two feet, I worked toward educating myself. Worked during the day. School at night. Relentless. Got my G.E.D. then went to college. That's when I met Nathan."

"Then everything changed."

Though she knew he was guessing, he was absolutely right.

"Yes, everything changed. I met someone who challenged me to be better, who set my heart on fire at the same time." She inhaled deeply and shook her head. "Who knew he'd prove to be the total opposite of what I thought he was."

"Was he then?" Naðr said softly.

Taken aback, her eyes shot to his. "He cheated on me from the moment we said, "I do," so yeah, I'd say he pretty much failed hard."

"Half of what drew me to my former wife, Aesa, was her absolute excellence at everything she did. She pushed me to be better, to rise up and be a better man, one who might rule well my people." Though sadness was in his eyes so too was something else. "Yet there was always strife between us…unrest. Passion? Yes. Love? Yes. But as a seer, as a free spirit looking for the world to bow down to her, Aesa always saw me as a fisherman's son born of dragon blood that she was determined to make into a king."

Megan looked at him for a long minute before she said, "Our circumstances aren't the same."

"No," he said gently. "There was no…cheating? But there was always a distance made of the different ways we looked at life. At our lack of a shared beginning." Melancholy met his eyes. "And I have missed her so much…until now…until you arrived."

His words, the look in his eyes, the soothing stroke of his hand on her arm, all swirled within her senses as the gap, one made of over a thousand years, closed between them. Naðr didn't need to say he loved her. It was right there in his unrelenting gaze. And while there were so many things left to say, there really weren't any at all when he again pulled her into his arms.

Passion didn't just flare but was compounded by the few words they'd shared as she rolled over him. There were no longer boundaries of control but freedom in the way she slowly sunk onto him. Their bodies worked in such unison that Megan moaned the whole time, or groaned, or plain old cried, she had no idea.

All she knew for certain was that she was free. The past was gone. The future was here. And she didn't want to let go of what she'd found. The world faded in and out, dimmed then brightened by the endless, varying sensations he made her feel. Yet he never let go. He made love to her over and over and she climaxed too many times to count, still…he was here.

And always would be.

Startled by the truth, she shot up.

Though dim light flooded the chamber, this time she wasn't alone.

"Megan," Naðr murmured, his hand wrapping around hers. "Come back."

Come back.

It almost felt like those two words were an echo of what was to come. A plea that might soon span over one thousand years. A lifeline...

When she didn't fall back right away, he pulled her into his arms and tucked her head beneath his chin. "Give me these last few moments with you by my side before I ready for war."

Megan frowned and ran her hand over his warm chest. "So soon then?"

"Yes. Now that Rennir is confident he won't be facing three dragons he will come swiftly."

"With Yrsa," she whispered and perched up enough that she could meet his eyes. Though she wouldn't have imagined saying such a thing a week ago now it seemed ridiculous not to. "It seems unfair that they're coming at you with so much magic when your hands are seemingly tied."

"We're warring men," he said easily. "If magic is used then we will deal with it."

While his answer frustrated her, Megan knew better than to push it. This was his territory. He knew what he was doing. But it was hard not to say more. Either way, it was soon taken out of her hands when Kjar stuck his head in and nodded at Naðr. After he vanished, Naðr kissed her temple then rolled away.

Megan wasn't about to lounge in bed when things needed to be done so she got up as well. "I need pants, not a dress."

Naðr opened the trunk he'd pulled the cylinder from the night before and nodded. "Everything you need is in here."

Alarmed, she dressed and eyed him as he pulled on pants then a light sleeveless vest of chain mail over his tunic. "Is Rennir coming today then?"

Naðr didn't answer straight away but slid on his boots. When at last he did give her feedback he was dressed in black, head to toe, much like when she'd met him, yet his expression varied. Though still imposing in a far-too-sexy way, now he was brooding and different. His cobalt eyes were dark and posture tense as he slid the sack that contained the cylinder and stone over her head. Strapped over one shoulder, across her chest and under the opposite arm, she barely felt its slight weight resting against her back.

He looked over her thoroughly before he nodded then took her hands, locking eyes. "It might be this day or the next but Rennir will be on us soon."

Megan nodded and kept her lips firm. Right now he needed to know she was all right. "I understand."

Yet it was tough to stay strong when he came close and cupped her cheeks, words soft. "We go to war soon. It is one that you cannot be part of."

Of course, because she didn't know how to fight with a weapon. Megan could argue this all day long but knew he was right. In this era, heck, even in her own she knew less than nothing about war. But she'd bet she could learn to use a dagger fast enough with a few instructions. She nodded, determined to appease him. "Sure. I get it."

"Get it," he murmured softly, frowning.

But his reservations didn't much matter when Kjar spat out a few words in Norse that had to be curses. Bad things were happening. Naðr eyed Megan once more then brushed his lips over hers, soft words hovering. "Stay with Meyla." Then he pulled back just enough to stroke his thumbs over her cheeks and look into her eyes one last time as he whispered, "Come back to me."

Come back to you? But I'm right here. The words died on her lips as he spun away and left.

Chapter Sixteen

Naðr could admit he'd made a few mistakes since Megan arrived.

The first? He should have focused less on bedding her and more on teaching her to fight. The second? He should have made damn sure she intended to return to him before he lost his heart. But in his defense it'd been a long time since he'd had to worry about feeling strongly for a woman. Right now, however, emotions like this would only prove harmful to his focus so he pushed them aside as Kjar updated him.

"The scouts have reported back. Rennir's making his move. Our men are already in position."

Though he'd kept bands of warriors on the outskirts of Rennir's land since he became king, Naðr had his best fighters planning for this attack since they'd returned from their last raid. Well-prepared bands were ready on the outermost vulnerable seaside locations and ships ready to close in. Though his brothers would have preferred meeting Rennir on his own territory, Naðr knew his plan was sound.

"I know it is not what you want to hear but you should keep Megan by your side," Kjar said, voice purposefully soft.

They both knew how much Rennir and Yrsa likely wanted her stone. A stone, unfortunately, that she needed to keep with her.

"No." Naðr shook his head. "She cannot defend herself."

"But you and your brothers can defend her."

"We'll be on the water. I won't have her in such a vulnerable position."

Kjar sighed. "Then I will stay here and protect her."

Naðr's eyes shot to his cousin. No warrior from here to Valhalla craved being sea bound as much as Kjar. Especially with war coming. Yet with the offer came a much needed sense of relief. None save him and his brothers were stronger and though it wasn't talked of often, Kjar had his own brand of magic. So he clapped his cousin on the shoulder and nodded his thanks.

After he spent ample time surveying the battle preparations and speaking with his people, who were more eager than anything, he made his way into the weapon's holding. Megan's voice drifted through the open windows as she and Meyla walked by, heading for the entrance that led into the adjoining room.

"I'm surprised Rennir wasn't already closer and waiting on word from Yrsa so that he could attack while the brothers were still on the mountain," Megan said.

"My father has men scouting the land just beyond Rennir's territory," Meyla informed as they walked into the building. "If there had been movement, my uncles would have stayed here."

"But not your father? The *king*?"

"You underestimate how much my father cares for you," Meyla said. "If it had been anybody else but you or even me, he likely would have stayed."

"Sweet mother of..." Megan's words trailed off before renewed awe lit her voice. "Look at all the gorgeous weapons, helmets and round shields. *Unreal*."

"Though the men keep their own weapons in their holdings, my father has always provided an ample amount of replacements. He doesn't want his warriors to ever be without a means to defend their families," Meyla responded.

Bemused, Naðr leaned against the threshold and watched Megan. She appeared to appreciate his weapons almost as much as his ships. Eyes wide, lips parted, she slowly spun, enraptured by the wide variety. Her dog, naturally, kept pace as she limped around her. But it seemed even such a display couldn't stop her eyes from finding his. Hel, every time she looked at him he experienced a lusty punch to the gut. Yet now it wasn't just physical but emotional.

And that wasn't safe during current circumstances.

So instead of pulling her into his arms, he inclined his head toward the daggers as he strapped on a sword. "Pick one out and Meyla will show you the basics of handling it."

"Actually." Megan eyed the opposite wall. "While I'll definitely grab a dagger, I think I might have more luck with those."

Naðr arched a brow at the bows and arrows. "Have you ever used one?"

"A few archery lessons when I was a kid," she murmured, looking them over carefully.

Impressed, he watched her take down a bow perfectly suited to her size. "I thought you didn't know how to use weapons."

"It's been a long time." She grabbed a bag of arrows. "And I'm not about bragging unless there's something to brag about."

Naðr strapped on several daggers and led her out the rear door to the archery targets. "I'm heading to the ship soon. Show me what you can do."

"Nothing like a little pressure," she muttered despite the confidence she radiated. Her competitive nature flared as she cocked an arrow and narrowed her eyes on the target. Unwavering, focused, she released.

Thwap. It sunk into the outer edge of the bull's eye.

"Well, look at that," Meyla exclaimed, grinning. "It seems you know how to use a weapon after all."

"I know how to shoot an arrow into a still object." Megan cocked another arrow, taking less time to focus before she released. This one hit dead center. "A moving object, a living person, now that's a different story."

So it seemed the gods had sent him another warrior woman after all. Megan was a natural with a bow and arrow and would likely be just as talented with other weapons. But she was absolutely right about the difference between shooting an arrow for sport versus shooting to kill. However, having such available to her would make both of them feel better.

"Take the bow and arrows with you but don't use them unless you have no choice." He strapped them to her back alongside the small sack then pressed the hilt of a dagger into her palm. "Keep this in hand and visible to others at all times."

"You're leaving now, aren't you?" she murmured.

"Yes, Rennir is coming. I'm taking our ship out."

"Our ship," she whispered, a ghost of a smile flitted then fell flat as she eyed the darkening skies. "Bad weather is coming. I want to go down to the docks and watch you depart."

Though tempted to tell her to stay here and use what precious time left to learn how to use the dagger, he understood her need to see the ocean. A seafarer by nature, she'd gauge the wind and water to surmise just how dangerous things would become...even before the battling. Besides, Megan was the sort of woman who would resent him for telling her what to do. So until it was truly a matter of life and death, she'd have her way.

As they headed toward the port, Naðr eyed Meyla. With several weapons strapped to her body and hair braided back, she was every inch her mother. "Are you ready daughter?"

Meyla snorted. "Every moment of every day when it comes to battling." But there was a miniscule tightening around her lips when her eyes met his. "Will you not reconsider taking Valan with you?"

Naðr would give her a lot but not that. Not yet. "He is not a seaman and needs more training. His strength lies on land."

"Protecting me no doubt," she mumbled.

"Damn good place for a husband to be." Megan glanced at the mountains. "Especially one used to fighting in the Scottish Highlands."

When Meyla frowned at her lack of support, Megan shrugged. "Sorry, but I'm with your father on this one. Very dangerous. Only those who understand the sea well should be out on it right now. Otherwise, the whole crew would be at risk and I know Valan wouldn't want that."

Meyla sighed then offered a relenting nod. "Perhaps you're right."

Naðr shot Megan a thankful look. The last thing he needed right now was his daughter upset with him. Not to say he hadn't grown used to such since Valan arrived. But he'd truly enjoyed reconnecting with her and had no desire to return to how things had been.

The majority of those too young, old or weak to fight were inside the fortress but still the shore and docks teemed with activity. Meyla strolled off but Megan remained by his side as he stopped along the way to speak with several groups of warriors. Naðr was pleased to see how well they were accepting her. Though most kept their silence, he didn't miss the approving nods they gave her when they saw the bow and arrows and dagger. It was clear in the set of her chin and body posture that she'd use them if necessary.

As they continued down the dock her frown deepened as she eyed the blackened clouds billowing low over the water. The wind had kicked up and the waters rougher than he would have liked. But what fun was there in calm seas? If it was his time to sit at Odin's table he'd do so with pride…even if it meant leaving her.

There was that *emotion* again.

"I can see by the look on your face you agree it'll be damn dangerous out there," Megan said.

"The wind's in my favor."

"The wind is unstable." Her lips thinned and eyes narrowed on their ship. "It'll switch on a dime and she won't like it."

"Worrying will do you no favors so set it aside and have faith in my abilities," he said. "I go into this with no fear. You should do the same."

"Some fear is good. It can save you."

"Respect. Caution. Remaining alert. These are things that will save me."

"Isn't respect born of a little fear?"

"My respect is for the sea and I have no fear of death." He stopped about a quarter of the way down the dock and turned to her. Something about the look in her eyes made him far more honest than he intended. "But I do have unrest when it comes to saying goodbye to you."

"Then don't." Her voice might be steady but what churned in her gaze wasn't. "Fight here. Not out there."

Light rain mixed with sea spray as he brushed his knuckles over her cheek and shook his head. "I can be nowhere else but the last line of defense before shore."

Megan grimaced, frustrated. "Then break the rules. Embrace the dragon. I don't care if I get stuck in this era."

"But I do," he murmured. "The gods wish that you have a choice and they're right. And I have no intentions of going back on my promise to the seers."

Kol had a wild grin on his face as he joined them. "Might be we'll be dining with Odin and Freyja this night, brother."

Naðr shook his head, took her hand and continued walking.

"Crazy," Megan said under her breath. "All of you."

Kol strolled alongside Megan and tossed a full blown smile her way. "You should join us. I know how much you like my brother's ship."

"It will be a wild ride," Raknar added, a tempered grin on his face as he fell in beside Naðr. "I have never been more eager."

"She stays with Kjar," Naðr grumbled.

"I might not be able to fight but I can row," she volunteered.

Naðr shot his brothers equally damning looks before shaking his head at Megan. "You will stay here. The conditions on the ship will be treacherous and the strength in rowing for only the strongest."

He knew as the words left his mouth that she wouldn't receive them well.

"So you're back to ordering me around."

"I'm back to keeping you as safe as I can."

"He's right." Raknar nodded.

"But not for the reasons he's giving," Kol offered. "He doesn't want you with us because you would be a distraction."

Raknar nodded. "Not only for the men but for him."

"And that would not be good," Kjar said from behind.

Megan glanced from brother to brother before her eyes settled on Naðr. "Is that true? Would a woman truly distract you from captaining a ship?"

Naðr scowled. "No."

Kol grinned at Megan. "See, you're already distracting him from being truthful."

Raknar intercepted his son before he could run by and crouched in front of him. "Take Megan's wolf up away from the battle. Keep her safe."

Though happy enough to see Guardian, Heidrek was crestfallen. "B..but I want to f..fight."

"And you *will*, son. Next time." Raknar cupped the back of his head. "For now, I need you to do this for me, yes?"

The sun rose and fell around his father so though eager for battle, Heidrek nodded and stood up a little straighter. "Y..yes. I will d..do this for you."

Naðr knew his brother would try to keep Heidrek as far away from Yrsa as possible.

Raknar nodded, kissed his son's forehead then pulled him into an embrace. "I love you."

"I l...love you too."

Meanwhile, Megan ruffled Guardian's head and kissed her on the muzzle. "Be good, wolfy girl."

Then Heidrek and Guardian were off down the dock.

Megan thanked Raknar and was about to say something more but the words died on her lips as they approached the ship's prow. She stopped walking and whispered, "Holy crap."

They all looked from her to the ship.

"What is it?" Naðr asked.

Wide eyed, she walked alongside the boat. "These Nordic symbols carved into the hull weren't here before."

"Kjar has been working on them," Naðr said with pride.

They were all taken aback when she swung on them, truly upset as her eyes whipped to Kjar. "Why would you do this? I don't understand."

"To protect the ship during battle."

Megan inhaled deeply. A haunted expression shadowed her face. "But that's not the only reason, is it?"

He should have expected Kjar would give nothing less than honesty...mostly. "No, they will protect against Yrsa's magic as well."

"They're identical," Megan murmured as she again looked over them.

"To what?" Raknar asked.

Naðr touched her arm when she didn't answer. "Megan?"

Startled, she jumped a little as her pained gaze met his, voice hoarse. "Now, with those carvings, this is every inch the ship I found at the bottom of the Atlantic." Her lower lip quivered slightly before she pressed it against her upper lip then nodded toward the ocean. "And this weather is far too similar to how it was in my vision."

Naðr clasped her upper arms and tried to lend strength as his eyes met hers. "Remember what I told you. I can handle this."

"I believe you also mentioned that you'd never sail a ship during this type of weather."

"We will not be raising the sail during the storm."

"I would think not." Her eyes narrowed. "But extreme situations make people do extreme things. I know you wouldn't normally but to protect your people...who knows."

"I will do as the gods will it," he ground out but he evened his features, truly having no desire to argue with her. "And I will stay safe."

His brothers had already boarded, Raknar bracing himself as he looked down. "We must go."

"I wish you'd let me come," she pleaded. "I know I could help."

Naðr pulled her close and decided that honesty was the only course of action. "My brothers were right. You would distract me.

Not because you're a woman but because you're no average woman. Whether or not you come back to me once you leave, you will always be mine and because of that I need to protect you. If there is a future for us, I will see you well trained and by my side in every battle, even if by sea." He cupped her cheek. "Until then, you coming with me now would be just as dangerous had I allowed Valan, even if for different reasons. Do you understand?"

"Well when you say it like that," she whispered, strained, eyes moist. "Damn you, Naðr Véurr."

"Hopefully not." He quirked his lips. "Loki wouldn't be my first choice to drink with this eve."

"How about you skip partying with the gods tonight and party with me instead?" she murmured.

While he might have urged her to come back to him when he left her earlier, he wouldn't do so again. Megan knew what lay in his heart and would carry that knowledge with her wherever she ended up. So he chose instead to kiss her soundly. A meaningful, tender gesture he hoped would not be their last. Only when Kol cleared his throat from above did Naðr realize a simple gesture would soon make movement near impossible.

Yet even after he pulled away, it was hard to let her go.

"I will see you after the battle." Naðr brushed his finger along her soft jaw one last time. "And if you end up battling, fight well."

Then he turned, climbed a few steps and leapt up onto the side of the ship. The wind blew at her fur cloak and reddened the tops of her cheekbones but not once did she look away. No, this was a woman who would only show strength. Naðr put on his helmet and nodded once before he at last turned away, ready to battle, even ready if a Valkyrie escorted him to Odin.

But even though he was ready for certain death, he wasn't kidding himself entirely.

He wanted more time in this life.

And he wanted her there waiting when he returned.

Chapter Seventeen

"Are you well, lass?"

Megan blinked against the sting of rain, sleet, salty sea spray and likely an untimely tear but was unable to rip her gaze from the longship sitting on the stormy horizon. "I don't think so, Valan. He's going to get himself killed out there."

"'Tis hard to imagine." Valan crossed his arms over his chest and eyed the ship. "He's a bloody good captain and warrior. Lads like that dinnae go down easy."

White-tipped grey waves rolled and lightning crackled across the inky sky. For a split second, images of the ship lolling to its side as it had in her vision flashed in her mind.

"I think his gods are eager to have him by their side," she grumbled.

"And he would be honored."

Megan frowned at Kjar as he joined them. "I'm surprised you're not out there with them."

"My king will fight better knowing you're safe."

"Ah, so he ordered you to protect me?"

Kjar offered no answer. "The battling has already begun. It is time to go to the shore."

Though there was no activity that she could see, Megan knew better than to doubt him. Yet she wasn't above trying to get more information as the three of them walked down the dock. "Those were some mighty intricate designs you carved into the hull. How did you accomplish so much in such a short amount of time?"

"With help from my men," Kjar grunted.

Megan eyed the man. If she wasn't mistaken he was paler than normal. Setting aside her curiosity, she said, "You don't look so well. Are you okay?"

Offering no answer, his sharp eyes scanned both ways as they approached the shore. "Loki's balls. They're coming too soon. Far too many. Yrsa and her tricks," Kjar growled. "Valan, go find Meyla. Now."

But the Scotsman was already gone.

"How are they here so soon?" Megan said. "I thought…"

Those were the last words out of her mouth before all hell broke loose. They'd just made it to the end of the dock when an explosion of warriors burst into the village in front of the fortress walls. Despite the chaos erupting, she was relieved to see the gates being shut. Naðr's warriors fought insanely, cutting down all until they were securely closed.

Then the battling was everywhere.

Though adrenaline rushed through her veins and her instinct was to panic, she pushed fear aside. If she didn't focus right now, it could mean certain death, even with hulking, vicious Kjar already downing several men before they could reach her. In fact, several men and a few women were taking up arms in a circle around her.

Then it suddenly occurred to Megan.

They were here for *her*.

But how could King Rennir have so easily fooled Naðr and his brothers? Three *dragons*? Or at least tricked them enough that they were out there when a great deal of the enemy were here.

The sharp, metallic scent of blood hit her nostrils as throats were slit open and guts were run through. Frustrated at being so helpless, she kept her dagger firmly in hand and spun slowly. An unsettling but much appreciated numbness settled over her as death reigned down on more enemy bodies than she could count. Or at least she hoped they were…assumed they were.

Then the worst happened.

A man broke through the ranks. Big, ferocious and *so* not her friend, he shot her a tooth-rotten grin and eyed her dagger with mad glee. He knew she had no idea how to use it. Then, if that wasn't enough, movement over his shoulder caught her attention. The gale-swept horizon now hosted not just her ship but several others.

Enemy ships.

But that's not what made her go cold. No, what made breath nearly impossible was the way her ship, Naðr's ship, *their* ship, not only had its sail raised but was turning back toward shore. Rolling uncontrollably in the waves, it listed precariously.

Just like in her vision.

Megan nearly cried out to Kjar but caught herself. The last thing he needed was distraction. Meanwhile, the big guy in front of her drew closer. He'd sheathed his weapon so he was looking to take her alive. When he lunged, she dodged. But he spun fast and before she knew it, he'd wrapped his arm around her waist and lifted.

Survival instincts kicked in.

Unlike the man that got ahold of her on the mountain, this one underestimated the few skills she had...and the weapon. Megan arched and drove her elbow back into his stomach. The second his grip loosened a fraction, she spun and kneed him in the balls. He lurched. She plunged the dagger into his side.

When his arms went slack and he stumbled back, she stared into his stunned eyes, frozen.

But a scream of rage soon pulled her free from her stupefied haze.

Heidrek?

Horrified, she saw what was happening further out on the dock. Raknar's son had clearly enraged a warrior three times his size. Though he should have been running for his life, the boy wasn't. Instead, he was standing his ground, glaring up at the monster with nothing but a small dagger and a barking Guardian trying her best to protect him. If that wasn't enough, two more enemy warriors were making their way toward them.

Absolutely *not*.

Megan didn't think about what she could or could not do, she acted.

Dodging left then right, she shot past the ring of warriors around her. All the while she drew her bow and arrow as she ran. The dock was long so she ran until she was as close as possible then stopped, cocked and aimed. Remain calm. Figure in the wind shear.

Release. *Thwap*.

The first guy was down.

Then she ran and pulled free another arrow, pacing the second guy before she stopped, cocked and shot again.

Missed.

But not by much.

Megan raced a few dozen feet then stopped and cocked again. This time when she released, the arrow slammed into the guy's upper back and he fell.

In the meantime, things had gone from bad to worse further out on the dock. The enemy warrior in pursuit of Heidrek had not only slashed the boy, or so said the blood trailing down his arm, but was tearing after a now retreating and very scared child.

Bastard. She'd see this guy dead, so cocked another arrow as she ran. Still, things were going downhill fast. They'd nearly reached the end of the dock. Aiming an arrow at him with Heidrek just beyond wasn't going to happen. She might have some skill but didn't trust it *that* much. Thank any god handy when Guardian locked on tight to the warrior's calf. Regrettably, the man was just close enough that he was able to snag the boy's wrist.

He yanked Heidrek back then kicked away Guardian. Fear turned swiftly to rage and the boy snarled. Suddenly, the man lost his footing and Heidrek was thrust into the raging sea. Horrified emotions suppressed, she got close and released an arrow into the enemy's gut. He went down hard.

Megan checked on Guardian. Her dog seemed good enough though upset as she barked down toward where Heidrek had gone over. Voice firm, she said, "No, wolfy girl. You stay here. I got this."

She tossed aside her bow and arrows, pulled off her boots then dove. All the while she prayed to any deity listening.

The waves were rough, brutal, but she plowed down beneath the water and searched. *Please, let me find you. Don't you dare die.* Though she wished she hadn't, Megan wasn't surprised when Guardian didn't listen and splashed down into the water. This time, however, she couldn't make sure her dog was safe but had to find the boy. He'd been through too much and didn't deserve a death like this.

Nobody deserved a death like this.

So she fought the undercurrent and searched, searched then searched some more. Her lungs burned and the water was frigid but still she kept her eyes wide as she dug through the turbulent, maddened froth. Both sharp relief and fresh pain seized her heart when she found him a few feet under against a dock post.

Heidrek was lifeless and unmoving.

Megan snaked her arm around his waist and swam to the surface. Trained to save a drowning victim, she wrapped her arms under his armpits, pointed her fingers back at herself and held tight. Then, as an acting floating device, she kicked them to an area safely between both docks then toward shore. No easy task considering the huge waves.

Guardian, still hanging in there despite her recent injury, swum alongside.

Though tempted to speak to him, rouse him if possible, Megan knew her breath needed to be saved for the arduous distance of water that ran along the docks. Even as her heartbroken gaze landed on Naðr's ship, she kept swimming. Even as tears burned her eyes, she kept swimming.

It was doing everything it had in her vision...everything that would lead to what she found in the future almost eighty feet below the sea. Trying to turn toward the shore, the ship's sail was already tearing. Wind howled, thunder roared across the sky and lightning flashed.

Naðr, you fool, what are you doing? You said you knew better.

But only he knew and there was nothing she could do to help him or his brothers. All she could do now was try to save Raknar's son. Then, just like in her vision, a particularly strong wind gust caught the ship at the same time as an overly large wave...

And it rolled.

Megan cried out and though it must have been the salt water stinging her eyes in combination with lightning flashes, she swore all the Nordic symbols Kjar carved along the ship's hull glowed. White. Bright. There. Then faded.

Hungry and desperate, the sea started to swallow their ship.

"Noooo," she wailed.

Though she continued swimming, it almost seemed the same wave that'd taken down the ship rippled across the water unnaturally and caught her. She tried desperately to hold on tight but Heidrek was ripped away by the current.

Again and again she attempted to grab hold of him but couldn't. The last thing she saw before water rushed into her mouth was Guardian locking onto the back of his tunic and swimming toward what she hoped was shore.

Then another wave caught her and she rolled.

Over and over.

Blackness came and went.

Chills came and went.

Then there was silence. So much silence. Empty space. Endless. Too much of it. A gaping tunnel that went on and on. Or did it? Was she in some sort of Heaven or even Valhalla? Though under the impression she was supposed to live a lifetime, was she the first to fulfill the seers' request?

"Naðr?" she whispered.

Because somebody had to be out there and she hoped it was him telling her everything was all right. Everyone was safe. Heidrek and Guardian had made it and so had his brothers and everyone else.

"We're right here, sweetie," came a soft feminine voice. "We're all with you and you're just fine."

"Water, she needs water," came another voice and her head was gently tilted forward.

Grateful, Megan sipped, sighed, and then murmured, "Meyla, where's your father?"

More silence…then, "Dad's not here right now, honey, but we are."

Confused by the terms 'Dad' and 'honey' but worried that Naðr wasn't there she whispered, "I saw his ship go down. Did he make it? His brothers? Are they okay?"

Again silence, which she would have worried over if darkness and exhaustion didn't steal her away. The next thing she knew warmth and sunlight covered her. Megan pried open her eyes and smiled when the first thing she saw was Guardian cuddled up against her. With a sigh of relief, she ran her hands down her fur, thankful that they'd made it.

Then her eyes drifted over Guardian.

To Veronica.

The feeling that rushed through her was indescribable as she jolted upright. Joy and exaltation were swiftly followed by fear and worry as she looked around. Veronica and Guardian had been laying on one side of her and Amber on the other. Both sat up abruptly when she did. So did Sean who had been sleeping in a chair in the corner of the room.

"Christ," she managed, emotions overflowing in tears. "I'm home."

"Hell yeah you are." Sean sat on the end of the bed. He squeezed her ankle, voice deeper than normal. "Alive and well, thank God."

The next thing she knew her sisters had their arms wrapped around her, Guardian more than happy to bask in all the love.

"I'm so glad you're okay, sis," Amber whispered.

"Don't ever scare us like that again," Veronica said sternly, grip just as tight.

Megan held them for a good long minute before she mumbled fondly, "I can't breathe. Need a little space."

Though Veronica pulled back, Amber clasped her cheeks, brown eyes full of anxiety. "You've been in the hospital, ICU even. You're only home because Mema Angie pulled some strings."

Intensive Care Unit? Negative. "I wasn't in the hospital. You wouldn't believe where I was but definitely not there."

"Yes you were, for two days, but that's beside the point. Now you're here and just fine," Veronica assured.

"She's right." Amber flicked her wrist as if to wave away any extra concerns. "It's all behind you now."

"Listen, are you hungry?" Sean intercepted. "Breakfast. Lunch. Dinner. You name it, I'll get it."

Their eyes met. His voice was strained. He was uncomfortable and that didn't happen often to Sean. Though it was obvious they were on a beautiful campaign to assuage her fears, Megan shook her head and frowned at him. "Sean, what happened to me…at least from your end of things?"

When he didn't answer immediately, she scrambled to the end of the bed, driving him back to a standing position. Megan stood but the room tilted and she plunked back down. Irritated, downright panicked, she glared up at him. "What *happened* to me?"

Sean crouched in front of her and braced his hands on the bed. "Tell you what, why don't you let your sisters help you crawl into fresh sweats while I cook up some food. Then we'll curl up on the couch downstairs and catch you up?"

Tempted to argue with him, Megan knew better. Sean had an unrelenting look in his eyes. So whatever had happened on their end had been intense. But what of her end…of Heidrek and Naðr and all that she'd left behind over a thousand years ago?

Caught in a moment, downright frightened, she grasped at her back. "Where's my pack?"

"Downstairs and safe." Concern flickered in Sean's eyes. "Shower. Relax. It'll be waiting for you."

"Did you open it?"

"No."

She hitched her jaw, unsure. "Why?"

"Because you asked us not to," Veronica said softly.

"I did?"

"You did." Sean helped her to her feet, making sure she was steady. "How do you feel now, sweetheart?"

"Honestly? Sad." She squeezed his supportive hands, thankful. "The dizziness is gone. I'm okay."

He cocked his head and peered at her. "You sure?"

"Yeah."

"Good. What do want to eat?"

"Coffee. Lots of it."

"Gonna eat the fresh grounds directly from the can?"

"You bet."

"Done."

"You remind me of Kol, smart ass."

"I know, sweetie." Sean handed her off to her waiting sisters.

"You do?"

But he gave no answer as he set out presumably to brew coffee. After that everything was a blur made of warm sluicing water then cozy sweats before she found herself with a blissfully hot cup of coffee in hand. Though she looked for Aesa's Valkryie perched on her deck railing, it wasn't there.

So she grabbed the manuscript waiting patiently on her desk, right where she'd left it.

A fire crackled on the hearth and a cold beer sat on the table beside her before they all settled down and made idle conversation. Not a fool, Megan knew what they were doing. Helping her ease into a reality that she wasn't altogether sure was hers. But they seemed to understand that too.

Thumbing her finger over and over Naðr's name on page-number-whatever of the manuscript, she'd finally had enough. "Okay, tell me what happened."

Amber and Veronica glanced at one another.

It seemed Veronica had been designated to speak first in what Megan didn't doubt was a pre-planned conversation. "You, Nathan and the divers never came up. We stayed out there until midnight but had to come in because of the storm."

Megan wasn't the sort to speculate on whether everything she'd experienced was a dream. She knew it wasn't. "Then?"

"It was stipulated in Nathan's will that all measures be taken to find his body in the case of his untimely death," Veronica said, the lawyer that she *should* be kicking in. "So when the storm abated, dive teams were sent out. Nothing was found."

"Nothing?" Megan said, her heart pounding a bit harder because she intended to hire her own team.

"Nothing," Veronica confirmed. "The ocean floor at our location and miles surrounding are clear of artifact, Viking or otherwise."

"You're wrong," Megan said.

"I'm telling you what I was told," she countered.

Megan brushed it aside. Of course she was. Veronica had no reason to lie. She'd follow up with her own team later.

"Are you all right, sis?" Amber murmured.

"I'm fine," Megan snapped and closed her eyes to the wounded look on her youngest sister's face. With a deep inhale, she met Amber's eyes and worked hard at a soft smile. "Just tense, sis. It's been difficult."

"No prob," Amber said easily but it was obvious this ordeal, whatever it'd been from their side, had put a lot of strain on her. Good thing Sean was a strong shoulder for her sister to lean on.

"Tell me the rest," Megan said, determined to stay stable, unwavering...determined to get the feel of losing Heidrek and watching Naðr's ship go down out of her head.

Veronica sat next to Megan and squeezed her hand while Sean continued.

"It's been almost seventy-two hours and no sign of Nathan," Sean said. "They'll keep searching but with the current water temperature it doesn't look good."

Because he died at the top of a Scandinavian mountain.

But she didn't say that.

"How did I survive then?"

Megan didn't miss the looks exchanged between them before Amber blurted out, "You washed up, nude, right in front of your house, sis. We found Guardian and the cylinder with you."

So there went the proof of Viking clothing.

She shook her head. "Impossible, Guardian was dragging Heid—"

"We know. Heidrek," Veronica offered, eyes gentle as they met Megan's. "You told us many times."

Megan's eyes watered but before she could speak, Sean cut in. "You said a lot when you were in the hospital. Though in and out, you spoke of a whole other world. Ninth century Scandinavia to be exact. Naðr Véurr and his brothers Raknar and Kol."

"Then there was Kjar. You called him a magic man," Veronica murmured.

"And Meyla and Valan." Amber grinned even though she didn't mean to. "I kinda like them…and Kol," she said as an afterthought. "Bonafide troublemaker that one."

But it was Veronica's words that ensnared Megan and she probably looked at her for the first time with genuine need for guidance. "How do I know Heidrek is okay? I tried so hard to save him."

Veronica's eyes filled with moisture but she quickly blinked it away, realizing she needed to be the strong one now. "Focus on those last moments you had together, that you stayed strong. He knew you were coming for him. That means everything. Hold onto that for now then we'll go from there, okay?"

Spoken from the heart, Veronica's advice was that of a woman who had lost a child. Megan leaned her head against her sister's shoulder. "You're right, sis."

From there her sisters and Sean let the conversation flow slow and easy.

Too easy.

Though happy to be in the present, every second of every minute her mind was on Naðr. The devastation of seeing his ship go down, of potentially having lost him, gnawed at her.

"Where's the cylinder that was attached to my back?"

The room fell silent as Sean left.

She looked at her sisters. "What?"

Amber handed her the beer. "Why don't you drink a bit."

The look on Megan's face had her sister setting it aside quickly and plunking down across from her, an unnatural frown on her face.

"She's just looking out for you," Veronica muttered under her breath.

"Looking out for me how?"

Though Amber might've seemed reluctant and borderline deflated moments before, she piped right up. "You told us whatever's in that cylinder would take you back to," she made quotation marks in the air, "Naðr Véurr." Then her little sister sounded downright incredulous. "Ever since your accident you're convinced that you traveled back in time to ancient Scandinavia."

Blindsided, she looked from Amber to Veronica. "We haven't had a chance to talk but...you both think I'm making this up, don't you?"

"All we've done is talk," Amber defended.

"When she was looped on medication," Veronica countered and sighed as she wrapped her arm around Megan's shoulders and met her eyes. "She's worried. As am I. Forgive us."

Fine. Whatever. Still.

Megan felt so lost, adrift, confused. She wished Naðr was here, that he was alive and could make sense of this. But he wasn't and couldn't...no...because he was long dead.

Sean rejoined them. "Here they are."

Megan launched from the couch and grabbed the pouch that had been strapped to her back. "The stone and the cylinder." She frowned at the box with the other two stones that had been in her garage. "Why that?"

"You asked for both items."

"I did?"

"Many times."

"Oh." She reluctantly took the box as well and nodded. "Thanks."

But Sean didn't let go entirely of the pouch, his eyes firm on hers. "I won't hand this over if you don't sit down right now and tell your sisters about what's in that box from start to finish."

She shook her head. "Not yet."

"Yes. Now."

Megan swallowed hard. Crap. He meant it...and he was right. But how could she tell them without sounding nuts? "They won't believe me."

"I barely believe you but here I am," he answered. "Give them the benefit of the doubt. Let them into the confusion and terror you've been feeling for far too long."

"Not terror really," she defended.

"Share," he reiterated.

"Fine," she huffed but Sean knew she meant no harm as he plunked down next to Amber. Megan sunk to her knees within feet of the fire. How was she supposed to go about this when even she was wondering what had happened? Truly, she'd gone out diving then maybe…just maybe…she had a dream…

But as Megan opened the box and poured out the contents of the bag that Naðr strapped to her back hours, a day, a thousand years before, she had a strong sense that her Viking king was forever by her side.

Her stone.

The cylinder.

Tokens that had been in his hands rolled onto the floor. Blinking away tears, she explained the stones, the symbols etched on them and all she'd learned in ninth century Scandinavia about the seers, even the dragon brothers. Either her sisters would believe her or not. She wouldn't blame them if they didn't. Because she sounded insane.

When she was finished, silence fell, long and heavy.

Veronica handed Megan the beer and she took a hearty swallow. Then her sister leaned forward, concerned. "Sweetie, you already shared all of this and we're still trying to figure out what to make of it." Her eyes went to the cylinder. "What we want to know is what's in that?"

Jaw set, Megan glared at them. "You could have told me that I'd already covered all this. What was the point in making me relive it all again?"

"We needed to hear it, all of it, from you," Sean said.

When Megan frowned, Amber shrugged. "Sorry sis, we just wanted to see if you'd say the same things now that you're off the drugs. You did."

Dumbfounded, Megan shot, "So does that mean you believe me, now? Does it make any of this real?"

"Open the cylinder," Sean said. "That will be real, Megan."

If she didn't love them all so much she might've told them to go to hell. But the people in this room cared about her and damn if she didn't know it. So, determined to keep thoughts of Naðr far from her mind, she nodded. "Fine."

But even as she twisted the cap on the cylinder she thought of the first time she'd found it on the longship settled beneath the Atlantic. Then Naðr strapping it to her back, worried over her welfare.

"Shoot," she whispered and hung her head. "I want to see what's in this...and I don't."

"Then I'll open it for you." Megan's eyes shot open as Veronica knelt in front of her and grabbed the cylinder. "Ready?"

Megan shook her head and snatched it back. "No, I'll do it. It's meant for me. My way back to him."

"I know."

This was it. A choice. Given to her. Take it or leave it.

She closed her eyes. As if it had just happened she was back on the longship, Naðr's words and actions echoing in her mind. *"Besides me, only Megan will ever know what's in this cylinder because it is hers alone."* Naðr's *tender hand closed over her shoulder, his fingers dusting her tattoo. "As to what she's been marked with, it is a claiming of the seers." His hand squeezed gently. "She is here for me."*

"Is it there still?" she asked, clasping at her shoulder.

"The hot new tattoo that magically appeared? Sure is." Amber grinned. "And it's fabulous might I add."

"Agreed," Veronica said.

"Aren't you curious where I got it?" she asked, seeing her chance to make them believe.

"You told us. In Scandinavia." Sean sat next to her. "Hun, this is a lot for us to swallow but trust me we're working on it. For all we know you could have gotten that tat before all this happened, especially considering your infatuation with the markings on the stone." He nodded at the cylinder. "Are you ready now?"

This was so frustrating but she couldn't blame them for being less than convinced. If she was in their shoes she'd feel the same way. It was time to open the cylinder. To see how she could get back to him...because one way or another, the concept of never seeing Naðr again seemed impossible.

So, hand slightly shaking, she removed the top.

For all the build-up to this she truly thought stars would burst over her head. Yes, magical stars. Maybe even little bursts of dragon fire. But no, nothing happened. Nothing at all. Megan couldn't help but grin. Her grand finale was pretty darn low key save for the others pouring over its innards.

But Megan supposed that was celebration enough and she was thankful for it as she waved their eager eyes away and tried her best to muffle a smile. "See. No fireworks."

"What's in it," Sean prompted.

Megan didn't hesitate to pull the tube of material out...and out...and out.

"Damn," she muttered, as far more material than should have fit in the small tube soon lay across the carpet. "What *is* this?"

"A sail," Sean murmured as he fingered the material. "A really well made one at that."

"As in for a boat?" Amber said as she helped unroll it.

"Usually what sails are for, sweetheart." But he shot her a wink before saying, "Help me push back the furniture. Let's see how big it is."

Even after couches, chairs, and end tables were pushed into far corners; it barely fit in her living room. Grin blossoming into a smile, Sean looked at Megan. "This is unbelievable."

Already running the dimensions in her mind as she crouched, Megan fingered the sturdy yet delicate material as she met his eyes. "This is sail material but," she rubbed her fingers, "different."

"But it's a sail." Sean eyed the square dimensions of what they could manage to lay out. His eyes met hers and he shook his head. "If I didn't know better..."

Suddenly Megan knew. "It's meant for the boat we built."

"Mostly you, Sea Siren," he murmured as an incredulous but small smile met his lips. "Meant for *you*...to sail back to *him*."

Chapter Eighteen

Two Weeks Later

Bundled up in a down jacket and warm boots, Megan sat on her back deck and stared out over Frenchman Bay. Though her sisters had stayed an extra week she finally managed to convince them to go home. She'd done her best to keep a brave face and to show them the strength they needed to see. Yet even when they left, both wore concerned expressions. They'd texted and called every day since to check on her.

"Hey," Sean said as he joined her. "It's too cold to be sitting out here."

He'd been over daily and though he said it was to do touch-ups on the boat she knew he was there to make sure she was okay. Unlike with her sisters, she didn't have to be strong for him which was a relief because she was miserable.

"I'm fine," she murmured. "Fresh air's good for me."

"Mm hmm." He sounded less than convinced. "You gonna come down to the bar tonight? They're throwing a Halloween party."

"Naw." She shook her head. "Probably just catch a movie with Guardian."

"It'd do you good to be around people. I hate seeing you so sad. You're too thin and all you do is sit out here staring at the ocean."

When she didn't respond right away he waited. The weeks since she'd returned had been painfully difficult and even more so once her sisters left. She had no way of knowing if Naðr had survived but that didn't keep her from constantly thinking about going back. What if he was alive? If so, was he missing her as much as she missed him? The dull ache, the absolute emptiness in her chest, wouldn't abate. If anything, her longing grew.

Eventually she murmured, "I just miss him so much. All of them. More than I thought possible."

"And I miss you," he said softly and sighed, eyes meeting hers. "You know that whether or not we can truly wrap our heads around it, your sisters and I *do* believe you."

It was sweet of him to say but she knew it was a half-truth at best. Time travel, dragon shifters, Vikings, magical ships, it all sounded way too far-fetched.

So she changed the subject. "How are you doing since Amber left?"

"I'm all right." He shot her a grin. "Wiped out."

"I'll bet." She rolled her eyes and matched his grin. "But she has a funny way of bringing out your charming side, Sean."

"I didn't think I had one of those."

"You don't. Usually." Then her grin fell away. It hadn't felt comfortable anyways. "Seriously though, you're okay?"

"I am," he admitted. "Believe it or not it gets easier every time she goes."

Megan sighed but gave no response.

"You've been reading the hell out of that manuscript. Pages are in rough shape," he commented. "Learn anything new?"

"No but I'll admit it all strikes me far more interesting now that I know it actually happened…time-travel, magic…" she trailed off.

Sean stared out over the harbor and grew silent for a time. He genuinely surprised her when he murmured, "Are you in love with him?"

Megan didn't need to ask who as she met his eyes and whispered, "I think I must be for it to hurt so much."

"Awe, hell honey." He stood and pulled her close for a big hug. "I'm so sorry."

Then he pulled away and studied her. "I've got to get some stuff done before the party. You sure you don't wanna come?"

"Positive." She plunked down in the chair again. "You go have fun, okay?"

Sean ran a hand through his hair and eyed her warily before nodding. "Yeah, okay. I'll catch up with you later."

"Sure thing."

Megan resumed staring at the sea when Sean paused at the top of the stairs, his words so soft she barely heard them. "My brother is in love with you too, Sea Siren."

"What?" Her eyes shot to Sean but he'd vanished.

Then Megan jerked awake. She blinked. What the heck? It was much later in the day. Had Sean even been here? He must've been.

That last statement had to have been a dream though because it had reminded her too much of...Kol?

A low sound came from nearby and Megan stopped breathing. The large raven was perched on the railing staring at her. Aesa's Valkyrie. It cried out once, twice, and then launched into the air.

Her eyes followed it as it sailed out over the bay. Thin layers of dark clouds blanketed the horizon. Suddenly, sunlight shot through a small break, casting both the sea and water into an even more brilliant blue.

The exact color of Naðr's eyes.

Her eyes rounded at what shimmered and flickered as it burst from beneath the water as a ghostly mirage. There was no other way to describe it. It broke the surface like a submarine would. First it was transparent then had more context as it did something no sailing vessel would ever be able to do after being submerged. Whole, sitting comfortably on the calm water, it was turning her way, sail intact.

Naðr's ship.

Their ship.

The wind kicked up as Megan stood and grasped the railing. Her heart surged and a tear slid down her cheek. *Please* don't let this be a dream. *Please* let this be real. Whether or not it was, she knew in that moment that she had to go back.

She *had* to know if he was still alive even if it meant being stuck back in time without him.

Guardian whined and followed her as she raced into the house and grabbed a few sheets of the manuscript and a pen before heading for the garage. When she opened the door she froze.

Not only was the boat on a trailer attached to her truck, but the sail that had been in the cylinder was now affixed to her little longship. All she had to do was raise it.

Awed, she stumbled forward and snatched up the note left on one of the bench seats.

Opening it, she read.

Hey Sea Siren,
Thought I'd get this set up for you just in case. Don't have to tell you but keep the extra oars in the boat and stay damn safe. I might

*be the sort to let love get away but you're not. Go get him. I'll keep
an eye on your sisters.*
    Sean

Hell, *really*? God, she adored that man.

Megan made sure the box with the remaining stones was left on
her workbench then penned out three quick letters. One for each
sister and one for Sean. She poured out her heart and let them know
how much she loved them all. As was habit, she'd kept her will
updated. Everything she owned went to her sisters save this house
and property. They belonged to Sean.

"Well, that's it then," she said to Guardian who smiled up at her.

Megan hit the automatic garage door opener, eyes wide and
hopeful as she searched the horizon. The ship wasn't gone! Not yet.
But quickly fading. Hopping in her truck, she pulled out and angled
the trailer down into the water alongside her dock. This wasn't the
first time she'd put a boat in the water alone.

By the time she had it tied off and pulled the trailer away, the
ship was a scant outline. Flying, she changed into appropriate
clothes, waterproof warm boots, a jacket, gloves and a hat. Stone
tucked safely in her pocket; Megan had just made it back to the boat
when Guardian barked at her.

Right. Her dog.

"Oh, sweet girl, you've got to stay," Megan murmured as she
crouched and hugged her. "I could be sailing straight to my death
right now."

Her throat thickened with emotion as she kissed Guardian's
muzzle then stood, voice firm. "Stay, wolfy girl. Sean will take good
care of you."

Then, unable to look her in the eyes again, Megan got into the
boat, untied it then pushed off, scooping the oars to thrust the boat
forward. The waters had grown a bit choppier so she rowed hard.
Then, against all odds, when waves should have pushed her in, the
current propelled her forward.

But not before a loud thunk sounded behind her.

Megan glanced over her shoulder. *Ugh.* "Guardian! Bad girl."
Still she couldn't help but grin when her dog wagged her tail and
woofed. The unnatural shift in tide was carrying them out fast and

the sail needed to be opened to allow for better control. "Well, I guess you're in it for the long haul then."

Yet the minute the sail was up, the weather shifted. It could change on a dime, but this didn't fit any criteria she was accustomed to. Though nothing was in the area, it felt more like a system moving down from the great lakes at rapid speed without the benefit of Vermont and New Hampshire's mountains to break it up some.

Megan pulled the oars in and held onto the rudder the second she saw veins of blue and gold light starting to form in the sail. Wide-eyed, she watched as the same runic symbols that Kjar had carved into Naðr's ship started to crawl through the entire sail. Then her tattoo started to burn. The Vegvisir, meant to help her navigate back to Naðr.

"It's really happening. Come here, baby," she whispered and gestured to Guardian. "We're going for a ride."

Her dog crawled over the bench and nestled between Megan's thighs. Certain that there was no point in holding the rudder anymore, she wrapped her arms around Guardian and started praying as the boat lurched forward. Feet braced, she held on tight as the wind increased and the waves swelled. A low rumble of thunder echoed across the sky and lightning zipped then jumped from cloud to cloud.

Then *whoosh*...the wind whipped them forward faster and faster. So fast that she thought for a moment the sail wouldn't hold.

But it did.

Cresting ten foot waves head on, it soon became what most would consider a terrifying rollercoaster ride. Not Megan. Perhaps because she knew this storm wasn't natural but more than likely because she loved being at sea. Rough, unforgiving, she was completely at its mercy. The only downside was that if she went over so did Guardian.

Still, she couldn't help but grin and shake her head. "I told you not to come, sweet girl."

Even so, though her dog stayed close, she wasn't whining. In fact, she didn't seem all that frightened. But that might be because Megan wasn't. No, she was too busy being impressed with how well her and Sean's boat was doing. She bit her lip and wished he could have been here. He would have *loved* this.

The runic symbols in the sail glowed brighter as the skies darkened and the seas grew rougher. Chuckling, Megan didn't look back once as the boat plowed on, cresting waves that might soon grow too tall. Some might think she'd lost it, who knows, maybe she had, but *this* was living.

Then something happened.

Shifted.

Megan couldn't explain it save the temperature changed by a few degrees and the wind howled and whipped differently than it had moments before. Sea spray thrashed at her face and she closed her eyes. Leaning forward, she grasped Guardian tightly as the boat climbed a wave larger than all the rest.

Up, up...up.

Salt stung her eyes so badly she couldn't open them.

However, she *could* laugh insanely when the boat crested the wave and they started flying down. What else was she supposed to do? She must have lost her mind when she set out like this.

Then another mild gush of seawater sprayed over her as a loud grinding noise met her ears and the boat dragged alongside something. Laughter died on her lips.

Then everything went still.

Too still.

Even the water beneath the boat.

Were they dead? Had they drowned and didn't know it?

But everything felt *so* real. The chill. The wetness. Everything. Still holding onto Guardian, she spit water from her mouth and rubbed it out of her eyes. Blinking rapidly, struggling to see, she peered around. Everything was blurry.

Until it wasn't.

But even then she had barely a moment to process anything before someone jumped into the boat.

And she was pulled into his arms.

Naðr Véurr.

"You came back to me," he murmured. "Thank the gods you came back."

Megan didn't have a chance to respond before his lips closed over hers. Desperate, she wrapped her arms around him, petrified she'd wake up just like she had the numerous times she'd dreamt about him these last few weeks.

But no.

She didn't wake up. And she knew she wouldn't.

He was *real*.

This was real.

At last, she broke the kiss, needed to look into his eyes. And they were right there. As gorgeous as ever as he stroked her cheeks, obviously making sure she was real as well.

"I've missed the *hel* out of you, beautiful," he said hoarsely, emotion ravaging his handsome face. "Not a moment went by that I didn't think of you, always praying to the gods for your safe return." He shook his head. "I even came damn close to breaking the pact with the seers and allowing my dragon to find you so that I might convince you to return."

"No need. I couldn't stay away," she whispered. "I missed you so much."

"Good to have you back, Sea Siren," came a voice from above.

Megan stared at Naðr for a good long moment before her eyes rose to Kol leaning over the edge of their longship.

"Yes it is," Kjar said with a crooked grin, eyes scanning her boat with appreciation. "Very nice vessel."

"It took you long enough," Raknar said with a smile as he shimmied down the ladder and wiggled a finger at Guardian. "Come on girl, my son's been looking forward to seeing you again."

"He's alive." Megan melted against Naðr. "Thank any god listening."

"Because of you and your dog," Raknar said, eyes grateful as he scooped Guardian and brought her up.

"A mighty Viking tigress queen rushing down the docks and shooting arrows to down the enemy some said," Kol enlightened.

"With the wind turning her hair to living spirals and her arrows to pure fire others said," Kjar added.

"How long have I been gone?" she whispered.

"Two fortnights." Naðr said. "Far too long."

Megan didn't have a chance to respond before Naðr ushered her toward the ladder. "Up. Then we'll talk."

More than content to be ordered around by him, for now, she complied. She'd only reached the top when Raknar of all people pulled her over the side and brought her down into a tight embrace.

"Thank you so much for saving my boy," he murmured. "I am forever indebted to you."

He'd no sooner pulled back when Kol swept her into a hug.

She laughed. "What's this for?"

He squeezed her tight then pulled back, dimples erupting as he grinned and winked. "They both got to hug you. Only seemed right."

Megan kept chuckling. "Of course it did."

"I'm going to have a few of my men bring your boat into port if that suits you."

When her eyes met Naðr's, everything else fell away except him. Tall, gorgeous, black fur cloak blowing back from his shoulders, she nodded, speechless. Though she knew she was here it all still seemed so surreal.

Him especially.

"You're soaked," he muttered and removed her jacket before wrapping his cloak over her shoulders. But not before she felt a tiny zip of warmth run over her and the rest of her clothes dried in an instant. Dragon magic then? Had to be.

Caught, ensnared, lost, she stared at Naðr's face and whispered, "I'm really here. I'm back." She blinked. "But how are you...alive? I watched you sink." Her eyes swung over their ship. "I watched this go down."

"Kjar." He smiled at his cousin. "Is more than you think he is and formed a bond with Adlin MacLomain when he helped us fight Rennir's brother years ago."

Lots of questions came to mind but she was curious about Kjar first and foremost. "What are you then?"

When Naðr nodded at him, Kjar explained, "My mortal grandmother coupled with Heimdall."

Before he could continue, she sputtered an interruption, "You mean the *god* Heimdall? The watchman of the Norse gods? The very one who guarded Bifrost, the Rainbow Bridge that connects the Nine Realms to Middle Earth?"

Kjar stroked one of his long goatee braids and shrugged a shoulder as if it was no big thing. "I suppose that'd be him."

Megan swallowed, eying Kjar. "So you're a...demi-god?"

"Guess so," Kjar said.

"One generation removed but yes," Naðr provided. "And the reason you're here now."

"Right," Kjar said as though an afterthought but she didn't miss the unmistakable twinkle in his eyes as he looked at her. "You really do know how to build a boat."

Raknar shook his head, clearly understanding that she needed more answers. "It seems when Adlin MacLomain was here he and Kjar became good friends. Adlin has a certain fondness for love so when the deal was struck with the seers and the gods became involved, he took it upon himself to steer things in a more beneficial direction."

"He loved my daughter, Meyla," Naðr reminded.

"More so, he loved her father and what he was willing to do to help the MacLomain clan." Kol grinned. "Enough so it seems to enlist the help of Kjar to make sure we three brothers didn't just fulfill an agreement made to the seers but that we might find true love because of it."

Megan's eyes found Kjar's. "What did you do?"

Kjar, not for the first time, struck her as far older than he looked when his steady eyes met hers. "I made sure you loved my king."

"Then?" she prompted.

The Viking eyed her for a long moment before he said, "Then I made sure to carve the symbols into this boat so that it might call you back to him."

"But," she started before Kjar cut her off.

"When the symbols were carved into this ship they were imprinted onto the sail in the cylinder. I am a shipwright and grandson to Heimdall. I've the ability to harness the power between realms and between time. I've the power to merge both."

Megan shook her head. "But what about this boat shipwrecked on the bottom of the Atlantic? What about the box of stones I found?"

"The box of stones was waiting on the ship when we pulled away from the dock to go fight Rennir," Naðr said. "No doubt left by the seers." He cupped her cheek, pained. "You don't know what I felt when I opened it. Even your stone was in there. In two places at once. So I engraved the inner lid with my name in case we went down."

"And you did," she whispered.

"No." He shook his head. "But the seas did grow rough and the box was lost overboard."

"But I watched the sail raise then tear when I was trying to save Heidrek. I watched this ship go down."

"The ship you watched sink was also the one you found on the ocean floor in your time. But it was always a mirror image of this vessel or a ghost ship. When you went under as you tried to save Raknar's son, the King's ghost ship followed," Kjar explained. "But you were crossing the Rainbow Bridge between times. As if sailing through two separate realities, one ship sunk and one stayed afloat. But the love that tied you together through time allowed the ghost ship to carry you back here to begin with. A time loop...until now."

The massive Viking smiled as he eyed the glorious ship. "Now she is truly both of yours. A ship that sailed rough seas from both above and below but found calm waters. A ship caught in time that followed its true path."

Seriously? "If the ghost ship followed me to the twenty-first century, why wasn't it on the ocean floor when I returned?"

Kjar looked as though she should have this all figured out. "Because it landed where you would find it when you went diving to begin with. It was always a means to bring lost love together across the centuries."

"So I traveled a bit further into the future than it did." Baffled, she cocked her head. "But it would have never traveled into the future to begin with if all of this hadn't happened. That seems impossible."

"The Rainbow Bridge and its time loops always do," Kjar agreed with a little smirk. "Gods and demi-gods alike do like to play their games."

So it seemed.

"And the cylinder...how was that beneath the ocean?" Megan said, voice thick with emotion.

A sly grin crawled onto Kjar's face. "Maybe the gods or maybe Adlin MacLomain." His eyes seemed well over a thousand years old when they met hers. "After all, did he not make sure you got a certain manuscript?"

Megan's mouth fell open a fraction when the Viking turned away and became busy manning the ship. She'd not told a soul that the manuscript about The MacLomain Series: Next Generation had been sitting untouched on the counter of Cadence's bookstore. And she'd felt horrible for taking it...especially when she went to go visit Leslie afterward.

But then something had always held her tongue.

"Meddlesome, devious wizard," Naðr muttered. But there was a grin on his face and a definite fondness in his voice when he pulled her close.

"He certainly sounds it," she said, so entirely happy. "But I'll admit I wouldn't mind meeting him one day."

"Nothing says you won't," Naðr murmured as he ran kisses up her jaw until he hovered over her ear. "Until then, would you like to sail on our ship?"

"I would," she said. "But first...what happened to Rennir. Did you win?"

"King Rennir is dead and we have won for now," he assured. "But Yrsa is not yet defeated. Because she is a seer she will supersede his son and rule as queen and we will all fight her together." Naðr tilted up her chin and gazed into her eyes. "Until then, let us have this moment."

That sounded damn good.

Naðr didn't have to say a word. The sail was already being raised as he took her hand and led her until he leaned against the center of the stern and brought her back against his front. "One of these days I'll let you climb the dragon head on the prow so you can ride her. But for now." He wrapped a strong arm around her waist and braced his legs on either side of hers. "This is the best place to be on the ship when she sets sail."

Not entirely sure she believed him, it didn't much matter when he brushed aside her hair and trailed kisses up the side of her neck until he whispered in her ear, "This is for a woman who was laughing when she arrived, who came back to me, one who'd clearly just sailed stormy seas. Are you ready?"

Megan was about to respond when the sail was released and the ship lurched forward. She yelped in surprise as it took off. Winds whipped them forward, the mighty sail billowing and proud as the dragon prow led the way.

Exhilarated, winded, she leaned her head back against his chest and laughed. This ship, *their* ship, was so much more unimaginably incredible than she ever envisioned it might be, even when she'd found it beneath the waters of the Atlantic.

Sun sliced down and the dragon prow glittered as she cut through the water. Majestic mountains loomed, waves danced, but nothing could slow the speed, the sheer power of their ship.

The sheer power of *them*.

Even the wind couldn't drown out his low growl as he turned her lips to his. "I love you, beautiful."

"And I you my Viking king," she murmured then kissed him.

Some might say they'd crossed a great distance to be together but she knew better.

All they did was sail straight into their future.

The End

Curious what happens next with the Sigdir brothers? Find out in Raknar's story, *Viking Claim*.

Interested in what initially brought Valan to ninth century Scandinavia? What was in the manuscript that Megan finally got her hands on? Then head over to medieval Scotland in *The MacLomain Series: Next Generation*.

Previous Releases

~The MacLomain Series- Early Years~

Highland Defiance- Book One
Highland Persuasion- Book Two
Highland Mystic- Book Three

~The MacLomain Series~

The King's Druidess- Prelude
Fate's Monolith- Book One
Destiny's Denial- Book Two
Sylvan Mist- Book Three

The MacLomain Series Boxed Set is also available.

~The MacLomain Series- Next Generation~

Mark of the Highlander- Book One
Vow of the Highlander- Book Two
Wrath of the Highlander- Book Three
Faith of the Highlander- Book Four
Plight of the Highlander- Book Five

~The MacLomain Series- Viking Ancestors~

Viking King- Book One
Viking Claim- Book Two
Viking Heart- Book Three

~The MacLomain Series- Later Years~

Coming late 2015

~Calum's Curse Series~

The Victorian Lure- Book One
The Georgian Embrace- Book Two
The Tudor Revival- Book Three

The Calum's Curse Boxed Set is also available.

~Forsaken Brethren Series~

Darkest Memory- Book One
Heart of Vesuvius- Book Two

Also available in the Forsaken Brethren Series Twinpack.

~Song of the Muses Series~

Highland Muse

About the Author

Sky Purington is the best-selling author of fourteen novels and several novellas. A New Englander born and bred, Sky was raised hearing stories of folklore, myth and legend. When combined with a love for nature, romance and time-travel, elements from the stories of her youth found release in her books.

Purington loves to hear from readers and can be contacted at Sky@SkyPurington.com. Interested in keeping up with Sky's latest news and releases? Visit Sky's website, www.SkyPurington.com to download her free App on iTunes and Android or sign up for her quarterly newsletter. Love social networking? Find Sky on Facebook and Twitter.

Made in the USA
Lexington, KY
22 August 2015